As an undergraduate or graduate, it is essential that you start your job hunting campaign before graduation. You should start the process early in your final year. Don't wait until you have taken your final exams when the competition for jobs is toughest.

商用英文 第二版

劉鴻暉　林秀璟　著

BUSINESS ENGLISH

五南圖書出版公司 印行

■ 前 言

　　公司內部任何人只要與顧客接觸，均可稱為「銷售人員」，這包含接應電話的總機、助理甚至到客戶端服務的維修工程師。所以，不要輕易判定商用英文跟你的工作屬性與內容無關，就卻步停止學習。直到親臨實戰場合，卻使不上力時就後悔莫及。

　　在全球化的商務環境中，商用英文儼然成為國際通用語言，商用技巧及商用書信英文日益重要。如果在商務場合中，專業英文表達方式與能力都不盡理想，顧客端對滿意期待將會大打折扣，並進一步影響商務之往來。

　　基於此，本書以深入淺出的方式，讓初學者循序漸進學習基礎商用英文，以克服剛入門或是實務經歷較少者在學習時的障礙與畏懼。此書不僅適用於在學學生的教學上，更可讓自學進修者輕易上手，提供了社會新鮮人初入社會或工作經驗少者，最佳的基礎商用英文學習選擇。

　　本書祈望能夠提供正確精簡的商用英文技巧與商用英文書信用法，讓在職者可以在涉外的商業環境上得心應手；而在校者可以提早學習模擬商務情境，以培養未來進入職場的競爭力。

學習目標：期望透過主題式教學，增進讀者對商用英文的熟稔，以案例方式帶入模擬商場情境。期盼讀者在職場應用或證照應考時，得以輕鬆應對進退。

本書摘要：商用英文課程將涵蓋商用技巧英文與商用書信英文；其中涵蓋商場實務、企業往來與商務處理等商業英文議題。為增進讀者學習效率，並於短時間內增進學習效果，除了於每節結束後，針對該節主題設計常用句子或模擬商務情境的練習題以增加學習成效外，也針對商用英文中較常用的單字或片語加以解析。最後於書末編列四回測驗卷，以提升應考實力。

學習必備：一顆學習的心──唯有如此，學習才能事半功倍！

> 與大家分享一個英文單字的故事：
>
> 如果每個英文字母都對應一個數字：A代表數字1，B代表數字2，C代表數字3，D代表數字4，以此類推，Y代表數字25，Z則代表數字26。有一個英文單字的字母數字總合是100，請猜猜是哪一個英文單字？
>
> 答案：這個英文字就是「態度」（ATTITUDE）。
>
> 　　　　書籍只不過是工具，唯有以用心的態度來學習，才能讓你的商用英文突飛猛進。

你的預期目標：(1)計劃從商用英文學到什麼？

　　　　　　　(2)期望看完本書後，商用英文專業程度可以達到什麼程度？

What are your goals in this subject? (Please write down)

_____

_____

目錄

前　言

Section ①

商用技巧英文
English for Business Skills

1.1 First Impression and Introducing Yourself
第一印象與自我介紹

　　每一位員工都是企業對外大使，對於企業聲譽的塑造扮演著舉足輕重的角色。員工對顧客或合作夥伴的態度與應對進退，攸關著企業整體形象。本節首先介紹人與人見面溝通與自我介紹的方式以及注意事項。

　　面對國際化的商業環境，如果無法以清晰和正確的英文介紹自己或表達意見，商業夥伴可能會對你的印象大打折扣，甚至可能拒絕進一步的交談。因此，如何在職場上擁有的正確態度，進而藉由充分準備個人履歷建立自信心是學習的重點。

First Impression：產生良好的第一印象

> 根據哈佛大學行為科學研究顯示，面對面溝通包含三大要素：肢體語言、談話內容和語調。肢體語言是一個成功溝通的最重要因素，它占了全部重要性的55%。其次是語調，它占了三分之一強的重要性。最後，便是談話內容，僅剩7%。在電話溝通裡，語調的重要性躍升至四分之三強，甚至比面對面溝通的肢體語言比重還重，談話內容也升至25%。上揚的語調易使受話者放下戒心、敞開心胸暢談，對顧客的誠心與尊重更是產生好語調的不二法門。

▶ Smile－微笑是國際通用的語言
Smiling is an international language.

面對面溝通（face-to-face communication）：

肢體語言	body language	55%
談話內容	words	7%
語　　調	tone	38%

Your attitude is the first thing people see in a face-to-face communication.
（面對面溝通中，態度是決定他人對你看法的首要關鍵。）

▶ Thanksgiving, appreciation, gratitude－感謝之情
Thanksgiving, appreciation and gratitude will make your business easier.
（心存善、感謝與感恩讓你在商場做生意更容易。）

■　〈tell about the water crystal story〉水結晶的故事

不知道大家對「水結晶」的實驗熟悉嗎？

十分震撼的故事是這樣開始的：1995年日本神戶發生大地震，當時嚴重的災情造成超過一萬人喪生。當時日本IHM綜合研究所所長江本勝博士，便針對神戶當地的自來水做水結晶實驗，卻發現水結晶是分崩離析、醜陋不堪的。但江本勝博士對實驗結果卻不以為意，因為當地的自來水已受嚴重污染，水中亦加入氯等許多消毒的化學物質。所以，有如此不堪入目的水結晶應是意料之中。數月後，江本勝博士再次取樣當地水質，重新做實驗，可是該次實驗結果卻令人震懾，因為水結晶竟是如此的不同於之前。這時神戶自來水的結晶是美麗的、是有形得像雪片般的迷人。於是，江本勝博士便大膽做一個假設──地震發生當時人心惶惶、失去親友的悲痛到處瀰漫，神戶的水也感受到了；三個月後，來自國內外的關懷與救援紛至沓來，而當地居民的內心也日漸平復，當然，神戶的水也感受到了。

接著，江本勝博士便展開一連串的水結晶實驗。對水說好話、讓水聽美妙的樂音，甚或觀看優雅的圖片，水結晶會呈現美麗的六角形狀並且繽紛燦爛。而讓水聽難以入耳的話語或重金屬音樂，水結晶就似身歷其境，變得醜陋、不成行。

人身為萬物之靈，體內有70%是水構成的，若是存善念說好話，那不僅是自身體內的水結晶呈現繽紛燦爛的六角形；受話者的一方也將同時感受到，其體內70%的水結晶也能美麗地呈現。

心存善念，凡事先想到別人是與他人融洽相處的根本之道，運用至商務場合更將讓你無往不利。心存善念，不僅僅是水感受得到，植物同樣感受得到，當然，在您身旁的每一個人也都感受得到。混沌喧囂的世間，現代人最需要的就是來自空谷深處的真誠與善念。善念如清泉不僅緩緩入喉、沁人心扉，更可引發廣大深遠的效益。如果善念對自然界都可以起到鼓舞的作用，那麼對於人類社會的影響力勢必無庸置疑、無遠弗屆！

（更多詳盡實驗訊息與精美圖片，請參考台灣大紀元網站：http://www.epochtaiwan.net/webpage/special/water/1.htm）

想看看，除了上述所提之外，要留給對方好印象還須具備什麼條件？

- always have *plenty* to say（不會語拙）
- have many amazing stories to tell（話題豐富與多樣）
- *maintain* eye contact（目視對方）
- be honest（誠實）
- never *interrupt*（不會插嘴）
- listen carefully to what others are saying（仔細聆聽對方說話）

「聽」在溝通中扮演非常重要的角色。如果只是一股腦兒地表達自己的想法，未曾給對方喘息的機會，對方可能會放棄表達心中真正的想法或需求。所以要避免說話時漠視對話內容，或是佯裝在聽（fake listening）、選擇性聽取訊息，這不僅讓溝通事倍功半，也是不禮貌的。在商務場合上，容易造成顧客對企業產生負面印象。

「積極聆聽」（active listening）是對方在講話時，專心聆聽（non-verbal communication），不插嘴或中斷談話（listening without interruption）；針對對方的問題先想再答，想從顧客端知道的訊息先想再問。而針對一個主題的討論也不會顧左右而言他；如顧客質問：「你們的產品很爛！」業務人員卻回答：「目前該產品正在做促銷，有沒有興趣購買？」這樣的對話是很難達成共識，唯徒增顧客的抱怨。

■ 單字解析

plenty (n)：充裕、大量

There are still *plenty* of product brochures in the Marketing Department.

（在行銷部門還有很多產品手冊。）

maintain (v)：維持、保持

Dely company *maintains* close relations with their loyal customers.

（德理公司與他們的忠實客戶保持緊密的關係。）

interrupt (v)：中斷、阻斷

Don't *interrupt* the speaker, ask your questions afterwards.

（勿打斷演說者的演講，待演講結束後再提問。）

【讀者筆記】：還有哪些重點是第一次見面時須注意的？

_____

_____

_____

_____

_____

_____

_____

_____

_____

_____

_____

_____

_____

_____

_____

_____

_____

_____

_____

_____

_____

_____

Introducing Yourself：自我介紹

　　自我介紹時，目光必須直視對方（look people straight in the eyes），這不僅是基本禮貌，而且代表對方是受到你的尊重的。如果你是一位內向（introvert）害羞的人，不妨多保持微笑，微笑總是可以打破僵局（ice breaker）、緩和氣氛。

　　如果已知對方的名字，在輪到你自我介紹時，重複對方名字，將有助於你熟記對方的姓名，也會讓對方感受到你的誠意。

　　自我介紹時，必須先告知對方自己的全名、公司名稱以及服務單位。若是商務拜訪，也要將目的與事由交代清楚。為了打破首次見面的尷尬與冷場，以寒暄的方式做開場白是個不錯的選擇，親近的溝通容易打破彼此的藩籬，在最短的時間內與顧客打成一片；而簡潔、好的問題可以很快吸引顧客的興趣。

▶ 見面時打招呼的英文表達方式

● Nice to meet you, Daisy. I am Orwell Chang. Please call me Orwell.

　＝ It's a pleasure to meet you, Daisy. I am Orwell Chang.

　＝ Nice to meet you, Daisy. My name is Orwell Chang.

　＝ Let me tell you a little bit about myself, Daisy. I am Orwell Chang.
　（黛西，很高興認識您！我叫張歐威爾，請叫我歐威爾。）

● Hello, This is Orwell Chang from Best Tech. It's nice to meet you.

　＝ It's my pleasure to meet you. I am Orwell Chang from Best Tech.

　＝ I *am* so *happy* to see you. This is Orwell Chang from Best Tech.

　＝ It's really my honor to have this opportunity to see you here. My name is Orwell Chang and I work with Best Tech.
　（哈囉！我是最佳科技的張歐威爾。很高興認識您！）

● I *am* so *glad* to have this opportunity to *introduce* myself to you. Currently, I am a sales representative at Annabelle Marketing.

= It's my great pleasure to be here in front of you to present myself. I work at Annabelle Marketing as a sales representative.

= I really welcome this opportunity to *introduce* myself. I am a sales representative of Annabelle Marketing.

（很高興有此機會介紹我自己給您認識，目前我是安納貝爾行銷公司的業務代表。）

■ 單字解析

表示「樂意、高興」的英文表達

be glad to ＝ be happy to ＝ be pleased to ＝ be delighted to

introduce (v)：介紹、提出

This new CEO *introduces* innovative ideas into business operation.

（新執行長把創新觀念引進至商務運作上。）

The chairman *introduced* the speaker to the audience.

（主席將演講者介紹給聽眾。）

Application Letter and Autobiography Writing：應徵信與自傳撰寫

自傳撰寫，不僅是求職的第一步，也將有助於豐富自我介紹時的訊息。自傳不僅可以讓用人單位了解你的背景，更可讓你獲得面試的機會，甚至雀屏中選。通常需要英文自傳的公司，多是外商公司、大型企業或涉外單位。在眾多求職者中，英文自傳扮演敲門磚的角色，必須用心撰寫。在有限的篇幅裡，除了成長背景與求學歷程之外，更須強調你個人的特殊性及其與應徵職位之相關性，才能吸引人事專員與用人部門的目光。

其實，自傳撰寫並沒有固定書寫的格式，但請記住自傳就如廣告傳單，必須具備簡明、清晰與具吸引力的原則，請加入創意為自己加分。以下提供撰寫應徵信和自傳時的五個步驟。

Stage 1: Starting Writing（開始）

● Gathering all the information you need
蒐集所有相關訊息：包括你的個人經歷（personal history）、學歷、工作經歷（job history）、成就（achievements）與技能（skills）。

● Putting your ideas on paper
寫下你的想法：自傳是屬於自己的行銷工具（marketing tool），認真誠實地闡述相關主題。

● Ordering and classifying all the ideas
排序所有訊息的先後次序。

Stage 2: Composing（撰寫）

● ***Transferring*** your ideas into words
將心中的想法訴諸文字。

● Emphasizing your competence and special events
強調能力與特殊事蹟：想看看你的能力或特殊事蹟可以讓你脫穎而出嗎？如果你是人事經理，願意給這封自傳作者一個面試的機會嗎？

● Thinking about who is going to read it
確認你的讀者是誰：撰寫自傳時，試圖將你自己置於雇主的角色，檢視你的內容是否引起或符合應徵公司的興趣與要求。

● ***Developing*** the words into phrases and sentences
潤飾文句：辭意通暢的文句顯然比辭不達意、錯字連篇的自傳更具優勢。

Stage 3: Revising（修改）

● Reading through what you have written
從頭至尾詳讀：順一順自傳內容的流暢度。

● Asking others to prove read it
邀請他人校閱：可以請老師協助檢閱，並給予寶貴意見。

● Checking! Does it make sense?
檢查！確認內容表達是否合理、正確。

Stage 4: Editing（編輯）

● Can you improve them?

是否可以寫得更好：想看看是否可以用更文雅、專業的用詞取代通俗、不雅的文字。

● How can layout and punctuation marks help?

格式：整體布局可以更完善嗎？或是適當的標點符號有助於整篇文章的表達。

● Are spelling and punctuation marks correct?

拼字與標點符號的使用正確嗎？切記：應徵信函與自傳要避免使用時下年輕人喜用的火星文。

Stage 5: Final Copy（完成）

● *Writing up* work for final presentation

成品：應徵信函或自傳完成後，請調整文件格式，讓整體外觀看起來更具吸引力。

● Using word or PDF file

打成 Word 或PDF檔案，以利閱讀：若是你的英文書寫字體工整雅致，不妨試試以手寫代替打字，這樣也可以讓面試者印象深刻喔！

As an undergraduate or graduate, it is essential that you start your job hunting campaign early. You should start the process early in your final year. Don't wait until you have taken your final exams when the competition for jobs is toughest.

作為一位大學生或是研究生，及早準備找工作是必要的。在求學的最後一年，就應該提早準備履歷。千萬不要等到過了畢業考，才倉促著手進行，因為那時機找工作是最競爭的。

■ 單字解析

transfer (v)：轉變成、移轉

Timo has *transferred* from the warehouse to the accounting department.

（悌莫已由倉庫調至會計部服務。）

develop (v)：發展、開發

EGA is *developing* a new business.

（EGA 公司正開展一項新的業務。）

The corporate strategy gradually *developed* in the general manager's mind.

（公司策略在總經理心中逐漸形成。）

layout (n)：布局、圖樣

The plant *layout* is impressive.

（工廠的布局令人印象深刻。）

write up (ph.)：寫成作品

To write something again in a complete and useful form.

eg: To *write* up your notes.

【Tips: eg = exempli gratia（拉丁文）例如】

　　應徵信函與自傳最忌洋洋灑灑長篇大論，它不是個人生活史（life history）的闡述，而是獲取面試機會的敲門磚。撰寫應徵信函或自傳時，切記謹守簡潔（brief）、有焦點（focused）、活潑的（dynamic）、清晰（clearly layout）與易懂（easy to understand）等原則。

　　此外，也不要以一份制式（a single purpose）的應徵信函或自傳適用於所有不同性質或產業的職務應徵上，應該針對不同工作屬性提出量身裁製（tailor-made）的應徵信函和自傳。建議讀者可以先撰寫一份完整詳盡的自傳，隨後針對不同的公司要求或工作內容刪修相關內容。

▌ Application Letter：應徵信函參考範例 ▌

I am so glad to have this opportunity to introduce myself to you. I hope the following information will help you to have a better understanding either on my academic background or **evaluating** my work experiences.

I was born on January 25th, 1985 in a **traditional family** in Taipei County where education was deemed as the priority for the next generation. Under this circumstance together with my own efforts, I am proud to say that my performance in school was excellent. In the meantime, I also joined some kinds of school and community activities, such as the Association of the Scouts and swimming group. I like to help people when they need. I enjoy my life and always try my best to complete every event.

In 2002, the same year of high school graduation, I passed the Joint Examination and chose Business Management as my major at Taipei College of Business. During the four-year college life, not only had I actively taken part in various societies, but also read all kinds of books and journals. In addition, I was granted the scholarship from college and local government. In the final year at Taipei College of Business, I was busy preparing the team dissertation. The title of our dissertation was "An assessment of Management and Corporate Social Responsibility", supervised by Professor Irene Pan. After one-year of devoted working, we won the first prize.

After college, I chose Taipei County Bank as my first job, where I was in charge of clerk services. From this position, I had learned some management skills and was able to apply the objection handling knowledge to my daily operation. I had been in this job for one year and received a customer satisfaction award. This gives you an example of my service ability.

I am quite sure about myself and always persist in carrying out my future plan. To **achieve** my goal, I decide to change my job orientation and choose a **forward-looking** company like yours to work with. Should you require any information, I would be pleased to provide anytime. Please also **refer to the** attached documents of my awards and certificates. I look forward to hearing from you soon.

▌應徵信函中文翻譯 ▌

　　非常榮幸有此機會向　貴公司介紹我自己，期待以下的訊息將幫助您更了解不僅是我的學術背景，而且得以評估我的工作經驗。

　　我生於1985年1月25日，在台北縣的一個傳統家庭，家中非常重視下一代的教育。在這樣的環境中，加上自己本身的努力，我很榮幸地說我在學校的表現一直很優異。同時，我也加入一些學校與社區社團，諸如：童軍社和游泳社。當別人需要幫助時，我樂意幫助他人。我享受生活，並總是盡全力完成每一件事。

　　2002年，也是我高中畢業那年，我通過了聯招考試，並選擇了台北商業大學的企業管理作為我的主修。在四年的大學生活，個人不僅積極參與各種社團，也廣泛閱讀了各式書籍與期刊。除此之外，我也榮獲來自學校與地方政府的獎學金。大四那年，我忙於準備小組論文。我們的論文題目是：「管理與企業社會責任之評估」，該論文由潘愛琳教授指導。在一整年的努力下，我們終於拿到第一名。

　　大學畢業後，台北縣銀行的櫃檯服務成為我的首份工作。在這份工作裡，我學到了一些管理技巧，並得以運用危機管理知識於每日的工作中。這份工作持續了一年，也榮獲一項客戶滿意獎。希望這個事蹟讓您了解我的服務能力。

　　我有自信，也常堅持實踐我未來的計畫。為達目標，我決定改變工作屬性，並選擇一家如　貴公司一樣有前瞻性的公司工作。如果您需任何訊息，我將很樂意隨時提供給您。請參考附件我的獎狀與證照。期待能很快地接到您的訊息。

■ 單字解析

evaluate (v)：評價、估價

Customer value is no longer *evaluated* by product price.

（客戶價值不再由產品價格來決定。）

撰寫履歷時，描述家庭背景的表達

傳統的家庭 traditional family ＝ conventional family

平凡的家庭 ordinary family ＝ normal family

achieve (v)：完成、達成

Handerson *achieved* his sales quota last year.

（韓德森去年達到業績。）

forward-looking ＝ future-oriented: 有前瞻的

refer to (v)：參考、談及

Please *refer to* below sales figures.

（請參考以下的銷售數字。）

練習題① 請寫下你的應徵信函

（Please write down your application letter.）

_____

_____

_____

_____

_____

_____

_____

_____

_____

_____

_____

_____

_____

_____

_____

_____

_____

_____

_____

_____

_____

_____

_____

_____

_____

_____

1.2 CV Writing 履歷撰寫

　　履歷是求職時最基本的文件，而英文履歷同樣無固定格式。履歷是讓對方可以在最短的時間內熟悉你個人背景的管道。所以，必須完整呈現個人的基本資料於履歷之中。撰寫之前同樣要蒐集自己相關資料，並以正確、條理的英文翻譯。通常有些單位要求英文的佐證資料，如：英文畢業證書、成績單等；有些國外單位或公司更要求有法院與外交部的認證，以杜絕佐證資料的造假，求職者可能要有被錄取後提供這些公證文件的心理準備。

　　基本的履歷必須具備個人資訊、學術背景、工作經驗與才能等四個部分。但是，請記得個人簡歷和廣告單一樣必須簡潔、清楚。研究顯示，履歷頁數最好維持在A4大小紙兩頁。個人資訊除要有姓名、性別、生日、地址與聯絡方式外，有時身分證件亦須一併提供。學術背景基本上要敘述受教育過程，但需要用到英文履歷的用人單位，大致上只要陳述專科以上學歷，包括學校、國別、求學期間、主修課程、學業成績以及論文等。工作經驗則須詳列之前曾經工作過的公司或單位，並描述該工作內容，及提供公司聯絡方式以做必要時之檢驗。才能項目則可羅列許多細項，包含語文能力、人格特質、擁有證照等等。當然你也可以依照工作特性詳列個人的傑出表現，例如：特殊榮譽或成就表現、實驗成果、獲得專利、表揚事蹟、展覽演出等等。

　　此外，有些公司或單位甚至要求應徵者提供推薦信（references），一般推薦人多為學校老師或是之前工作的主管。所以，及早準備推薦信是必要的，好的、具說服力的推薦信絕對可以為求職加分。

Curriculum Vitae

Name:	Male/Female	
Date of Birth: Month/Date/Year		
Address:		
		除非應徵公司有特別規定，否則無需在履歷上放上大頭照。
E-mail:	Tel: Mobile phone:	

Curriculum Vitae：簡歷，可以縮寫成ＣＶ，或以美語常用的 resume來代表簡歷。

英文姓名的表達：名在前、姓在後。如：Susan Powell，Susan是名＝first name、given name，Powell是姓＝surname、family name、last name。也可以姓在前、名在後，但是姓後必須加逗號，如：Powell, Susan。

Date of Birth（出生日期）

　　Date/Month/Year（英式英文表達方式，BrE）

　　Month/Date/Year（美式英文表達方式，AmE）

地址的表達：□□□□□（郵遞區號zip code/postcode/postal code）地址撰寫從最小單位至最大地方。

如：台北市103大同區承德路二段133巷76號8樓之2

1️⃣0️⃣3️⃣8F-2, No.76, Lane 133, Chen-De Road Section 2, Da-Tung District, Taipei, Taiwan

【其他地址的英文說法】室 <u>Room</u>；樓 <u>Fl.</u> 或 <u>F</u>；號 <u>No.</u>；棟 <u>Building</u>；弄 <u>Alley</u>；巷 <u>Lane</u>；街 <u>Street</u>；段 <u>Section</u>；路 <u>Road</u>；

鄰 Neighborhood；里、村 Village；區 District；鄉、鎮 Town；市 City；縣 County；省 Province

手機：*BrE*多使用mobile phone，*AmE*較多使用cell phone或cellular phone。

Academic Background

Date	University graduated and degree received（碩士學位、畢業學校）
（your major or dissertation title，說明主修學程，或是碩士論文題目，或是獲獎細項。）	
Date	University or College graduated（畢業學校）
（your major or records of awards，說明獲獎細項。）	
Date	School graduated（畢業學校）
（records of awards，說明獲獎細項。）	

■ 單字解析

Academic Background：學術背景

If you want to apply for a good job, it would be necessary to describe your *academic background* in relation to the job.

（若你想找份好工作，描述與工作相關的學術背景是必要的。）

學校與學位的表達

elementary school/primary school 小學

junior high school 國中

senior high school 高中

college 專科／學院：畢業後所授予的學位叫「學士」。

B. A.（Bachelor of Arts）文學士

B. Sc.（Bachelor of Science）理學士

專科（五專、三專、二專）文憑叫 *College Diploma*

university 大學：畢業後所授予的學位叫「學士」。

B. A.（Bachelor of Arts） 文學士

B. Sc.（Bachelor of Science） 理學士

大學生叫 *"undergraduate"* 或 *"college student"*

graduate school 研究所：畢業後所授予的學位叫「碩士」。

M. A.（Master of Arts） 文學碩士

M. L.（Master of Laws） 法學碩士

MBA（Mater of Business Administration） 企業管理碩士

MSc（Master of Science） 理學碩士

Ph. D.（Doctor of Philosophy） 博士

post doctoral / post doc 博士後研究

研究生叫 *"postgraduate"* 或 *"graduate student"*

Work Experiences

Date	**Company Name**, Job Title（公司名稱、職稱） Job descriptions:（工作內容簡述） Address:（地址）
Date	**Company Name**, Job Title（公司名稱、職稱） Job descriptions:（工作內容簡述） Address:（地址）

　　在工作經驗欄目中，涵蓋所有支薪或是義務的職位，花點時間寫下從事這些工作你學習到的技能和專才，以及從中所獲取的成就與傑出表現。另外，專家並不建議在履歷中寫下你的薪資所得。

■ 單字解析

work experience：工作經驗

Our manager has plenty of *work experiences*.

（我們的經理擁有豐富的工作經驗。）

MBA students with limited or no *work experience* need to highlight their potential.

（僅有有限或是無工作經驗的企管碩士學生，必須強調他們的潛力。）

Competence and Qualifications

> Please write down your personality and core competences.
> （請寫下你的人格特質與核心能力。）

　　通常履歷中能力與資格的呈現是不可或缺的，學歷與畢業科系符合徵才需求是必要條件，而能力與資格則是充分條件。在不造假的情況下，列出你所擁有的「優勢」，才能從求職者中脫穎而出。如果你驚覺在這方面仍「不具競爭力」，就要在求學時或想要轉業前，好好規劃如何提升自己的競爭優勢。

　　對於能力與資格的描述，可以關鍵字方式條列，應避免長篇大論式的細數家珍。

■ 單字解析

Competence (n)：能力、優勢

Competence is a standardized requirement for an individual to properly perform a specific job.

（能力是指一個人可以稱心地執行一項工作之標準條件。）

擁有「聽、說、讀、寫」的語言能力，這些語言可能含有：

Taiwanese台語、Mandarin/Chinese中文、English英語、
French法語、Deutsche/German德語、Japanese日語、Korean韓語、
Spanish西班牙語、Italian義大利語、Portuguese葡萄牙語、
Indian印度語、Thai泰國語、Russian俄語、Swedish瑞典語、
Hebrew希伯來語。

擁有個人的「優勢」，這些強項可能指擁有以下的人格特質：

- interpersonal skills - ability to put people at ease 人際關係處理的智慧
- dependable 可靠的
- organized 有組織能力的
- efficient 有效率的
- team worker 具團隊精神
- self-starter 自動自發
- adaptable 適應能力強
- client focused 以客為尊
- communication 溝通能力
- creative problem solver 創意危機處理
- drive to achieve 達成目標
- passion for the business 工作熱忱
- take ownership 負責任、主動參與各項任務
- trustworthy 可信賴

擁有「商業技能」，這些可包含：

- word processing 電腦文書處理
- presentation skill 演說能力
- negotiating skill 協商能力
- objection handling skill 危機處理能力

qualification (n)：資格證書、執照

What are the *qualifications* for a sales specialist?

（什麼是當一名業務代表須具備的條件？）

擁有國家或國際認可之「證照」將爲你的履歷與求職加分，這些可能是：

外語證照：GEPT全民英檢、TOEIC多益、TESL國際英語師資、TESOL國際英語教學、TEFL英文師資認證、JLPT日語檢定。

電腦證照：<u>作業系統</u> → CSA、LINUX、LINUX LPI、RHCE

　　　　　<u>網路管理</u> → CCDA、CCDP、CCIE、CCNA、CCNP、CCSP、CNA、ITE、NCIP、CNE、Master CNE

　　　　　<u>程式設計</u> → Embedded 微軟、ITE、SCAJ、SCJD、SCJP

　　　　　<u>多媒體</u> → 3D Studio Max、AutoCAD、SolidWorks、3D動畫應用、MAYA 動畫設計、電腦輔助製圖技術士、電腦遊戲動畫認證、影像動畫特效

商管證照：PMP專案管理、WBSA商務策劃

職業證照：CAD建築機械製圖、中餐技術士、中華民國甲乙丙技術士證、電腦技能基金會TQC認證

財經證照：<u>國家</u>→不動產經紀人、保險證照、證券期貨

　　　　　<u>國際</u>→CFA美國特許財務分析師、FRM風險管理師

▍撰寫履歷時的注意事項

職場上並沒有所謂完美的履歷表。當求職者求職、轉業或試圖升遷時，常會發現要書寫一封十全十美、看了令雇主滿意的履歷並非易事。專家建議，最佳的履歷表就是將求職者描繪成能解決問題的人，證明你能解決他們的痛，那你被僱用的機會就相對提升。

以下附上美國人力資源公司 RL Stevens & Associates, Inc. 執行長史蒂文斯的「十個最糟履歷表缺點」，協助讀者在撰寫履歷時，儘量避免犯這些讓雇主厭惡的錯誤。

1. 與雇主的需求脫節

讓雇主感受到你的求職是滿足他們的需要，而非你自己的需求。推銷與雇主需求相關的工作經驗；進行該公司所處產業的研究，並對雇主需求做SWOT分析：找到企業內部的優勢（strength）與劣勢（weakness），以及外部環境的商機（opportunity）與危脅（threat）。

對潛在雇主的兩個最大的競爭友商做類似的SWOT分析，以展現你不僅能快速理解雇主的需求，更清楚這一行業的挑戰。當你轉換到缺乏經驗的新產業時，這對你特別重要。你的履歷表必須使用該行業的專業術語，否則你的履歷只能石沉大海。

2. 不尊重雇主的時間

讓招聘經理愈容易讀懂你的履歷，你就愈可能成為他手下的一員。看履歷表對招聘決策人來說，就像昨日的咖啡一樣無味。你的履歷表必須在二十秒之內，讓招聘人員能清晰地感受到你會幫公司賺錢或省錢、開發新的商機、留住既有客戶、建立並擴展客戶關係，或將他們的工作環境變得更安全和宜人的場所。

3. 缺乏重點與方向

　　成功的行銷活動將產品與顧客配對，此一原則亦適用在求職上。要有戰略思維，不要漫無方向，且目標要明確。你的履歷應該展現出企圖心、有智慧以及富有意義的貢獻。即使經常轉換工作跑道，你的履歷表必須突出你曾用來達成工作計劃的技能，把資格證照或特殊表現總結在履歷表的最前面，這能顯示出你的職場生涯不是漫無目的。

4. 未顯示出對雇主產業知識的了解程度

　　你的履歷必須回答招聘人的主要問題：「我能為你做什麼？」當你選擇轉行時，因缺乏該行業的實際經驗，雇主因而認定你將無法勝任。為了平息雇主的疑慮，你應當描述過去的事業成就與可轉移的技能，讓雇主感受到你所擁有的技能與他們習習相關。

5. 不連貫又無條理的敘述方式

　　一份寫得很好的履歷表能傳達相關技能、有關職業知識、具備處理所有人和情況的能力。確定你的履歷表看起來連貫且符合邏輯；一個不連貫的工作歷史，缺乏職務升遷，或無法展現出情緒穩定或適應能力的人，雇主將不會對你產生任何的興趣。請記住，將最重要的部分放在履歷表的最前端。

6. 缺乏實質內容

　　重要的不是你做過了什麼，而是你有什麼成就。關鍵的細節是什麼？過度使用「管理」或「負責」等詞彙，顯示出求職者懶得動腦筋。成就可能也包括相關的工作外的活動，特別是那些能使你展示領導、機警和組織能力。證明給雇主看，為什麼你適合某個職務。

7. 難以閱讀的履歷表

可讀性等於易於接受。簡化專門術語和縮寫，使任何人都能很容易看懂你的履歷。自工作責任中找出獨特的成就，把重心放在可轉移到任何行業的技能。如果你都無法說清楚，那你自然也就無法說服雇主。以重點條列，凡是段落密集、句子冗長，保證會使雇主興趣缺缺。

8. 過時的內容和呈現方式

避免履歷看起來和其他人的履歷表同出一個模子。也不要將個人網站、部落格等網頁連接置入。要有專業的設計，用字遣詞能展現出你的成就、核心價值、職場表現與領導能力。

9. 誇大不實的履歷

編造或誇大的資歷將產生嚴重的後果，個人誠信與可信都將瀕臨危機。絕對不能在履歷表中撒謊，也不要歪曲訊息，或填塞以提高個人行銷作用。履歷表中的謊言包括：言過其實的工作成就、學術成就，甚至造假的學經歷。招聘決策人經常進行背景調查和網上搜尋來核對簡歷。

10. 用相同的履歷表申請所有工作

至少準備十種不同的履歷表，包括按時間順序的、按照功能的，和那些專為現場面試的，每一種都有它具體明確的目的。所有履歷撰寫的最終目的無非是獲得優質面試。拋棄制式的、一種尺寸適合所有履歷的表格，以證明你走在現實路上。如此一來，你的履歷將成為能夠推銷你長期價值的行銷文件。

（本文節錄自大紀元網站2008年8月13日訊息，作者為大紀元記者陳新生先生 http://news.epochtimes.com.tw/8/8/13/91437.htm）

 請撰寫自己的英文履歷表

Curriculum Vitae

Name:	Male / Female	
Date of Birth:		
Address:		
E-mail:	Tel: Mobile phone:	

Academic Background

Date	University graduated and degree received
Date	University or College graduated and degree received
Date	School graduated

Work Experiences

Date	Company Name, Job Title Job descriptions: Address:
Date	Company Name, Job Title Job descriptions: Address:
Date	Company Name, Job Title Job descriptions: Address:

Competence

Please write down your personality and core competence.

Qualifications

Please write down your qualifications and certificates.

1.3 Interview English 面試英文

　　如果你應徵的工作是外商公司、大型企業或者是負責對外的職位，那面試時多以英文進行。在無法得知面試者的提問時，只能自己多加練習，平時培養使用英文的習慣，因為口語英文是很難在短時間內完全提升。

　　本節僅羅列一些面試時通用語句，以協助讀者有練習的範本。這些句子大概在一場正式的面試不同階段都派得上用場，但針對專業問答及隨機提問，讀者就須長期培養。

▶ 面試應徵時的英文

● Good Morning, Sir and/or Madam. I am *grateful* to be here to present myself.
（早安！各位女士先生，很榮幸在此介紹我自己。）

● Good afternoon, Sir and/or Madam. I am very happy to have this opportunity to introduce myself.
（午安！各位女士先生，很高興有此機會介紹我自己。）

● Good day, Sir and/or Madam. It is my pleasure as an interviewee to meet you.
（日安！各位女士先生，很榮幸身為面試者與您見面。）

■ 單字解析

grateful (a)：感激的、感謝的
I am *grateful* to have you help me get the job.
（承蒙幫忙取得該職，我非常感激。）

▶ 面試時自我介紹並說明應徵職位

● My name is James Chang, and I am applying for the position Sales Specialist in the Marketing Department.
（我叫張詹姆士，我要應徵行銷部門的業務專員。）

● My name is Winland Lee, and I am a candidate for the job － applied engineer.
（我是李溫嵐德，是應徵應用工程師一職的候選人。）

▶ 剛畢業無工作經驗者

● Even if I never have any work experience in this job, I will try my best to learn fast if you give me this opportunity.
（即使沒有此工作的任何相關經驗，但如有機會獲得此職位，我將盡全力學習。）

● I just graduated from the university, but I shall utilize (＝*apply*) my skills and knowledge when I get this position.
（雖然剛從大學畢業，但是當我被錄取時，將全力運用我的技能與知識。）

● My work attitude and learning ability will get me into orbit in a short time.
（我的工作態度與學習能力將於短時間內步入軌道。）

● I think your company/this job can provide me a great opportunity to learn and grow.
（我認為貴公司／這份工作可以提供我很好學習與成長的機會。）

● This position will be a great chance of learning experience and a challenge to my first job in my career. I will definitely *benefit* from it under your supervision.
（這份工作將是學習經驗的好機會，也是我職場生涯中第一份工作的挑戰。在您的指導下，我將從中獲得許多。）

● If you could grant me this opportunity, I should *devote* myself to work *in return*.

（倘若您賜予我這個機會，我會全力投入工作以做回報。）

■ 單字解析

apply (v)：應用、實施、使起作用

I will *apply* my skills and hard-work for the achievement of Mercia Technology.

（我將應用我的技能與努力工作，一起成就莫西亞科技公司。）

benefit (v, n)：有益於、利益、好處

Sales will *benefit* from this comprehensive action plan.

（業務將受益於本次的全面行動計畫。）

devote (v)：奉獻、專心

The CEO *devoted* himself to social work.

（執行長為社會工作付出貢獻。）

in return (ph.)：回報

The builder offers more discounts *in return* for buyer's sincerity.

（建商以更優惠的折扣回報買主所釋出的誠意。）

▶ 面試時要強調自己是合適人選（有經驗者）

● My educational background and three years hands-on experience have perfectly matched to this position.

（我的教育背景以及三年的實務經驗，讓我成為該職位的最佳人選。）

● I had several case experiences of project management in the past few years by which I am ***tailor-made*** to become the team leader of your new project.

（在過去幾年，我擁有許多專案管理的實戰經驗，所以我是貴公司新專案團隊主管職位量身訂作之人選。）

● My major in accounting for both undergraduate and postgraduate degrees is just what you need for this open position.

（我的學士與碩士主修都是會計，正好符合貴公司徵才的條件。）

● I had a successful experience of introducing the products of Hi-Capacity Corporation into the European markets, and it is good enough to meet the requirements for this position.

（我在Hi-Capacity公司時，成功將公司產品銷售至歐洲市場，正好符合該職位的徵才條件。）

■ 單字解析

tailor-made (a)：量身訂作

Roster Chemical provides *tailor-made* products to its clients.

（羅斯特化工提供客戶裁身訂作的產品。）

▶ 獲得錄取

● The pleasure is mine to become one of you in Mactan Machinery.

（能在馬克坦機器公司上班是我的榮幸。）

● I can't wait to devote myself to Codova Trading Co.

（我迫不及待想為科多發貿易公司貢獻我的專才。）

● I welcome this opportunity to work with Lapu Metals.

（我很高興接受在拉普金屬公司工作。）

1.4 You are the Actor! 演說與報告

一場成功的演說，不僅要言之有物，同時也須兼顧重要的演說技巧，如清晰和抑揚頓挫的語調或者是善用肢體語言等等。商場中有眾多演說和報告的機會，如果一些常用技巧不能練習好，會導致當眾出糗。

商務報告時，多佐以簡報檔的放映，以吸引聽眾的注意力，並藉此活潑化演說，有些公司甚至提供與會者每人一份簡報內容，讓客戶對該公司有更深刻的印象。此外，演說時避諱不適或粗俗的言語及笑話，也不得任意批評或指責競爭友商的產品或服務。

本節提供演說和報告的一些常用說法協助讀者運用。當然，如果有機會做一場演說或主持會議，請記住熟能生巧（Practice makes perfect），事前多加練習絕對有意想不到的好處。同時記住不要太緊張，演說開始前先深呼吸（deep breaths），穩定自己的表現，並儘量以詼諧的口吻帶動現場的氣氛。在這種特殊場合表現出色，很容易獲得上司或老闆的嘉許與讚賞喔。

以下英文表達方式皆為演說時常用佳句，建議讀者熟記，親臨戰場時將受用無窮喔！畢竟事前流汗練習，總比事後表現不佳獨自流淚好。

Presentation Skills 演說技巧

　　在英文演說中，如果掌握好「起、承、轉、合」的關鍵句表達，不僅讓聽眾清楚了解你所表達的內容，更可讓整體演講加分。茲將一個演說，所將涉及之基本句子分述如下：

▶ Getting attention（演說即將開始）
　　演說即將開始，主席或司儀希望大家注意的說法如下：

● May I have your attention, please!
　（請大家注意了！）

● Ladies and gentlemen. Shall we start!
　（各位女士、先生，我們要開始了！）

● Alright everyone? Are we ready to begin?
　（好了嗎，各位？我們可以開始了嗎？）

● Let's get down to business, shall we?
　（咱們可以開始了嗎？）

■ 單字解析

吸引某人注意 ＝ have somebody's attention

　　　　　＝ attract somebody's attention

　　　　　＝ catch somebody's attention

　　在演說或報告之前，要引起聽眾注意可搭配一些動作，如：輕輕敲打麥克風，以引起與會者的注意。在餐會場合則可以餐具輕敲水杯發出聲響，來引起注意。

shall（助動詞），否定為**shan't**

(1) 與「I」和「we」連用，表示將做某事或意圖做某事。

　　如：We shall have to go right now.（我們將必須馬上離開。）

(2) 與「you」、「he」、「she」、「it」或「they」連用，表示某事必定發生或承諾讓它發生。

　　如：The murderer shall be caught and punished.（謀殺犯必須繩之以法。）

(3) 「Shall I」禮貌問句

　　如：Shall I close the door?（我把門關上，好嗎？）

(4) 「Shall we」建議做某事

　　如：Shall we dine out today?（我們今天去外面吃飯，要不要？）

▶ Introducing a speaker （主持人介紹演講者或來賓）

主持人於開場白，應該正確地介紹演講者或來賓的姓名與相關背景，表達對演講者、來賓或與會者參與的謝意，並致歡迎詞：

● I'm very pleased to *welcome* our speaker Dr. Ben Bagadion.

= It's a pleasure for me to welcome our speaker Dr. Ben Bagadion.

= I'd like to extend a warm welcome to our speaker Dr. Ben Bagadion.

= I'd like to introduce our speaker Dr. Ben Bagadion.

（很榮幸歡迎我們的演講者Ben Bagadion博士。）

● Our guest speaker today is Mr. Robert Spears.

（今天蒞臨的來賓是Robert Spears先生。）

● Please give a warm round of *applause* for the General Manager Mrs. Donna Decena from Mercy Corporation.

= Please give a big hand for the General Manager Mrs. Donna Decena from Mercy Corporation.

= Please join me in welcoming the General Manger Mrs. Donna Decena from Mercy Corporation.

（讓我們熱烈歡迎來自梅西公司的總經理Donna Decena女士。）

● It's a *privilege* for me to introduce Ms. Cora Hennz to all of you.

（很榮幸介紹來賓Cora Hennz女士給各位認識。）

● I welcome the *opportunity* to present Manager David Chen to you.

（很高興介紹David陳經理各位認識。）

■ 單字解析

welcome (v, a)：歡迎、受歡迎的

You are *welcome*.

（不客氣！你是受歡迎的！）

You are *welcomed*.

（不客氣！你是受歡迎的！）

　　以上兩個句子皆表示「不客氣！」的意思，但使用上仍有些微差異。"You are welcome."用於你回覆對方達謝你給予的協助、恩惠或東西。而"You are welcomed."此句很少用，意指你歡迎對方到此地來，即使如此，當歡迎某人蒞臨某地時，也須慎用此句。建議此時可以改以："Welcome to my party."（歡迎蒞臨我的派對！）表達。

applause (n)：鼓掌、喝采

a burst of applause ＝ a round of applause ＝ a big hand

Please give a around of *applause* for our outstanding achievement.

（請為我們傑出的表現鼓掌！）

privilege (n)：殊榮、恩典、特權

It is a great *privilege* to know you.

（認識你真是莫大的榮幸。）

opportunity (n)：機會、良機

Now is a good *opportunity* to enter overseas markets.

（現在是進入海外市場的好時機。）

▶ Staring a presentation gracefully（闡明會議主要議題）
　這時主持人可從獨特的觀點（unusual angle）簡述演講的內容：

● Let's start by looking at this *agreement.*
　＝ We are here today to look at this agreement.
　（咱們先看這份協議。）

● Why don't we first go over the contract?
　（讓我們先看看這份合約吧。）

● Before I begin, I would just like to mention that our department has achieved our sales quota this month.
　（在我開始之前，我想提一下本部門此月已達銷售業績。）

● First I'd like to say a few words about this research proposal.
　（首先我想說一下這份研究提案。）

● Today, I shall be *dealing with* the final arrangement of this *joint venture.*
　＝ Our main goal today is to deal with the final arrangement of this joint venture.
　（今天我將處理這樁合資案的最後協議。）

● I'm here to tell you about the full contents of marketing strategy.
　＝ I have called this meeting in order to tell you about the full contents of marketing strategy.
　（在此我要告訴你們有關市場策略的所有內涵。）

● I plan to say a few words about this report.
　（我計劃要談一點這份報告。）

● I'm going to talk about the *corporate social responsibility* today.
　（今天我將談論有關企業社會責任的議題。）

● The subject of my *talk* is the sustainable development of an enterprise.

　= The theme of my *presentation* is the sustainable evelopment of an enterprise.

　= The topic of my *speech* is the sustainable development of an enterprise.

　= The field of my *lecture* is the sustainable development of an enterprise.

　（我的演講題目是企業的永續經營。）

● I would like to give you an overview of international business.

　（我想讓你們對國際企業有個概括的認識。）

● I've divided my talk into three parts.

　= My talk will be in three sections.

　（我的演講題目將分成三個部分。）

■ 單字解析

agreement (n)：協議、同意

New Zealand's prime minister will sign a groundbreaking free trade *agreement* with Vietnam.

（紐西蘭總理將與越南簽訂一項開創性自由貿易協定。）

deal with (ph.) 處理、應付

This little girl has learnt to *deal with* all kinds of complicated situations.

（這位小女孩已經學會處理各種複雜的情況。）

The article *deals with* an important concept.

（這篇文章處理一個重要的概念。）

joint venture (ph.)：合資企業、創投公司

A *joint venture* (often abbreviated JV) is an entity formed between two or more parties to undertake economic activity together.

（合資企業，常縮寫成JV，是指由兩個或以上的單位所組成的一個實體，以共同從事經濟活動。）

corporate social responsibility (ph.)：企業社會責任

Company should align *corporate social responsibility* strategy to business objectives.

（公司應該將企業社會責任策略與企業目標相結合。）

talk = presentation = lecture = speech：演講、演說

▶ Length（演講時間的說法如下）

● My talk will take about twenty minutes.

（我的演講約二十分鐘。）

● The presentation will take about two and half hours, but there will be a twenty minute coffee break in the middle.

（我的演講是兩個半小時，但中場會有二十分鐘的休息時間。）

● We'll stop for lunch at 12 o'clock.

（演講十二點結束，並可用餐。）

▶ Making a transition（當展開一個新主題的說法如下）

● Next, the distribution networks will cover the following topics.

（配銷網絡將會是接下來的主題。）

● Now, we will be looking at how this relates to *profit-making*.

（現在讓我們看一下這和賺取利潤之間的關係。）

■ 單字解析

transition (n) 轉變、過渡

There is a successful *transition* to the new information technology system in this company.

（這家公司轉換到新的資訊系統很成功。）

profit-making (ph.) 營利的、有利可圖

How does a company turn inventions into *profit-making* assets?

（一家公司如何將創意發明轉為可以營利的資產呢？）

▶ Making the summary or conclusion
（強調重點與結論的說法如下）

- I'd like to end by emphasizing these main points.
  = I'd like to end with a summary of the main points.
  （我想以強調這些重點做演說結束。）

- That finishes off my presentation.
  （以上就是我的演講內容。）

- Does anyone have any question?
  （有人要提問嗎？）

- Comments or questions are welcomed.
  （歡迎評論或提問。）

- I hope you found the talk informative.
  （我希望你們覺得這個演講對你們有用。）

- Thank you very much for listening.
  （非常感謝聆聽。）

▶ Asking for clarification or explanation
（若你是聽眾，聽不清楚演講者的演說內容時，問法如下）

● Excuse me, could you explain how this project is done?
（不好意思，能否請你解釋這方案如何完成？）

● *Excuse me*, could you just *go over* the statement again?
（不好意思，能否請再解釋一次該聲明？）

● Would you mind briefly *clarifying* how to complete this plan?
（能否請你簡單闡明如何完成這項計畫？）

● Would you please explain this process?
（能否請你解釋這個流程？）

● *Sorry* to interrupt, but I didn't quite understand when you mentioned the second argument.
（抱歉打擾，我不是很清楚你描述的第二項論點。）

■ 單字解析

excuse me 和 sorry 的差異

Excuse me 是禮貌語詞，用法有：(1)引起他人注意；(2)請人讓路；(3)打擾他人或失禮以表歉意；(4)婉轉表示不認同；(5)婉轉要求離開或與他人講話；(6)因推擠他人或做錯事表原諒（AmE）；(7)沒聽清楚對方的話，要求再說一遍（AmE）。

"Excuse me" 一詞在美國比英國更常使用。若說這句話時，現場不止一人，可以 **"Excuse us"** 表達。如：Excuse us for a moment.（容我們失陪片刻。）

Sorry 可表示：(1)對某事感到歉疚、難過或惋惜；(2)於道歉時使用，表不好意思或抱歉；(3)遺憾；(4)沒聽清楚對方的話，要求再說一遍（BrE），或使用Pardon一詞。

【例句】

A: "Would you mind opening the window?"
　　（請將窗戶打開好嗎？）

B: "Pardon!"（抱歉，請再說一次。）
　　= Pardon me.（請原諒，請再說一次。）
　　= I beg your pardon.（請原諒，請再說一次。）
　　= Excuse me!（抱歉！美國較常用。）
　　= Sorry!（抱歉！英國較常用。）
　　= Would you mind repeating that?（請再說一次。）
　　= What did you say?（較不禮貌的問法。）
　　= What?（較不禮貌的問法。）

go over (ph.) 重溫

Stella *went* over this report again.
（史泰拉再讀一次這份報告。）

clarify (v) 闡明、澄清

William *clarified* his stand on this issue.
（威廉闡明在該問題上的立場。）

從自己親身演說與他人演說中，你學到了什麼？
是不是下一次有機會再演說時，會做得更好！

Memo

練習題③ 請寫下身為主持人，你將使用的介紹語詞
（If you are a host and chair, write down your opening.）

_____

_____

_____

_____

_____

_____

_____

_____

_____

_____

_____

_____

_____

_____

_____

_____

_____

_____

_____

1.5 Telephone Techniques 電話溝通技巧

　　電話是商業往來中經常使用的溝通方式之一，乃是透過電話通訊進行交談與聯繫，屬於較不正式的溝通。一般企業對企業有關報價與下單都還是以書面方式進行，以避免未來交易時爭議的產生。

　　通常接受電話下單多屬於零售業或網路行銷業，這種電話交易方式都會錄音為證，以免未來有爭議或麻煩。本節主要是一些慣用電話溝通時的英文技巧，熟練之後面對交易對象才不會結巴或不知所云，讓自己隨時擁有職場競爭力。

　　在正式的商務場合中，打一通成功的陌生拜訪電話並不是件簡單的事。不過，如果能掌握一些基本用詞，其實在最短的時間內，找到對的人是容易的。以下列出電話溝通中開啟的實用語詞供大家參考。

Telephone English：電話英文範例

● **Operator:** Hello, Interactive Consulting, How can I help you?

（接線生：Interactive顧問公司您好，我能幫您嗎？）

● **Dick:** This is Dick Peppers. Can I have extension 7539?

（狄克：我是狄克‧派伯斯，能幫我轉分機7539嗎？）

● **Operator:** Certainly, hold on a minute, I'll *put* you *through* to extension7539.

（接線生：沒問題，請等一下！我幫轉分機7539。）

● **Don:** Ernan Roman's office, Don speaking.

（當：爾納‧羅馬辦公室，我是當。）

● **Dick:** This is Dick Peppers calling, is Ernan in?

（狄克：我是狄克‧派伯斯，請問爾納在嗎？）

● **Don:** I'm afraid he's out of the office *at this moment*. Can I take a message?

（當：很抱歉他現在不在辦公室，我能幫您留言給他嗎？）

● **Dick:** Yes, Could you ask him to call me back at 0915-245242. I need to talk to him about the Food Taipei Show, it's urgent.

（狄克：是的，能請他打我的電話0915-245242，我必須與他談論台北食品展，這很緊急。）

● **Don:** Could you repeat the mobile phone number, please?

（當：請您再說一次手機號碼，好嗎？）

● **Dick:** Yes, that's 0915-245242, and this is Dick Peppers calling.

（狄克：電話是0915-245242，我叫狄克・派伯斯。）

● **Don:** Thank you Mr. Peppers, I'll make sure Ernan gets this *as soon as possible.*

（當：謝謝派伯斯先生，我會儘快讓爾納知道。）

● **Dick:** Thanks, bye.

（狄克：謝謝，再見。）

● **Don:** Bye.

（當：再見。）

■ **單字解析**

put through (ph.) 轉接

I will *put you through* to Brown now.

（我現在將你的電話轉給布朗。）

at this moment (ph.) 此刻

What are you doing *at this moment*?

（你現在在做什麼？）

as soon as possible ＝ ASAP (ph.) 儘快

He was noticed to submit the proposal *as soon as possible*.

（他被通知儘早繳交提案。）

Telephone English：電話英文例句

● 你好，我是 XYZ 公司研發部的考瑞忠。

Hello, this is Corazon calling from XYZ R&D department.

（電話溝通中，I am 要改為 This is。）

● 請問大衛在嗎？我是Stone公司的布蘭達。

Is David available, please? My name is Brenda from Stone company.

＝ Is David in the office?

● 您好，我想與大衛談話。

Hello, I'd like to speak to David.

＝ Hello, may I talk to David, please?

＝ Hello, may I speak to David, please?

● 我就是大衛。

This is David.

＝ David speaking.

● 請您將您的名字拼給我好嗎？

Would you please spell your name for me?

● 我能知道您貴姓大名嗎？

May I know your name, please?

＝ May I have your name, please?

＝ Can I ask who's calling, please?

＝ Excuse me, who is this?

● 請稍後！

Hold on a moment, please.

＝ Hold on, please.

＝ Hold on.

＝ A moment, please.

＝ Can you hold the line?

＝ Can you hold on a moment?

● 抱歉，您打錯電話了。

Sorry, you have the wrong number.

＝ Sorry, you dialed the wrong number.

● 喔，抱歉！我打錯電話了。

Oh, dear. I think I've dialed the wrong number.

● 不，這裡是財務部，我幫你查分機號碼。

No. This is the Finance Department. I will check the extension number.

● 不好意思，他忙線中。

Sorry, his line is busy now.

＝ His line is engaged now.

＝ He is engaged now.

● 不好意思，他在開會。

I am afraid he's in a meeting.

● 不好意思，他不在辦公室。

I am afraid he's not in the office.

＝ Sorry, he is out at the moment.

＝ I am sorry he isn't in.

● 不好意思，他現在不方便。

I am afraid he's not available just now.

● 不好意思，本部門業務主管史帝夫已經離職了。

I am sorry, but Steve, our Sales Director, is no longer with us.

● 可以請您稍後再撥嗎？

Would you please try later?

＝ Could you ring later?

＝ Could you call later?

＝ Could you telephone later?

＝ Would you mind calling back?

● 有什麼我可以為你效勞（服務）？

Is there anything I can do for you?

＝ Is there anything else I can do?

＝ May I help you?

＝ What can I do for you?

＝ What can I do to help?

● 需要我幫你安排約會時間嗎？

Would you like me to fix up an appointment for you?

● 艾德琳的分機是229。

Adrin's extension number is 229.

● 我將你轉接至美姬。

I will put you through to Maggie.

● 能幫我轉分機326？

Can I have extension 326?

＝ Could I speak to extension 326?

＝ May I speak to extension 326?

＝ Can you connect me to extension 326?

● 請問你的分機是？

What is your extension number?

● 請問你的傳真是？

What is your fax number?

＝ May I have your fax number?

● 請問安東尼的電子郵件是？

Could you tell me Antony's email address?

● 我將請她回來後儘速與您聯繫。

I will ask her to call you back as soon as she is back.

● 可不可以請她回我電話？我的電話是：531477。

Could you ask her to call me back, please? My number is 531477.

＝ Could you ask her to call me at 531477, please?

＝ Could you ask her to call me back, please? She can reach me at 531477.

● 我能留言給他嗎？

May I leave him a message?

- 我能幫您留言給他嗎？

 May I take a message?

  ＝ Could I tell him who is calling?

  ＝ Would you like to leave a message?

- 我今天晚一點再打來。

 I will call again later today.

- 知道了！

 I see.

  ＝ I got it!

- 好的！

 Okay

  ＝ Sure

  ＝ Certainly

  ＝ 100% sure.

- 請問他幾點回來？

 What time do you expect his back?

  ＝ When will he come back?

- 你知道他何時會開完會嗎？

 Do you know when he will be out of his meeting?

- 讓我查看一下他今天的行程表。

 Let me check his schedule for the day.

- 你可以告訴他我有打電話來？

 Could you tell him that I called?

● 他大約一小時後回辦公室。

He will be back in office about an hour.

● 他沒有專線，請撥總機。

He doesn't have a direct line, please try our switchboard/operator.

● 我想如果您能留言或試著今天下午晚一點再打過來，會比較好。

I think that it would be better if you leave a message or try to call back this late afternoon.

● 他有你的行動電話號碼嗎？

Does he have your mobile number (＝cell phone number)?

● 讓我重複你的訊息，確認無誤。

Let me repeat your message, just to confirm.

● 您的意思是指貴公司可以接受付款條件，對嗎？

What are you saying is that you can accept the payment term. Is that right?

● 我最好將它寫下。

I'd better write it down.

● 湯瑪斯先生，我可以寄一封簡訊給羅絲，但是很抱歉我無法保證她能夠及時收到。

Mr. Thomas, I can send Ross a message, but I am sorry that there's no guarantee that she'll get it in time.

● 我一定會轉告他的。

I will be sure to pass the message to him.

● 你聽得到嗎？

Hello, can you hear me?

● 電話通訊不良，我再重撥。

We have a bad connection (signal). Let me call you back.

● 不好意思，電話有雜音，請再說一次好嗎？

Excuse me, there is some noise on the line. Could you repeat that, please?

● 聽起來似乎你很沮喪，能告訴我發生什麼事嗎？

You seem upset. Do you want to tell me what's wrong?

● 陳先生，這聽起來很急，是嗎？

This sounds urgent, Mr. Chen. Doesn't it?

● 艾爾比女士，讓我為您解決問題。我將打電話給本公司的工程師確認一、兩件事情，然後馬上回電給您。

Mrs. Elbe, let me save you the trouble. I will give our engineer a call and check one or two things. I'll call you right back.

● 假如你需要協助，請讓我知道。

If you need any help, just let me know.

● 讓我試著總結我們今天的談話內容。

Let me just try and summarize where we've got to.

● 感謝您的協助！

Thank you very much for your kind assistance.

● 我希望能夠協助您，但是這已經超乎我的專業領域，所以我已經安排專家與您聯繫。

I'd like to be able to help, but it's outside my professional area, so I've arranged for expert to contact you.

● 很抱歉造成您的不便。

I do apologize for any inconvenience this might have caused you.

Telephoning skills：電話溝通技巧

企業內部一通專業有效的電話溝通可以迅速提供來電者服務，亦可鞏固或提升顧客滿意度和忠誠度。完整的電話溝通包括「起、承、轉、合」，茲附如下，供讀者於實務職場上參考。

1. 起（Open a Call）

電話開啟時，首先自我介紹、告知名字、公司名稱、服務單位以及去電事由。為了打破首次通話的尷尬與冷場，以寒暄的方式做開場白是個不錯的選擇。親近的溝通容易打破彼此的藩籬，在最短的時間內與對方打成一片。

若顧客主動打電話進來，最好在三至四個鈴響內接通，以避免緊急的顧客需求無法被及時地解決或滿足。假如一位顧客緊急需要的產品訊息或報價資料，無法被及時滿足，可能該心急如焚的顧客就會轉向該企業友商尋求解答與支援，影響所及公司可能損失一個潛在的商機。

電話開啟十分關鍵，猶如面對面溝通的「第一印象」。溝通開啟無須冗長，簡潔、好的問題可以很快地吸引顧客或對方的興趣。大部分的人是禮尚往來，只要態度謙和些，常常會有意想不到的收穫。

2. 承（Identify Customer's Pains and Requirements）

在溝通開啟後，就正式進入主題——傾聽顧客的心聲。若是你主動撥出電話，除完整傳達並交付去電目的外，就是提供顧客服務。

在互動的過程中，顧客可能會適時地表達他公司所面臨的困境、亟待解的問題或未來的需求讓你知悉。若是顧客直接來電，可能只是「正面的」、單純表達採購需求或想知道某些產品訊息；也可能是針對某一次不滿交易的抱怨，這些「負面的」抱怨可能是不良的產品品質、過高售價或是售後服務差等等。

面對憤怒的顧客，必須使用正面的語辭，儘量緩和當時的緊張氣氛，避免與顧客直接發生衝突，找出他真正不滿的原因並儘速協助解決。假如事情處理得當，顧客的問題能夠確實被解決，就能將危機（crisis）變成轉機（turning point），進而成為未來的潛在商機（business opportunity）。

顧客需求與抱怨是一體的兩面，全賴你用心處理和解決；當面對顧客的抱怨時可以理性思考其原委，然後感性回應。

3. 轉（Propose Solution）

在了解顧客的想法與需求之後，便是幫顧客找到合適的解決方案。若是顧客的需求簡單，便立即處理；若是顧客的問題必須跨部門才能解決，這時找到企業內部對的資源或決策者益顯重要。此刻可採「三方通話」，邀請相關人員至談話中，及時在線上幫顧客解答疑問，以提高顧客滿意度。

若是無法立即解決的問題，承諾顧客何時前給予答案是必要之舉。處理顧客的不滿，必要時找高階主管與顧客對談，讓顧客有被重視的感覺。

　　幫顧客解決問題，是建立個人信用（credit）的好時機。解決問題的過程中，必須以客為尊、以解決顧客的問題與需求為優先考量。在提出解決方案時，亦不忘與顧客確認解決方案是否符合他公司真正的需要。針對顧客提出的每一個問題，要找出問題背後的根本起因，才不會徒勞無功，不至於提出的解決方案無法滿足顧客的根本需求。

4. 合（Close a Call）

　　掛斷電話前，必須再確認顧客需求與抱怨是否都已被滿足或解決，所提出的解決方案是否能解決顧客的最終問題。當時未決的也要告知顧客給予答案的期限，讓顧客得以對其老闆或公司交代。

　　大多數人認為服務開始與結束在顧客眼中同樣重要，但有些研究顯示結束時更舉足輕重。在電話溝通結束後，建議詳實記錄談話內容與重點，這些訊息都將成為企業商業智慧（business intelligence）的信息來源。

　　根據商業智慧分析結果，企業主動提供顧客高附加價值（value-added）的產品、服務或解決方案。這種將顧客的來龍去脈融入企業業務中，以了解「顧客情境」（customer scenario）建立更深遠的關係，讓企業在顧客心目中將日漸重要，最後成為不可或缺的夥伴關係（partnership）。

練習題④　電話禮儀

　　請兩人一組，一人扮演打電話的人，另一人為受話者，彼此練習打電話與接電話的禮儀。

▶ 情境一：找的人接電話（請翻譯成英文）

Elly：您好，我是Goody食品公司行銷部的Elly，請問David在嗎？

David：我就是，有什麼可以為您效勞的嗎？

Elly：David，你好嗎？好久不見！

David：Elly，我很好，您呢？是呀，從去年台北食品展到現在都沒碰面。

Elly：我也很好，只是最近忙著準備食品展。

　　　對了，我想和你約個時間見面以討論本次展覽的細節。

David：好的。請等一下，我拿一下我的工作日誌。

　　　（約略30秒）

　　　回來了，我6月11日到22日會去台北。

Elly：太好了！您6月12日下午能到本公司來討論嗎？

David：沒問題！

Elly：好，會後我請您去陽明山用餐並享受溫泉浴。

David：我已經迫不及待地想去台北了！

Elly：我會在您出發前，以e-mail與您討論細節。謝謝您！

David：不客氣，台北見。

Elly：再見，台北見囉。

David：再見，保持聯絡。

▶ 情境二：找的人開會中，不方便接聽。收話者請對方留
　　下姓名與聯絡資訊（請翻譯成英文）

Ariel：你好，我是Perkins科技的Ariel。請問維修部門的工程師
　　　　Joey在嗎？

Coreson：對不起，Joey外出開會，不在辦公室。我能幫妳嗎？

Ariel：下午他會進辦公室嗎？

Coreson：我想他今天應該不會再進辦公室了。

Ariel：我可以留個訊息給Joey嗎？

Coreson：沒問題，請說。

Ariel：我們的網路系統不穩定，想請他來檢查。我是Perkins科技
　　　　公司的資管經理Ariel，手機號碼是0910-000888。

Coreson：我已寫下，並將請Joey儘快與您聯繫。

Ariel：謝謝。可以請教你的名字嗎？

Coreson：我是Coreson。

Ariel：麻煩你了，Coreson。再見！

Coreson：不客氣。再見！

1.6 Memorandums, Notes and Information Exchange 備忘錄、筆記、訊息交換

It's important to take notes in business conversation, rather than rely on your memory. The main points need to be clearly recorded so that another person can make sense of them and you have a permanent record.

在正式的商務場合中，做筆記或是備忘錄是必要的。如果僅依賴記憶力，很容易就會遺漏談話內容，或是忘記交辦事項。一般商務人士會使用PDA或工作日誌來記事，而大部分的業務代表都使用筆記型電腦記事，當然新款手機也都有記事功能。無論使用何種方式，備忘錄或筆記就是要協助你記住一些重要細節，千萬不要僅依靠記憶。勤作筆記可減少在正式場合出錯的機會，這種簡短的資料記實並無固定格式，可以使用電子裝置所提供的格式，或是筆記本上的記事欄以及隨手貼（post-it）。

本節將談論備忘錄和筆記的呈現方式以及應答訊息時的英文語句。各位讀者也要隨時記得本節中所提到八個Ws。

Exchange Information 訊息交換

與商務對象進行往來時，經常需要針對訊息進行詢問與回答，本節即針對這種狀況詳列英文的正確用法。

▶ If you require some information, you could say
欲知某訊息的問法

● Could you tell me if the meeting will be held on time?
（能否告知會議將準時召開嗎？）

● Could you tell me when the new product will be *launched*?
（能否告知新產品何時推出？）

● Could you please tell me how much this MP4 player costs?
（能否告知這台MP4的價格？）

● Could you please tell me why this project had been cancelled?
（能否告知該計劃被取消的原因？）

● I wonder if you could tell me the procedure of setting this *server*.
（能否告知設定該伺服器的步驟？）

● I'd like to know the final price your company will offer.
（我想知道貴公司可提供的最後價格。）

● I'd like some information about your *terms and conditions* of the contract.
（我想知道貴公司合約的服務條款與細則。）

● Have we made progress in this discussion?
（我們在討論中有進展嗎？）

● Have we resolved the problems?
（我們解決問題了嗎？）

● Have we given you what you were looking for?
（我們已經給了您所尋找的東西了嗎？）

■ 單字解析

launch (v)：推出市場、開始從事

Airspace Corporation *launched* today a new class of information security products.

（Airspace公司今天推出新資訊安全產品系列。）

An improved product *launch* process results in faster time-to-market and time-to-profit.

（改進後的產品發表步驟將帶來更快速的上市與獲利時間。）

server (n)：伺服器

Cizko may be looking to enter the blade *server* market this quarter.

（Cizko本季可能進入刀鋒伺服器市場。）

terms and conditions (ph.)：服務條款與細則

If you are dissatisfied with any Amazing Bandwidth's *terms and conditions*, your sole and exclusive remedy is to discontinue using Amazing Bandwidth.

（假如您不滿Amazing寬頻的任何服務條款與細則，唯一且全部的作法便是停止使用Amazing寬頻。）

▶ **When someone give you some information, you could comment or reply**

（針對他人所提供的訊息，回答方式如列）

● Oh, I see.

（我懂。）

● Thanks for letting me know.

（謝謝讓我知悉。）

● Thank you very much for your useful information.

（非常感謝您有用的訊息。）

● Your reply is highly *appreciated*.

（非常感謝您的回覆。）

■ 單字解析

appreciate (v)：感激、感謝、賞識、察覺

We *appreciate* your long-term support.

（我們感謝您長久以來的支持。）

It will be highly *appreciated* if this flyer could be circulated as widely as possible.

（若此份廣告傳單可以儘可能地廣泛發行將十分感激。）

▶ **If someone asks you for information, you could reply**
（假如他人詢問資訊，你的回答方式如下）

● As far as I know, the board meeting is rescheduled on Wednesday.
（就我所知，董事會改到星期三。）

● Well, I can tell you that our new desktop PC will be put on the market in the 3rd quarter.
（嗯，我可以告訴你，我們的新型桌上型電腦將在第三季推出市場。）

● I'm afraid I don't know.
＝ I've no idea, I'm afraid.
（很抱歉我不清楚。）

● I don't have that information available just now, can I call you back later?
（我現在沒有那方面的訊息，能晚一點再回您的電話嗎？）

● I'm not sure. I'll have to find out. Could I let you know tomorrow?
（我不確定，我必須找出答案。能明日再讓您知道嗎？）

● I'm afraid that I cannot tell you that, it's *confidential*.
（很抱歉，由於商業機密無法奉告。）

■ 單字解析

confidential (a)：機密的、獲信任的

We needed to find a *confidential* shredding company that would offer absolute destruction of all sensitive and *confidential* information.

（我們需要找一家信得過的碎紙公司，可以提供將所有敏感與機密文件完全銷毀。）

▶ **If you want to give someone information, you could say**
  （告知對方訊息的表達方式）

● I would like you to know that the last date of ***promotion*** was yesterday.
  （想讓您知道促銷最後一天是昨日。）

● I think you should know that the head of marketing department will join
  our coming ***planning session*** meeting.
  （我想你應知道行銷部主管將參加我們下一次的行動策畫會議。）

● Did you know that Commark will end up its ***dealership*** in Taiwan?
  （您知道康馬克公司將結束在台灣的代理權？）

■ 單字解析

promotion (n)：促銷、推銷

Sales *promotion* is an initiative undertaken by an organization to promote an increase in sales.
（促銷是組織提增銷售量的方案。）

planning session (ph.)：行動策劃

Yearly business *planning session* is sometimes a time-consuming ordeal.
（有時候年度商業行動策劃是一件很費時的折磨。）

dealership (n)：代理權、經銷權

Sterling, Inc. is one of the best auto *dealership* in Taipei Area.
（Sterling公司是台北地區最好的汽車經銷之一。）

▶ If someone hasn't given you enough information, you could say（欲獲取更多訊息的問法）

● Could you tell me some more about the *decision-making* process?
（能否請您告知更多有關決策過程？）

● What can we do to help you manage the risks in this project?
（我們怎麼協助貴公司處理該計劃的風險？）

● I would like some more information about the *payment terms*.
（我想知道更多有關付款條件的訊息。）

● I'd also like to know your e-mail address and mobile phone number.
（我也想知道您的電子郵件信箱與手機號碼。）

● When can your institution issue this *certificate*?
（貴機構何時能核發證書？）

● How much will it cost when my *purchase* is over US$ 1,000?
（當我的採購超過一千美元時，該付多少錢？）

● Why exactly did the World Trade Center *collapse*?
（世貿中心倒塌的真正原因是什麼？）

● There is something else I'd like to know.
（還有一些事我想知道。）

● Can you give me some more details about this *shipment*?
（能否告知更多此次出貨的詳細？）

■ 單字解析

decision-making (n)：決策

The employees have some voice in *decision-making*.

（員工可表達在決策上的意見。）

payment term (ph.)：付款條件

Payment terms can include a discount percent for early payment.

（付款條件包含了提前償還的折扣百分比。）

certificate (n)：證書、執照、憑證

Use this calculator to find out how much interest you can earn on a *Certificate* of Deposit.

（使用該計算表來算出你的定存單可賺取多少利息。）

purchase (n, v)：購買、獲得

In any transaction, the Sale and *Purchase* Agreement represents the outcome of key commercial and pricing negotiations.

（任何交易，買賣合約代表了主要商業協商與議價結果。）

collapse (v)：倒塌、瓦解、崩潰

The *collapse* of Lehman Brothers sends shock wave around the world.

（雷曼兄弟的破產對世界造成衝擊。）

（註：雷曼兄弟是美國第四大投資銀行，擁有158年的歷史。）

shipment (n)：裝運、裝船

There are only three basic types of *shipments*: land, air, and sea.

（有三種基本的裝運類型：陸路、空運以及海運。）

筆記與備忘錄格式參考範例

【Notes 1】

> *Notes on the Infoprinta Exhibition*
> *To: Sales Manager (Cindy Won)*
> *From: Lind (Marketing Assistant)*
> *Subject: Record of consultation at Infoprinta*
> *Date: Dec 8, 2008*
> *Company: Warm Greeting Cards Co., Ltd*
> *Person met: President Tim Brown*
> *Nature of enquiry: About L73 Laser Printer*

【Notes 2】

2. ROTAP plc   32 Campus Highway Hsin-Chu City 300

During my duty on the company stand, I was approached by a company's CEO named Tim Brown. He enquired about our laser printer. It was the L73 he was interested in. In particular, he asked whether the machine was able to deal with.

【Memo】

```
3. Record of Conversation at Proprinta
   Date: Dec 8, 2008
(1) Met Mr. Brown from Warm Greeting Card company
(2) He expressed his interests in 10ca L73
(3) He wanted 12% discount on large order
(4) He said our competitor, PRINTIX Inc, would give him
    12% off
```

　　當記錄note或memo時，掌握以下的八個W原則，讓內容資訊更充實與完整，而重要的訊息也不至於遺漏：

1. what——會議或交談的主題與重要內容為何？
2. who——事件的關鍵決策者或相關人士是誰？
3. where——事件發生的地點在哪？
4. when——事件發生的時間何時？
5. why——找出關鍵決策者的顧慮或事件發生的主要原因。
6. how——事件發生過程，或是關鍵人物的決策程序。
7. while——永續經營的概念：思考一個決策或是訊息的執行或告知，將會對公司或顧客起到的作用。
8. whom——做這個決策或是訊息告知，將造成公司或顧客的影響為何？

練習題⑤　請依據下列狀況編寫一份備忘錄

　　2009年9月24日你出差到德國漢諾威（Hannover）參加Computex，遇到義大利廠商Vespian Computer的採購經理Mr. Lucas Pavaradi，詢問本公司Tiny Notebook的規格與報價，並把此備忘錄寄回台灣，請業務助理Tata Tsai與工程師Willy Tu協助後續事宜。（請自行運用8 Ws。）

1.7 Meeting and Conference 開會與會議

　　對組織而言，開會是部門與部門之間、主管與主管之間、員工與員工之間溝通聯繫的重要、且最常見的管道。會議召開在企業運作中司空見慣，舉凡公司策略制定、部門方針確定等等皆透過相關主管與公司員工共同開會。另外，通過與顧客的正式會議，除加深彼此的合作關係之外，亦可達成雙方的交易買賣。

　　以下範例模擬會議場合，一企業主與遠道而來的客戶之開會場景。

▌會議參考範例▐

Wyncasina Liu: *First of all*, I'd like to thank you, Mr. Hockman, for accepting our invitation to come to Taiwan. It's our great *pleasure* to have you here and you will find this business trip valuable.

Jason Hockman: The pleasure is mine, and I will enjoy my experiences here.

Wyncasina Liu: As you know, our company has been in the market for over 50 years. We know how to *harness* our customers' competencies. Customers are always the foundation of our success. Therefore, we have been *engaging* in an active dialogue with customers than many companies *are used to*.

Mary Cheng: We started this business half a century ago with a limited capital 0.3 million New Taiwan dollars. At that time, we had only 12 employees in a small factory *located* in Taichung County. However, not only is our *turnover* 1.5 billion US dollars, but also we own a big, well-equipped and high-technology *embedded* factory in the Hsin-Chu Science Park. The sales team with twenty-three members is working in our Taipei office, including General Manager, Wyncasina, R&D Director, Bingley and me.

Jason Hockman: I am so impressed. When you mailed me your *company profile* two years ago, you were two third the size you are now.

Wyncasina Liu: That's true. Thanks to our devoted unit heads and employees, efficient management process as well as the outstanding product quality, we can grow rapidly.

Jason Hockman: What's the percentage of your gross profit?

Wyncasina Liu: For the fiscal year 2007, our annual gross profit margin was slightly higher than 20%

Jason Hockman: That sounds great! By the way, I have noticed that you've just launched a brand new product last week. When do you plan to start mass production of this model?

Wyncasina Liu: I am surprised that our new MP4 has drawn your attention. Since the technology is almost mature, it is estimated to *hit the market* in the coming month.

Jason Hockman: I think I shall place a trial order then.

Mary Cheng: I have some samples of the new model MP4 at hand. I can give you one right now to experience its high performance. By the way, it's already time for dinner. I have made a reservation at Shin-Shin Restaurant near the Shilin Night Market, which is famous for Taiwanese local dishes.

Jason Hockman: That's very kind of you.

Wyncasina Liu: In fact, it's time for us to start off, otherwise we'll be struck in a traffic jam.

Jason Hockman: Well, Okay. Let's go!

▌會議參考範例中文翻譯 ▌

劉總：首先，我想謝謝赫可曼先生，接受我們的邀請到訪台灣。您的蒞臨讓我們榮幸備至，您將發現此行是有價值的。

赫可曼：我能拜訪貴公司是我的榮幸！我也將有個愉快的旅途。

劉總：正如您所知的，本公司歷史已超過五十年。我們知道如何駕馭客戶的能力，顧客永遠是本公司成功的基石。因此，與許多公司相比，我們一直都與顧客維持積極互動的對話。

鄭特助：本公司在五十年前創業時，僅有三十萬新台幣資本。當時，我們在台中縣的一家小工廠，只有十二名員工。然而今日，我們不僅僅擁有十五億美金的營業額，在新竹科學園區還有一個很大、設備先進和高科技的廠房。我們在台北辦公室的業務團隊有二十三人，在這還有劉總、研發主管賓立和我。

赫可曼：真令人印象深刻！當你在兩年前，郵寄貴公司簡介給我時，當時的規模還是現在的三分之二而已。

劉總：確實是這樣子的。拜本公司的高階主管和員工們的努力、有效率的管理流程以及高產品品質之賜，我們才得以快速成長。

赫可曼：請問貴公司的毛利是多少？

劉總：在2007年財報，我們的年毛利率約略高於20%。

赫可曼：真不錯！順道一提，我注意到貴公司上週推出一項全新的產品，該產品計畫何時開始大量生產？

劉總：您注意到本公司的新產品——MP4，我感到非常訝異！因為該技術已接近成熟，所以預計上市時間是下個月。

赫可曼：我想我會下個試用訂單。

鄭特助：我手邊有一些MP4新產品的樣本，可以馬上給您一個試用看看它的高效能。順便一提，現在已經是晚餐時間了，我已經訂好了在士林夜市旁，以台菜著稱的欣欣餐廳。

赫可曼：你真好！

劉總：實際上，我們也該出發了，否則我們將陷於車陣之中。

赫可曼：好！咱們出發吧！

■ 人物側寫

Wyncasina Liu：台灣廠商的總經理
Jason Hockman：遠道而來的外國顧客
Mary Cheng：Wyncasina Liu總經理的特別助理

■ 單字解析

first of all (ph.)：首先

First of all, I would like to thank you for putting in so much time and effort into developing this masterpiece.

（首先，我想感謝你們付出這麼多的時間與努力開發這項傑作。）

pleasure (n)：榮幸、愉悅、高興、娛樂

It's my *pleasure* to announce (that) Mr. Mick has been promoted to the Regional Manager.

（宣布米可先生晉升區經理是我的榮幸。）

harness (v)：駕馭、控制、利用

Scientists believed *harnessing* ocean energy would become an emerging business.

（科學家相信利用海洋能源會成為新興產業。）

engage in (ph.)：使從事、忙於

Jason has *engaged in* the enterprise resources planning for 10 years.

（傑生從事企業資源整合已經十年了。）

be used to (ph.)：（現在）習慣於、一向
used to (ph.)：（過去）習慣於、經常

Sales team and marketing team *are used* to working together.

（業務團隊與行銷團隊一向一起工作。）

In this company, managers *used to* work late.

（這家公司的經理通常工作到很晚。）

locate (v)：座落於、設置於

Chedi Hotel *located* its branch office in Bali.

（翠迪飯店將它的分公司設於峇里島。）

Our Sales Department is *located* in New York.

（本公司的業務部門位於紐約。）

turnover (n)：營業額、銷售額

We had a *turnover* of NT \$80 million, and a net profit of NT\$ 13 million last year.

（去年我們的銷售額為八千萬新台幣，純利達一千三百萬新台幣。）

embed (v)：嵌入、埋進

It is not recommended to use the *embedded* code.

（並不建議使用嵌入式編碼。）

company profile：公司簡介

hit the market (ph.)：在市場開賣、上市

This company announces that their new product will *hit the market* next quarter.

（這家公司宣布新產品將於下季上市。）

Meeting and Conference in English：會議英文例句

▶ 應出席者未到場時的表達方式

● Manager Harber is in another meeting and will join us around 2 pm.

（哈伯經理正出席其他會議，他將從兩點起加入。）

● His phone is engaged now and should be with us by 10 o'clock.

（他正電話中，十點前應該會加入我們。）

● I am afraid that Manager Cheng cannot be with us today since he is *out of* country this week.

= Unfortunately, Manager Cheng will not be with us today because he is out of country this week.

（鄭經理今天恐怕無法出席會議，因為他本週出國。）

■ 單字解析

out of (ph.)　缺乏

out of country　出國

out of date　過時、不流行

out of office　不在辦公室

out of order　故障

out of paper　沒紙

out of question　毫無疑問、無庸置疑

out of range　超出範圍（通常指電子產品的錯誤訊息）

out of stock　無現貨

out of time　不合時宜

out of touch　不熟識的、不諳時勢的

out of town　出城

out of work　失業

▶ 在會議開始時，打算中途先離開的表達方式

● I shall leave in the middle of the conference in order to visit a customer.
（我將於中途離開，赴約拜訪客戶。）

● I'm only available until 4:30.
＝ I'll have to leave by 4:30.
（我會在四點半前離開。）

▶ 感謝與會者參加會議

● Good morning/afternoon, ladies and gentlemen, may I have your attention, please?
（早安／午安，各位女士先生，請注意。）

● Thank you for your time to participate in this meeting.
＝ Thank you for your time to join this meeting.
（感謝各位參與會議。）

● We appreciate the time and effort you have put into this.
（感激您對此所投入的時間與精力。）

● Thanks for coming here.
（感謝蒞臨。）

● It's good to see you all again.
（再次見到你們真好。）

● Good morning/afternoon, ladies and gentlemen, let's get started.
（早安／午安，各位女士先生，讓我們開始吧！）

▶ 回顧上次會議記要

● In the beginning, I'd like to quickly **go through** the minutes of our last Monday's meeting.
＝ First, let's go over the report from the last meeting, which was held last Monday.
＝ Here are the minutes of our last meeting, which was on Monday.
（首先，我想快速回顧上週一的會議紀錄。）

▶ **會議記錄**

● Patricia, would you mind taking notes today?

= Patricia, would you mind taking the minutes of the meeting today?

（派翠亞，妳能擔任今天的會議記錄嗎？）

● Could you take the meeting minutes and e-mail them to us afterwards?

（會議記錄完成後請寄給我們？）

● Patricia, could you please send out a summary of today's meeting after it is over?

= Patricia, could you please send us the meeting notes of today's meeting?

= Patricia has kindly agreed to give us a report after the meeting.

（派翠亞，會議結束後，請給我今天的會議紀錄。）

● I will take notes during this meeting and e-mail them to you.

（我會做會議記錄，隨後以電子郵件寄給各位。）

▶ **會議目的**

● Please let me clarify the objectives of today's meeting.

（請讓我確認今日會議召開的目的。）

● There are a few questions I'd like to ask today.

（今天我想問一下一些問題。）

● I called this session to address the crash issue.

= I requested for this meeting to talk about the crash issue.

= The purpose of today's meeting is to discuss the crash issue.

（今天會議召開的目的是討論當機事件。）

▶ 請對方再表達一次

● Can I just make sure I understand that point?
（我能確認我了解意思嗎？）

● Could you explain the operational process more simply?
（你能更簡潔地解釋操作流程嗎？）

● Could you illustrate this slide in detail?
（你能詳細闡明這張投影片的意思嗎？）

● Could you please demonstrate this new product again?
（你能再示範一次新產品的操作嗎？）

● Could you please speak slowly?
（你能講慢一點嗎？）

● Could you please speak more loudly?
（你能說大聲一點嗎？）

● Excuse me. ＝ Pardon.
＝ I couldn't catch that, could you repeat it?
（不好意思，能再說一次嗎？）

● Please clarify the point you've just mentioned.
（請闡明您剛剛提到的論點。）

● I don't get what you've said.
＝ I don't get your point.
＝ Sorry to interrupt, but I'd like to confirm what you just said.
＝ Let me make sure that I understand what you said.
（我並不了解您剛剛所說的內容。）

　　在不清楚對方所表達的含意時，如果使用「I don't understand」，有時是表示不認同對方所提，故使用時要特別小心。

▶ 說明問題

● Could you summarize the basic problem for us?

（您可以為我們總結問題的癥結嗎？）

● Could you hold on a second? We Sales Team would like to discuss the payment term first.

　= Please give us a few moments to discuss the payment term among ourselves.

　= Please give us a few minutes to talk about the payment term as a team.

　= Let us talk about the payment term among ourselves.

（您可以等一下嗎？我們業務團隊想先討論付款條件。）

● **Excuse us**, we're going to discuss this issue in Mandarin.

（對不起，針對此問題我們想以中文討論。）

　　當會議成員來自各國時，如同一團隊成員想以中文交談，此刻，若能先說此句話，就會讓與會者有受到尊重的感覺。並於討論完畢後，以"Thank you for your waiting. We decided that..."回到會議主軸。

● Does this make sense?

　= Is that clear?

　= Do you get the meaning?

　= Do you understand?

（你可以了解剛剛我所說的嗎？）

● Fascinating, Mike! What you are saying is that this is one of those breakthrough technologies that make such an incredible difference to an organization.

（麥克，太棒了！你所指的是這是那些突破性的技術之一，可以帶給組織驚人的差別。）

▶ 開啓新議題

● Let's move onto the next subject.

　＝ Now that we've discussed the technological issues, let's talk about marketing strategies.

　＝ The next topic on today's agenda is marketing strategies.

　＝ Now we come to the question of marketing strategies.

　（讓我們跳到下一個議題。）

▶ 詢問對方的看法

● Jackie, what do you think about the environment-friendly project?

　（傑克，你對環保計劃的看法為何？）

● Would you comment on the environment-friendly project?

　（你對環保計劃的意見為何？）

● Do you have any advice（＝recommendation ＝suggestion）?

　（你的意見、建議為何？）

● Do you have any comment from the marketing point of view?

　（你從市場行銷的觀點來看，建議是？）

● How is the environment-friendly project coming along?

　（環保計劃的進展如何？）

● John, have you completed the testing report on the new accounting software?

　（約翰，你完成新會計軟體的測試報告了嗎？）

▶ 會議結果

贊成→ We are fine with that.

　　　= That seems reasonable.

　　　= That makes sense.

　　　= It sounds good.

　　　= We all agree about that.

　　　= I cannot agree more.

反對→ I disagree with those agreements.

　　　= I object those agreements.

　　　= I just don't like those agreements.

● We are hoping for a different answer. I understand that you've tried. But this strategy will not be workable in our department.

　　（我們期望不同的答案，我了解您已經試了，但是此策略在本部門是行不通的。）

　　陳述反對意見時，可先以 "I understand that..." 表示理解，再以But說明反對理由。

● That might work, but I'm afraid there will be a better solution.

　　（這似乎可行，但恐怕會有更佳的解決方案。）

　　This is a good idea, but we need an official statement, not a workaround.

　　（這是一個好主意，但是我們需要一個正式聲明，而不是應急方案。）

● Oliver, I am still left with a concern. If I was in your position, I'd be thinking about what I wanted from Executive Committee next Monday.

　　（奧莉薇，我還是有個顧慮。假如我從你的立場出發，我會思考下週一我想從主管委員會得到的是什麼。）

▶ 會議中提問

● Richard, this is Susan. May I raise a question?

（李查，我是蘇珊。能提問嗎？）

> 　　提問時，先報上自己的名字是基本禮儀，另外也可讓與會人士更了解你的提問內容與所屬公司或單位的關聯性。

● What does everyone think about this?

（各位的意見為何？）

● Let's put this to the vote.

（讓我們投票決定。）

● I agree with the suggestion because it is a feasible scheme.

（我同意此建議，因為它是可行的方案。）

● I don't quite agree with that point because it is infeasible.

（我不同意此觀點，因為它是不可行的。）

● In my humble opinion, the timetable of this proposal should be modified again.

（依我淺見，該計畫時間表應再次修正。）

● That's a good question. But I cannot answer it right now. Let me look into it and I'll get back to you as soon as possible.

（那是個好問題，但我現在無法回答。讓我深入研究之後，再儘速回覆你。）

● I think we have fully discussed this issue. Let's <u>move</u> (= go on) to next subject.

（我想我們已充分討論過此議題，讓我們移到下個主題吧。）

● We are stuck now. Shall we table this issue till next meeting and go to the final subject?

（目前我們的討論陷於膠著，讓我們將此議題留到下次會議、跳到最後一個主題吧？）

● O. K., Let's go on to next subject since we don't have much time left.

（好了！時間不多了，換到下一個主題吧。）

● We have got off track.

＝ I think we are getting a bit off-topic now.

（我們已經偏離主題。）

● We should get back to the subject at once.

（我們應該馬上回到原來話題。）

● Can we review the situation?

（讓我們稍微整理一下。）

● Okay, everyone, let's calm down.

（不要急，慢慢來。）

● I am trying to put myself in the position of your customers. Won't they want to see the next step forward?

（我試圖從你的客戶的角度看問題，他們不想看看下一步怎麼走嗎？）

▶ 會議結束

● Well, I think our decision covers everything.

（我認為我們的決定涵蓋所有項目。）

● I think that's about all for the time being.

（我想這暫時就是所有的討論內容。）

● Is there anything we should discuss?

　＝ Is there any other business?

　（還有沒有其他我們應該討論的呢？）

● Before we close today's meeting, let me summarize the main points.

　＝ Let me quickly go over today's main points.

　＝ OK, why don't we quickly summarize what we've done today.

　＝ In brief, following are today's main points.

　（結束會議前，讓我總結一下重點。）

● Let me just try and summarise where we've got to and the actions we agreed in the meeting.

　（讓我試著總結我們今天的會議結果，以及我們在會議中同意的行動。）

● Let's bring this to a close for today.

　＝ The meeting is closed.

　＝ I declare the meeting closed.

　（今天會議到此結束。）

● The meeting is finished, we'll see each other next month.

　（今天會議到此結束，下個月見。）

● Thank you for attending.

　＝ Thank you for your participation.

　＝ Thank you for your joining.

　＝ Thank you very much for your precious time to come.

　（感謝參與。）

1.8 Business Etiquette: Good Manners, Good Business 商業禮儀

公司內部每一位員工與顧客之間的互動是非常重要的，雙方都希望對交易往來感到滿意，並不期望因為彼此不了解，而有誤解、不被尊重，甚或有被欺騙的感覺產生。擁有商業禮儀，基本上可以讓雙方處於和諧的情境下，避免不必要的衝突。

商業禮儀涵蓋範圍廣泛，非僅限於與顧客在餐桌上的刀叉用餐禮儀。假如在商務往來中，事先搞懂商業夥伴的文化與社會背景，並對自己的行為舉止能稍加留意，就可以避免矛盾發生。若是在正式場合窘態百出，無法展現出適度的自信，或是讓周遭的人們感到不舒服、不自在，就是未具備商業禮儀。

很不幸的，各個不同國家、文化對禮儀的定義皆不盡相同。不經意冒犯顧客，輕則造成不好的印象，重則失去談判的機會甚至一位既有的客戶。在商務場合中，有時我們很難解釋失去訂單的原因，可能僅出於產品或價格問題，也有可能是在喝開胃酒時，一句言者無心的評論，冒犯了聽者有意的商業夥伴。

有時候特殊的舉止可以達成交易，卻也有可能失去生意。謙恭有禮備受讚許，虛心（open mind）、真誠與為對方著想的溝通態度，將帶給你在商務場合上的無往不利。當然，最重要的還是行為舉止必須符合「道德」（ethics）。不同的國家有著不同的民情風俗（local culture），也深藏著相異的做生意方式。要記住針對來自不同國家的人民，要給予不同的問候與做生意方式喔！

商業禮儀對企業的重要性

American Companies Find Manners Still Matter

（Source: The Epoch Times, http://en.epochtimes.com/news/5-6-28/29917.html）

Businesses are turning to *etiquette* training to boost their *bottom line*, according to the coaches who train employees on everything from shaking hands to buttering bread. Simply put, better-behaved employees are more valuable than *brutish oafs*.

"Etiquette is saying that it's really OK to be nice," said Peter Post, a writer and lecturer on business etiquette. "We've had an attitude in this country that being nice was somehow *counterproductive* to good business, to being successful," he said, adding, "In fact, being nice is a way to be much more successful in business. It has real bottom-line, dollar value."

He's seen demand for etiquette training boom in recent years. "We've heard *over and over* from corporations who have employees with all these skills but can't let them take a client out to lunch," Post said.

About the Etiquette

An etiquette coach answers *an array of* etiquette questions:

—What accessories do people notice first? Watches and pens.

—Where should empty foil butter wrappers go? Fold the foil wrappers in half and place them under the bread plate.

—How does one eat spaghetti at a business dinner? Don't even touch spaghetti; it's too messy.

—Should a man be told that his *fly* is open? Yes, people should be always informed of zipper failure.

In a telling development in the world of business etiquette, Post said he has just added a chapter on *ethics* to the business etiquette book he first published six years ago. Not paying attention to ethics, he said, can be costly. Just look at Tyco International's Dennis Kozlowski, facing prison for stealing the company's money. "We teach people to think before they act. My guess is he wasn't thinking. He was doing. But unfortunately we're responsible for our actions, and now he's responsible for his," Post said.

Experts say modern etiquette is different from just a few years ago. Women's roles have changed, families spend less time in such settings as sit-down meals, children of working parents often *fend for* themselves and television and movies glorify *profanity* and *rough-and-tumble* behavior. In many ways, we're missing a lot in our informal society and loss or tradition.

Back to Basics

Remember to say "please" and "thank you." Somewhere between childhood and adulthood, people stop using those words. A study of people who experienced *incivility* at work, conducted by the *University of North Carolina at Chapel Hill's Kenan-Flagler* Business School, showed how costly it can be. One in five said they worked less hard as a result of rudeness at work, and one in 10 spent less time at the office. Nearly half considered changing jobs, and more than 10 percent did so, the study found. "It's more than just telling a person the rules," said Post. "Etiquette does have value for people. Etiquette makes you a successful person."

▌文章翻譯 ▌

▶ 美國企業發現禮儀仍然十分重要

　　根據禮儀訓練師指出，美國企業正不斷增加員工的禮儀訓練，以加速達到公司預設結果。這些訓練師訓練員工所有的商業禮儀，其中從如何握手到怎麼在吐司麵包上塗奶油。看起來很簡單的一件事，但是好的行爲舉止總比愚昧無知的俗子更有價值。

　　身爲作家同時也是商業禮儀講師的彼得‧普斯特表示：「禮儀就是舉止優美。在美國，禮儀存有毫無建設性一直到能帶來好交易、成功的說法。實際上，好禮儀就是達到企業成功的途徑。禮儀眞的是企業的底限，它的確可以爲企業帶來無限的價值。」普斯特看到了這幾年企業對商業禮儀訓練的增長。他提到：「我們一再聽到即使企業員工擁有所作技能，但是還是無法帶客户出去吃飯。」

▶ 商業禮儀

　　以下列舉禮儀訓練師對禮儀提問的回答：

　　—什麼是人們首先注意到的配件？手錶和筆。

　　—空的奶油包裝紙應擺在哪？將包裝紙對折後放置麵包盤下方。

　　—在商務晚餐中該如何食用義大利麵？建議不要點義大利麵，因爲用叉子食用時吃相不佳。

　　—應告知他人忘了拉拉鍊嗎？是的，當他人忘了拉拉鍊，是應該被告知的。

　　普斯特在他六年前的初版著作《商業禮儀》一書中，加進了一個有關「道德倫理」的章節。他說如果商業禮儀不重視道德，那將付出極高的代價。就像泰科國際的前執行長科茲洛夫一樣，因為挪用公款而入獄服刑。普斯特指出：「我們教導人們三思而後行，我猜想科茲洛夫在作奸犯科時，並未仔細思考犯錯的後果。但不幸的是，我們必須為自己的所作所為負責，現在科茲洛夫也為他的所為負責。」

　　專家指出現代的禮儀與幾年前的禮儀不可同日而語。女性的角色已經改變了，家庭在教養方面所花的時間變少了，諸如：餐桌禮儀。職業父母的小孩通常自行外食，取而代之的是電視、電影輕蔑、草率的行為影響了小孩的行為舉止。很多方面，我們正失去社會上所傳承下來的許多好的文化資產與傳統。

▶ 回歸根本

　　切記將「請」和「謝謝」掛在嘴邊。有時候，小孩和成年人都不再使用這些美好的字眼。一項由北卡羅萊納大學查佩爾希爾分校商學院所執行的研究顯示，無商業禮儀的工作場合企業相應付出高的代價。報告中發現：五分之一的人指出，因為工作環境的魯莽，讓他們工作不認真；十分之一的人不想花太多時間在辦公室。有將近一半的人想換工作，並且已經有超過10%的人已經離職。普斯特說：「禮儀不僅僅只是告訴一個人遊戲規則，它將帶給人價值，更能使你成為一個成功的人。」

■ 單字解析

etiquette (n)：禮儀、禮節、規矩

Business *etiquette* is fundamentally concerned with building relationships founded upon courtesy and politeness between business personnel.

（商業禮儀基本上是商務人士在謙恭與禮貌的基礎上，建立往來關係。）

bottom line (ph.)：底限、概要、結果

The company's *bottom line* is a good profit margin.

（公司的基本要求是好的獲利率。）

brutish oaf (ph.)：粗魯、愚蠢的人

counterproductive (a)：毫無建設性、達不到預期目標

Violation of the company regulation would be *counterproductive*.

（違反公司規定將產生不良結果。）

over and over (ph.)：一再、反覆

civic group (ph.)：民間團體

Civic groups based on the different political stances should be guaranteed the freedom of speech and association.

（由不同政治立場所組成的民間團體，應該被保障言論與結社自由。）

an array of (ph.)：一系列

fly (n)：衣服拉鍊或鈕扣的遮布

ethics (n)：道德、倫理

It is very important to build business *ethics* and corporate social responsibility into the developing organization.

（將企業倫理與企業社會責任注入組織發展是很重要的。）

fend for (ph.)：供養

You have to learn to *fend for* yourself.

（你必須學會自我謀生。）

profanity (n)：不恭敬、侮慢、輕瀆

The use of *profanity* is becoming more and more common and managers are bringing it into the workplace by using it themselves.

（使用輕蔑的言語變得愈來愈常見，經理人自己也在工作場所使用輕蔑的言語。）

rough-and-tumble (ph.)：草率、混戰

incivility (n)：沒禮貌、不文明

Incivility is any action that interferes with a harmonious and cooperative working atmosphere in business.

（沒有禮貌包含任何干擾商業和諧與合作工作氣氛的舉動。）

University of North Carolina at Chapel Hill's Kenan-Flagler：北卡羅萊納大學查佩爾希爾分校

分享區 英國人、美國人、日本人與德國人在大街上掉了一塊錢的故事

　　若是在大街上遺失一元錢，英國人絕不驚慌，至多聳一下肩就依然很紳士地往前走去，好像什麼事也沒發生一樣。美國人則很可能喚來警察，報案之後留下電話，然後嚼著口香糖揚長而去。日本人一定很痛恨自己的粗心大意，回到家中反覆檢討，絕不讓自己再遺失第二次。唯獨德國人與眾不同，會立即在遺失地點的一百平方公尺之內，劃上座標和方格，一格一格地用放大鏡去尋找。

　　還有一則笑話是說，如果啤酒裡有一隻蒼蠅，美國人會馬上找律師，法國人會拒不付錢，英國人會幽默幾句，而德國人則會用鑷子夾出蒼蠅，並慎重其事地化驗啤酒裡是否已經有了細菌。

（以上故事摘錄自大紀元網站，更多文章內容請參閱http://news.epochtimes.com/b5/6/11/28/n1538076.htm）

打招呼方式

Greeting plays an important part in smoothing oral communications.

　　打招呼方式在商務禮儀上占一席之地，但世界各地人士於首次見面時的打招呼方式皆不盡相同，事先搞懂對方的打招呼禮儀是相當重要的。以下是主要的幾種打招呼方式：

1. 握手（handshake）

　　握手是一種很常見的禮儀，某種程度上是自信（self confidence）的表現。一般禮儀上握手是以右手握住對方手掌約兩秒鐘，雙目注視對方，面帶微笑，身體稍微往前傾。握手時舉動應文雅，適度施力，切忌過分用力。

2. 臉頰貼著臉頰（cheek to cheek）

　　臉頰碰臉頰多見於西方、東歐或是阿拉伯國家，是親密朋友間表示親暱的一種見面禮。

3. 擁抱（embrace, hug）

　　擁抱禮較流行於歐美，通常與臉頰碰臉頰同時使用。擁抱禮通常是右臂挾住對方的後肩、左臂挾住對方的後腰部。雙方頭部與上身先向左擁抱，再向右擁抱，最後再次向左擁抱，禮畢。

4. 鞠躬（bow, reverence）

　　鞠躬禮常在中國、日本與韓國使用。一般用於下級對上級、晚輩對長輩，亦用於服務人員對賓客致謝。

5. 微笑（smile）

　　微笑是國際通用的語言，可以縮短人與人之間的距離，為深入溝通創造良好的氛圍。

6. 雙手合十（press the hands together in front of the chest）

合十禮多見於南亞以及東南亞信奉佛教的國家。行禮方式為：兩手掌在胸前對合，略向外傾，掌尖與鼻尖相對。

▶ 常用打招呼的英文句子

- It's so nice to see you.
- It's my great pleasure to meet you today.
- Nice to meet you.
- How are you?
- How are you doing?

（以下是適用於較熟悉的朋友或顧客）

- How have you been?
- How's everything?
- How's it going?
- Long time no see.
- What's up?
- What's going on recently?

商務往來英文
English for Business Communication

2.1 Business Letter Format 商用書信寫作

　　商用書信收件對象不外是企業顧客、經銷商、配銷商、供應商等合作夥伴，此外也可能是公司同事或者是一般消費者。所以，在準備或撰寫商用書信時，想看看如果你是收信者，你期待收到什麼樣的信件內容？交辦事項都詳列清楚或解決了嗎？要傳遞的訊息明確表達了嗎？信件格式正確嗎？設身處地為對方著想時，企業要建立起良好的顧客關係就輕而易舉！

Golden Rules for Business Letter：商用書信撰寫準則

- **Heading**—give your letter a heading which will make it easier for the reader to understand your purpose in writing.
  下標題：在書信起始時，下一簡潔標題，例如：「報價」，以表示去函目的或緣由，讓對方在最短的時間內就可以一目了然來信目的。

- **Plan ahead**—decide what you are going to say before you start to write a letter. Because if you don't do this, the sentences are likely to go on and on until you can think of a good way to finish.

計畫書寫內容：書寫信函時先草擬大綱，列出去函目的與交辦事項，哪些重點該提，哪些內容可以省略。事前擬稿可避免龐雜無章的內容。

- **Short sentences, short words**—use short sentences and short words that everyone can understand.

儘量使用簡潔有力的句子與單詞，讓對方可以很快了解來意。

- **Number each paragraph**—put each separate idea in a separate paragraph. Number each of the paragraphs which will help the reader to understand better.

段落分明：商用書信忌不分段落，將所有想表達的內容一股腦兒宣洩。建議為了讓讀者更了解書信內涵，不同主題必須分段闡述。

- **Think about your reader.**

書信內容與出發點永遠以客為尊，時時奉「顧客至上」為圭臬。

▶ 撰寫書信時，須注意內容是否符合下列5Cs

1. CLEAR（清晰）

- your reader can see exactly what you mean.

意思表達須明確。

2. COMPLETE（完整）

● make sure all the necessary information is included.

商業信函內容必須完整，如：邀請函應詳細說明時間、地點等。

3. CONCISE（簡潔）

● your customer is probably a busy businessman with no time to waste.

想看看：或許你的客戶是一位忙碌的生意人，他的寶貴時間是不容恣意浪費。所以，一封簡潔易懂的書信，對他而言就益顯重要。

(1) 簡潔語句的運用

● We wish to acknowledge the receipt of your letter...

可簡潔為：**We appreciate your letter...**（我們感激您的來函……）

● Enclosed herewith please find two copies of...

可簡潔為：**We enclosed two copies of...**或**Please find enclosed two copies of...**（隨函附上兩份……）

(2) 短句或單詞的運用

Enclosed herewith → **enclosed**

at this time → **now**

due to the fact that → **because**

a draft in the amount of \$2,000 → **a draft of \$2,000**

4. COURTEOUS（謙恭）

● make sure the letter is written in a sincere and polite tone.

寫信時要多從對方的立場考量，而非僅從自身想法出發，語氣上將可更尊重對方。措詞要有禮且謙恭，及時地回信也是禮貌的表現。

【例句】

◯ We have received your letter of 26 July **with many thanks**.

（我們很感謝收到您於7月26日寄出的信函。）

◯ **It's our great pleasure** to send you our latest catalog.

（能寄給貴公司最新型錄是本公司最大的榮幸。）

◯ You will be particularly interested in a special offer on page 2 of the latest catalog **enclosed**, which you requested in your letter of 26 July.

（您將特別對附上的最新型錄中第二頁的特別優惠有興趣，該型錄是您於7月26日的來函中索取的。）

◯ You earn 3% discount when you pay cash, and we will send you the brochure next month.

（當您付現時，可享九七折折扣。我們將於下個月寄目錄給您。）

✕ We allow 3% discount for cash payment. We won't be able to send you the brochure this month.

（我們允許客戶付現時享九七折，我們無法於本月寄目錄給你。）

5. CORRECT（正確）

● avoid any mistake in grammar, punctuation mark or spelling.

應避免犯任何文法、標點符號以及拼字上的錯誤。為有效杜絕拼字錯誤，可以利用word所提供的「拼字檢查」作全面的核對。

(1) 避免用詞錯誤

✕ As to the steamers sailing from Kaohsiung to San Francisco, we have **bimonthly** direct services.

此處bimonthly用法會產生歧義：可以是twice a month（一個月兩次）或者every two months（兩個月一次），建議改寫為：

○ 1. We have **two** direct sailings **every month** from Kaohsiung to San Francisco.

（每個月從高雄到舊金山有兩次直航班。）

○ 2. We have **semimonthly** direct sailing from Kaohsiung to San Francisco.

（每半個月從高雄到舊金山有一次直航班。）

(2) 注意詞語所放的位置

● We will be able to supply 6 cases of the item **only**.

（我們將只能夠供應六箱商品。）（可能有多項商品。）

● We will be able to supply 6 cases **only** of the item.

（我們將只能夠供應該項商品六箱。）（只有一項商品。）

(3) 注意句子的結構

● We sent you 5 samples of the goods yesterday which you requested in your letter of May 20 **by air**.

（我們昨日已將你於5月20日寄出的航空信件中所要求的五個樣品寄出。）

● We sent you, **by air**, 5 samples of the goods which you requested in your letter of May 20.

（我們已將你在5月20日信件中所要求的五個樣品，以空運寄出了。）

【Remember】A dull or confusing layout makes a letter difficult to
read.
（一封辭不達意或格式不清的商用書信將讓對方不易讀懂。）

商用書信書寫步驟

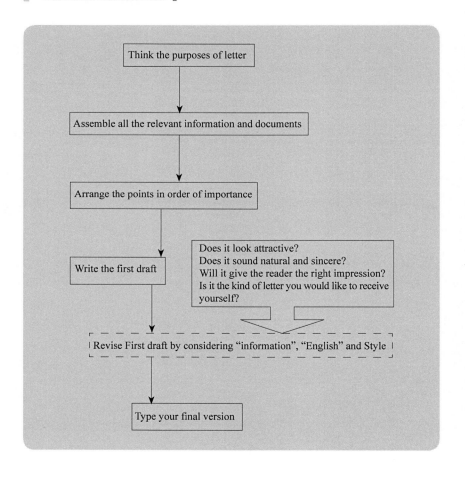

　　本節提供撰寫商用書信的流程（如上圖所示），供參考。首先思考書信的主題與目的，然後找出相關資訊與文件，並將所有訊息內容消化整合，再依照其重要性安排先後次序。之後，以「起、承、轉、合」的寫作方式撰寫一份初稿。完成後，依訊息內容、英文文法、拼字與商用書信格式加以潤飾；看看此篇書信內容是否具吸引力？所表達的陳述是否正確無誤？表達方式是否自然與真誠？該封信件是否能帶給讀者好的、正面的印象？如果你是收件人，是否願意收到這樣的一封信？如此種種面向都考慮完全後，那一封完備的商用書信便大功告成。

　　另外，除了書信內容，正式完整的商用書信尚須包含下列子項目：寄件人公司名稱與聯絡方式（地址、電話、傳真、e-mail）、收信人的公司名稱與聯絡方式（地址、電話、傳真、e-mail）、書信撰寫日期、收信人名字與稱謂、信函主旨、主文（撰寫流程如上所述）、問候語、寄件人姓名與職稱，若是有附件的話，請再加上附註。

　　如果知道對方的名字與職稱，儘量於信件開啟的稱謂表明。如果是紙本信件，應以原稿寄出，避免使用原稿的影本，以示正式與尊重對方。如果企業以大量印刷制式的信件廣發顧客群，這樣要建立進一步企業客戶良好關係是很難的。

　　一般的商務信函是以二十磅紙張為主，重要信件多使用三十二磅紙張。信函紙張以白色最為正式，雖然有些公司也開始使用淡色彩紙張，可是要避免使用色彩過於鮮豔或強烈的紙張作為書信用紙。排版時，文字以單行間距（single space）為主，若信件內容較少，可使用兩倍行高（double space）。段落與段落間的區隔可以空一行分開，讓收件人容易閱讀，結尾敬辭前可以空兩行，另外別忘了留三到四行的空間供簽名使用。

商用書信的呈現方式多樣，以下提供較常用的格式供參考。

【信封範例】

【內文範例】

RESORT & HOTEL

EGI

company name, logo, contact details

inside address

subject

date

body of letter/
main message

complimentary close

signature
position, company name

enclosure direction

▎ 商用書信參考範例 1 ▎

WORLDIGITAL CORPORATION

262 BACAL AVENUE, HIWAY
MAMBALING, CEBU CITY 6000
PHILIPPINES

Dear Sir / Madam,

WORLDIGITAL CORPORATION is a fully integrated technical service company that provides high quality services in the area of **troubleshooting, maintenance** and at the same time, we also offer product or items assistance at a very reasonable price. We work with our clients to make the most effective technical service output as much as possible.

We provide brand new computer parts or items such as Monitor, Motherboard, Processor, Memory, Video Card, Hard Disk, Mouse, Keyboard, DVD Rewriter, Headset, Microphone, Cables, Networking parts, Ink Cartridges, UPS, Toners, Speakers, Windows & Office License, Router, and etc. **In addition to** this, we also have Computer Sets, Laptop, Printer, and Office Supplies. At the same time, we deliver items and give a 30 days term.

For more inquiries and updated price, purchase order and **quotation** information, please call or fax our office and look for JUVY - 417-4955.

We trust that you will find our proposed system suitable and responsive to your needs. We look forward to a mutual business relationship with you.

Respectfully yours,

JUVY Bacayas

Sales In-charge
Tel No.: (032) 417-4915 Fax : (032) 417-8203 / 417-8613
Email: juvy@worldigital.com.ph

▌商用書信參考範例中文翻譯 1 ▌

WORLDIGITAL CORPORATION

262 BACAL AVENUE, HIWAY

MAMBALING, CEBU CITY 6000

PHILIPPINES

敬啓者,尊鑑:

　　WORLDIGITAL公司是一家完全整合技術服務廠商,我們提供疑難排解、維修等高品質服務,同時也提供價格合理的產品與零件。我們儘可能地提供我們的顧客最有效的技術服務。

　　本公司提供全新的電腦周邊與零件,如:螢幕、主機板、處理器、記憶體、顯示卡、硬碟、滑鼠、鍵盤、DVD燒錄機、耳機、麥克風、電纜、網路設備、墨水匣、不斷電電源供應器、碳粉匣、喇叭、微軟產品、路由器等等。此外,本公司也銷售桌上型電腦、筆記型電腦以及辦公室設備。同時,我們提供產品宅配與三十天的付款條件。

　　如欲知更多訊息與最新價格表、訂貨單或報價資訊,請打電話或傳真到我們的辦公室。請找朱碧,電話是417-4955。

　　我們確信您將發現我們所建議的系統將符合並回應您的需求。期待與貴公司建立雙方生意往來的關係。

恭敬的

朱碧‧巴卡雅斯

業務負責人

Tel No.: (032) 417-4915 Fax: (032) 417-8203 / 417-8613

Email: juvy@worldigital.com.ph

■ 單字解析

troubleshooting (n)：疑難排解

Troubleshooting is a process of eliminating potential causes of a problem.

（疑難排解是一種解除問題潛在導因的過程。）

maintenance (n)：維護、維修、保養

System *maintenance* is performed by engineers.

（工程師執行系統維護。）

in addition to (ph.)：除……之外

In addition to foreign language, the job position also requires good communication skills.

（除了外語能力之外，此工作職位尚須良好的溝通技巧。）

quotation (n)：報價單、估價單

Please find attached our latest *quotation*.

（請參考附件本公司最新的報價單。）

respectfully (adv)：恭敬地

Everybody stood *respectfully* when the general manager entered the office.

（當總經理進辦公室時，每個人都恭敬地站好。）

商用書信參考範例 2

ANEBELLE MARKETING

71 Sap Road, Bally Down, Ireland BT24 8LU

Tel/Fax: 01238-561085

12/10/2008

Miss Cliare Chuang
Hi-Speed Co., Ltd
8F No.276 Chin-Kuo Road
Taichung , Taiwan 407
Your reference : HS/501

- -

Dear Claire,

Just to let you know I received your shipment today in good order.

Thank you for your **prompt** service and **courtesy** in this manner. It is much **appreciated** as the product was needed to facilitate a major customer of this company.

In the meantime some items from that delivery have gone on day one, so this product may have some potential if it is presented to the market quickly. What are your company thoughts on this subject? Please let me know. Please send me any relevant marketing information and promotional materials or drafts on this if they are available.

Please also let me have the prices of cameras and other products ASAP. It will be highly grateful if the information of the rest of your product range can be also provided.

Thank you very much for your kind attention. I hope to hear from you soon.

Best Regards,

Sean Maguire

Marketing Manager

▌商用書信參考範例中文翻譯 2 ▌

安納貝爾行銷公司

71 Sap Road, Bally Down, 愛爾蘭　BT24 8LU（郵遞區號）
電話／傳真：01238-561085
Miss Cliare Chuang（收信人：克萊兒・莊）
Hi-Speed Co., Ltd（公司名稱）
8F No.276 Chin-Kuo Road（地址）
Taichung , Taiwan 407
Your reference: HS/501（信件主題：有關Hi-Speed公司 HS/501型號的產品）
12/10/2008（寫信日期）

親愛的克萊兒，妳好：

　　想讓妳知道我們已於今日收到妳寄來完好無缺的貨物。謝謝妳迅速與禮貌的服務，真的感謝！因為這批貨是要交付給我們一位重要的顧客的。

　　此時，這批貨的某些產品項目也在第一天就銷售一空。所以，也許當這個產品快速推出市場時，將具有某種銷售潛力。請讓我知悉貴公司對此產品市場反應的看法。請寄給我任何與該項產品有關的市場行銷訊息以及促銷資料。

　　也請妳儘快地告知相機與其他產品的價格，如果貴公司還能一併提供其他產品系列的訊息，將十分感謝。

　　謝謝妳的留意。期待能很快接到妳的消息。

致予最深的問候

妳誠摯的朋友

史恩・馬奎爾（行銷經理）敬上

■ 單字解析

prompt (a)：迅速的、即時的

Our clients are truly impressed by our *prompt* service.

（本公司的即時服務深深地打動了我們的客戶。）

courtesy (n)：慇勤、謙恭有禮

We got free advertisement through the *courtesy* of the local newspaper.

（透過地方報社的提供，我們得到了免費的廣告。）

▌ 商用書信參考範例 3 ▌

LEAMINGTOM FLAVOURS

No.186 Best Road
HsinChu Science Park
HsinChu 300
Taiwan
Tel: 886-3-5577888
Fax: 886-3-5577889

Susan Powell
Sterling Trading
37 Ally Drive
Spring Technology Park
Melbourne 30011
Australia

13 October 2008

Your reference: 20081012

Dear Susan,

You asked us to send you our price list and catalog for the new season. I am sure that you will be interested in our brand new products. You will notice that every single product is made from 100% natural ingredients. We use no artificial additives at all.

This year, for the very first time, the samples of our top ten popular aromas have been included for your trial. I think you will agree that our product is second to none and is an outstanding value for money.

Should you have any enquiry, please do not hesitate to contact me. I look forward to hearing from you soon.

Very truly yours,

James Hsieh

Sales Manager

Enclosed: catalog, price list, order form

▌ 商用書信參考範例中文翻譯 3 ▌

列明頓香料

No.186 Best Road
HsinChu Science Park
HsinChu 300
Taiwan
Tel: 886-3-5577888
Fax: 886-3-5577889

Susan Powell（收信人）
Sterling Trading（公司名稱）
37 Ally Drive（地址）
Spring Technology Park
Melbourne 30011
Australia

13 October 2008

Your reference: 20081012（信件主題：回覆收件人在2008年10月12日寄的信件）

親愛的蘇珊，妳好：

　　妳要我們寄去最新一季的產品目錄與價目表，我確定妳將對本公司全新的產品感到興趣。妳將發現我們每一項產品都是100%天然成分製成，完全不使用人工添加物。

　　今年本公司首度附上銷售最佳前十名的香料給貴顧客試用，我想妳會同意我們的產品絕對是首屈一指，且物超所值。

　　若有垂詢，請不要猶豫與我聯繫。期待很快收到妳的訊息。

妳最真誠的

詹姆士・謝（業務經理）敬上

隨信附上：產品目錄、價目表與訂單。

■ 商用書信開啓的稱謂（salutation）

(1) 如不知對方姓名與性別，可以"Dear Sir/Madam,"表示，亦即中文書信「敬啟者」的意思。

(2) 若知道對方的性別，但未知姓名，男士以"Dear Sir,"表示，女士以"Dear Madam,"表示。

■ 收信人與相呼應的結尾敬辭（complimentary close）

(1) 如以"Dear Mr. Roman,"或"My Dear Ms. Champell,"稱謂，原則上結尾敬辭使用**"Yours sincerely,"**呼應。**"Yours sincerely,"**，是相識者之間最適宜的結尾敬辭。

(2) 至於熟悉的好友，如"Dear Lily,"或"My Dear Tony,"，相對應的結尾敬辭可使用**"Yours ever"**或**"As ever"**。

(3) 若以"Dear Sir/Madam,"或"Dear Sir,"或"Dear Madam,"的稱謂，配合使用的結尾敬辭是**"Yours faithfully,"**，這是商業書信中最正規的結尾敬辭。同時也可以**"Yours truly,"**表達。也有愈來愈多人以"Yours sincerely,"作為結尾敬辭，當然也可以使用**"Yours very sincerely,"**來表示彼此的更親近。

(4) **"Yours faithfully,"**和**"Yours truly,"**的用法多適用於彼此相識的律師、醫師、銀行職員或證券交易員等。

(5) 另，除**"Yours..."**之外的結尾敬辭，也可以使用**"Best regards,"**、**"Kind regards,"**、**"Warmest regards,"**或只用**"Regards,"**代替，另也可以寫成**"Best Wishes,"**。

(6) 在書信開啟時，稱謂中每個英文單字都必須大寫，如**"Dear Mr. Bush"**。而結尾敬辭中第一個英文單字也要大寫，句尾要加逗點，如"Yours faithfully,"，"**Best regards,**"。再者，以"**Yours...**"帶出的敬辭也可以表達成：如"Yours faithfully,"→"**Faithfully yours,**"，"Yours sincerely,"→"**Sincerely yours,**"，"Yours ever,"→"**Ever yours,**"等。

■ 商用書信中常見各國公司的寫法

(1) **Co., Ltd** ＝ Company Limited是「股份有限公司」的意思，台灣的公司英文名稱多用Co., Ltd表示。

(2) **Inc.**是Incorporation的縮寫，根據法律所組成的公司，是「有限公司」的意思。在美國常用Inc.一詞。

(3) **Pty., Ltd**則是 Private company limited的簡寫，也是「有限公司」的意思。

(4) **LLC**是Limited Liability Company（有限責任公司、股份有限公司）的縮寫。LLC並不像Inc.正規、組織規模龐大，Inc.除了向政府繳交公司所得稅外，股東還要繳納紅利所得稅，屬雙重稅收制。但LLC則享有公司稅收優惠，股東所得可直接以個人收入繳納個人所得稅，避免了雙重稅收。

(5) **GmbH**（Gesellschaft mit beschränkter Haftung）為德文「公司」的意思，直接翻成英文是company with limited liability，「有限責任公司」的意思。

(6) **S. A.**在法國、西班牙皆表示「股份有限公司」的意思。

(7) **S. P. A**是義大利文「股份有限公司」的意思。

2.2 The Sample Sentences 商用書信例句

　　本節節錄不同商務流程上英文句子的表達方式，使讀者先熟悉商用英文的模式。後面章節將針對重要的商務往來階段英文用法做更詳細的介紹，內容包括電子郵件撰寫、詢價與報價、銷售、經銷與契約、客戶抱怨與處理等。本節最後一部分羅列一般企業各種職務職稱的中英文對照表。

▍禮貌開啓語

- Thank you for staying with us at Plantation Bay Resort. We hope your stay has been most delightful.

  （感謝您入宿森林海灣渡假村，我們希望您於住宿期間有最愉快的假期。）

- Your company has been highly recommended by the Taipei World Trade Center.

  （台北世貿中心極力向我們推薦貴公司。）

- Having your contact information from the Bureau of Foreign Trade of Taiwan, we now avail ourselves of this opportunity to write to you and see if we can establish business relations by a start of some transactions.

  （我們從台灣國貿局獲悉貴公司聯繫訊息，想藉此機會向您介紹敝公司並期望建立生意往來。）

- From the Taipei Representative Office, we have obtained your company details and understand that you are experienced importers of computers. Therefore, we have great interests in setting up a business relationship with you.

  （從台北代表處獲悉貴公司專營電腦，我們有極大興趣想與貴公司開展業務關係。）

● We learn from Barkin Companies, Inc. that McGrow specializes in motor parts, and would like to build business relationships with you.
（承巴金公司的介紹，獲悉貴公司麥格洛專精於汽車零件，我們想與貴公司開展業務關係）。

● We have heard from the Economic Division, Taipei Representative Office in the Federal Republic of Germany that you are the best in the market for Home Appliances.
（駐德國台北代表處經濟組向我們推薦貴公司，貴公司執家電用品牛耳。）

● Through the courtesy of Davidson Corporation located in Sydney, we have learned that you are one of the leading exporters of body care.
（承雪梨大衛遜公司告知，貴公司是當地身體保養產品的重要出口商之一。）

● The Sity Bank in your city has been kind enough to inform us that you are skillful at bicycle-manufacturing and interested in trading with Taiwan in this field.
（承蒙貴地史悌銀行告知，貴公司專精於自行車製造並有意與台灣進行該方面的貿易。）

● We are given to know that you are potential buyers of stationery made in Taiwan, which comes within the frame of our business activities.
（據悉貴公司是台灣文具潛在買主，而該商品正屬於我們的業務範圍。）

▌建立生意關係

● We are well-known in trade circles.
（我們在貿易界很有名望。）

● Our company mainly trades in arts and crafts.
（我們公司主要經營手工藝品。）

● Norbain is a worldwide supplier of security products and provides a first class sales and support service.
（諾班是一家世界級安全器材供應商，並且提供一流的銷售與支援服務。）

● Our purpose is to explore any possibility of developing trade with you.
（我們的目的是開發彼此發展貿易的任何可能性。）

● We plan to develop direct contact with the Continental buyers.
（我們計劃與歐陸買主建立直接的生意往來。）

● We make a great progress in our business with Japan.
（我們在日本業務推廣上有很不錯的進展。）

● We have been doing quite well in our business and are willing to open an account with you.
（我們的生意一直很好，希望能與貴公司建立生意往來的關係。）

● We have been interested in making an investment in Australia.
（我們一直對在澳洲投資很感興趣。）

● Being one of the largest manufacturers of electronic products in Hsin-Chu city, we wish to set up business relationships with you.
（我們是新竹市最大的電器製造商之一，希望與你們建立生意往來關係。）

● Because of the rapid growth of our business in Asia, it is necessary to open branches at the following countries.

（鑑於本公司在亞洲地區業務的迅速成長，有必要在下列地點設立分公司。）

● If you agree with our proposal of a barter trade, we'll give you paper in exchange for your timber.

（如果你方同意我們進行易貨貿易的建議，我們將用紙與你們交換木材。）

● Shall we sign a triangle trade agreement?

（我們簽訂一個三角貿易協議好嗎？）

● A triangle trade can be carried out among the three of us.

（我們三方可進行三角貿易。）

● If you're interested in the leasing program, please fell free to let us know.

（如果你們有意做租賃方案，請隨時告訴我們。）

● We'll try our best to widen our business relationship with Ayala Corp.

（我們將盡全力擴大與Ayala公司的生意往來。）

● We have been working on expanding our scope of cooperation with Leeds, Inc.

（我們一直努力擴大與里茲公司的合作範圍。）

● We look forward to reactivating our business relationship.

（盼望我們的生意往來重新活絡起來。）

● We shall welcome a chance to renew our friendly relationship.

（很高興能有機會來恢復我們的友好關係。）

● When will you introduce your branch office to us?

（什麼時候把貴公司的分公司介紹給我們？）

● Would you please recommend some reliable handicrafts exporters in Thailand?

（請推薦我們一些可靠的泰國手工藝品出口商好嗎？）

● If you are interested in distributing our other products, please kindly inform your requirements as well as the special terms and conditions (＝ T&C).

（假如貴公司有意經營本公司其他產品，請告知您的需求以及特殊的服務條款與細則。）

▋通知和邀請顧客

● We would appreciate if you could inform us of your departure time so we can update our records.

（我們將感謝您，假如您可以告知您的離開時間，讓我們得以更新紀錄。）

● I would like to inform you that our factory has moved to the above new address.

（特此通知，本廠已遷移至上述的新地址。）

● We are pleased to notify you that our business will be turned into a limited company from 1st of September.

（很榮幸通知貴公司：本公司將從9月1日起變更為股份有限公司。）

● Notice is hereby given that the annual general meeting of the stockholders will be held at the Waterfront Club on March 7.

（特此函告：年度股東大會將於3月7日在水濱俱樂部召開。）

● By this, you are advised that Mr. Martin has been paid US$ 12 million today.

（據此：今日我們已經付給馬丁先生一千二百萬美元。）

● Please do not hesitate to contact our Duty Manager through our service center at extension 0, should you need any further assistance.

（假如您需要任何進一步的協助，請不要猶豫透過打分機0與我們服務中心的值班經理聯繫。）

● Welcome to Taipei, may you had a pleasant flight and hope you will enjoy your stay here in Taiwan. Soon as you're rested, may I request the pleasure of your company either lunch or dinner at your most convenient time today.

（歡迎蒞臨台北，期待您有個愉快的飛行，並且希望您將享受待在台灣的這幾天。當您充分休息後，期望今天得以榮幸地邀請您，在您最便利的時間，一起享用午餐或是晚餐。）

● Please help us in our pursuit for excellence by sharing your thoughts with us.

（請提供您寶貴的意見，讓本公司得以繼續追求卓越。）

▎答覆顧客來函或詢問

● We are so glad to answer your inquiry concerning Sterring Company.

（我們很榮幸告知您有關史德霖公司的情況。）

● In answer to your inquiry for coal, we can offer you 20 tons.

（有關貴公司詢問煤一事，我們可提供貴公司二十噸煤。）

● In response to your letter of the 26th of October, we are sorry to inform you that we are unable to take the price offered.

（回覆貴公司10月26日來函，本公司無法承購貴公司開價的產品。）

● Replying to your letter of the 17th respecting the payment, I will send you a cheque (= check) shortly.

（關於17日付款信函一事，我將馬上寄支票給你。）

● Kindly excuse our not replying to your letter of January 8th until today.

（請原諒我們至今才回覆貴公司1月8日的來信。）

● We are offering a sound product with competitive price.

（我們提供貴公司物美價廉的商品。）

● To keep you informed of our latest range of digital cameras, I have enclosed a product catalogue for your information.

（為了讓你更清楚我們最新的數位相機產品，茲附上產品型錄供參考。）

● We are happy to acknowledge the receipt of 2nd June letter.

（很高興6月2日來函已收到。）

● The goods will be dispatched by air immediately.

（這批貨物將馬上空運給貴公司。）

● Please give us the forwarding instructions as soon as possible.

（請儘快告知船務事宜。）

● Kindly acknowledge receipt, and have the goods sent by the last steamer in December.

（產品已於12月最後一輪船航班寄出，貨到時惠請告知。）

● We would like to confirm our call last week regarding the offers.

（想與您確認上週透過電話討論的報價內容。）

● It's our pleasure to confirm the order which you had just placed with us yesterday.

（很榮幸與您確認昨天您向我們下的訂單。）

● Please find enclosed the related documents.

＝ Please find the enclosed related documents.

（請查閱附加相關文件。）

● We would like to place the following orders with you.

（我們想跟你們訂貨。）

● Referring to our telephone conversation this morning, we enclose an advertising brochure.

（據今早的談話內容，隨函附上一份本公司廣告冊。）

● With reference to our sales representative, we are pleased to tell you that we have found the receipt for the goods.

（在敝公司業務代表的協助下，我們已經找到貨物收據。）

詢問顧客

- What can I do to help?
  （我能幫什麼嗎？）

- How do you feel about the new proposal?
  （您對新企劃案的看法為何？）

- Do you mind if I ask why you decide on 50 people in Phase I?
  （您介意假如我請教您為什麼第一階段您決定五十人呢？）

- Why is the new service being pioneered in this region?
  （為什麼在該地區開始這項新的服務呢？）

隨函附件

- Please find enclosed our brochure for your reference.
  （隨函附上敝公司產品簡介。）

- Enclosed you will find an invoice of 30 cases of goods.
  （隨信附上三十箱貨物的發票。）

- A stamped envelope is enclosed for reply.
  （隨函附上回郵信封，請回覆。）

- We enclosed an account statement for your remittance at your earliest convenience.
  （隨函附上對帳單，希儘速匯款。）

- To avoid delays, please verify your bills by reviewing the attached folio.
  （為避免耽擱您的時間，請檢視附件單據以確認您的帳單金額。）

- We appreciate if you fill out the attached Guest Questionnaire and present it to the Front Desk when you check out.
  （感謝您可以為我們填寫附件的顧客問卷調查表，並請於退房時繳到我們的接待櫃檯。）

▌道歉

- At this moment, I could only ask you to accept my apologies.
  （此刻我僅能請求您接受我的道歉。）

- We do apologize for any inconvenience this might have caused you.
  （非常抱歉可能造成的不便。）

- We received your fax dated 3rd of April, and regret informing you that it is impossible for us to deliver the goods on time.
  （4月3日來函已收到，但無法準時交貨甚感抱歉。）

- We are sorry to learn that your manager is still dissatisfied with the payment terms.
  （很抱歉知悉您的經理仍對付款條件感到不滿。）

- I've tried every effort but I'm afraid we cannot do it in the timescale you want. I am sorry, but on this occasion we have no alternative.
  （我已經盡力了，但是我擔心我們無法在您期望的時間表內完成。很抱歉，在此情況下我們別無選擇。）

- I regret to inform you that two cases of the goods are in bad condition.
  （我們遺憾通知您：有兩箱貨物品質不良。）

▌感謝顧客

- We thank you for your inquiry.
  （感謝您的詢問。）

- Thank you very much for your courtesy.
  （感謝您的好意。）

● Thank you for giving us the opportunity to quote.

（感謝貴公司惠賜機會讓我們報價。）

● Thank you so much for your order.

（謝謝下單。）

● Thank you very much for your cooperation.

（謝謝你們的合作。）

● Your attendance to our booth during the Taipei Trade Show is grateful.

（感謝貴公司出席本公司在台北貿易展的展覽席。）

● Your kind assistance is deeply appreciated.

（非常感激您熱心的協助。）

● We are delighted to serve you at any time.

＝ We are glad to be at your service.

（我們隨時樂意為您服務。）

● While thanking you for your support in the past years, I wish you have a continuous confidence in our new company.

（在感謝您過去支持的同時，希望對新公司也繼續給予支持。）

● In the past ten years, we have done a lot of trade with each other.

（在過去的十年裡，貴我雙方做了很多生意。）

● We sincerely thank you for your valued cooperation on this matter and assure you the best service.

（我們誠摯地感謝您對此事具價值的合作，並且確保提供您最佳的服務。）

● Thank you once again for giving us the opportunity to serve you and we hope to welcome you back very soon.

（再次感謝給我們機會為您服務，本公司期望您的再次光臨。）

Company Organization公司組織

▎Job Position 工作職稱 ▎

工作職稱	英文說法	工作職稱	英文說法
董事長	chairman	總經理／執行長	CEO (Chief Executive Officer)
董事會	board of directors	財務長	CFO (Chief Financial Officer)
總裁	president	營運長	COO (Chief Operation Officer)
副總裁	vice president	資訊長	CIO (Chief Information Officer)
總經理	general manager（美式）	人資長	CKO (Chief Knowledge Officer)
	managing director（英式）	秘書／幹事	secretary
副總經理	deputy general manager	主任秘書	chief secretary
總經理特助	general manager assistant	協理／主管	executive / director
	special assistant to GM	處長	director
顧問	consultant	廠長	factory director / factory chief
發言人	spokesman	公關經理	PR manager
律師	lawyer	經理／主任	manager
專案經理	project manager	業務經理	sales manager
副理	assistant (＝ deputy) manager	襄理	junior manager
課長	section manager	組長	supervisor
管理師	administrator	專員	specialist
資深專員	senior specialist	高級專員	advisory specialist

業務代表	sales/client representative	法務部	legal department
記者	reporter	人力資源人員	HR administrator
品管人員	quality controller	工程師	engineer
研發工程師	research and development engineer (R&D)	技術支援工程師	field application engineer
稽核員	auditor	操作員	operator
辦事員	clerk	職員	staff
出納員	cashier	技術員	technician
櫃台接待	receptionist	總機	operator
研究員	researcher	助理	assistant
業務助理	MA = marketing assistant	行政助理	AA = administrative assistant
研究助理	RA = research assistant	教學助理	TA = teaching assistant

練習題① 中翻英

1. 本公司從安全雜誌上看到貴公司的廣告訊息，想藉此機會與貴公司建立生意往來關係。

2. 據悉貴公司正在找尋太陽能電視的供應商，很榮幸通知您本公司的產品正屬於此範疇。

3. 特此通知，本公司自下個月起將移至新廠房辦公。

4. 很抱歉至今才回覆貴公司上週三的來函。

5. 茲附上本公司最新產品目錄，以供參考。

6. 想與您確認貴公司剛剛寄來確認訂單的電子郵件內容。

7. 隨函附上本月的貨款明細。

8. 非常感謝您的協助。

9. 謝謝貴公司訂貨。

10. 我們一直對在北歐投資感到興趣。

練習題② Write a reply letter in accordance with enquiry from overseas customer

　　請練習撰寫一封完整的英文信函，描述Mercia Tech公司的業務經理Helen Wu答謝Roster公司副總裁Fred Dabenson於2009年3月18日來函決定下訂五萬台最新款的數位相機。Helen Wu並於信中允諾可以優惠價格並於兩週之內交貨。

▶ 信件中必須涵蓋

1. 公司名稱、公司的聯絡方式（地址、電話、傳真、e-mail）
2. 顧客的公司名稱與聯絡方式（地址、電話、傳真、e-mail）
3. 書信日期
4. 顧客名字與稱謂
5. 信函主旨
6. 信函主文
7. 問候語
8. 寄件人姓名、職稱
9. 若有附註，可自行加入

2.3 E-mail Writing 電子郵件撰寫

　　網際網路的普及對全球商業環境產生極大的影響，以往的商業書信郵寄往返與傳真已經大部分被電子郵件所取代。目前在商業流程上的溝通多透過電子郵件傳達，以節省時間與成本。但讀者在商場上使用電子郵件的方式可不行與和朋友通電子郵件慣用的方式相比，本節將告訴你如何慎用此一新興的商用書信模式。

　　一封成功的電子郵件常常取決於清晰的表達與具說服力的內容，一封令人印象深刻的電子郵件，可讓讀者在最短的時間內了解全文意涵。以下列出九個使用電子郵件時的要點，包含：落標言簡意賅、一目了然的主題、謹慎使用「緊急」一詞、小心使用「cc」功能、郵件內容切中主題、明列對不同收信人的交辦事項、簡潔精要的郵件主文、謙恭的語句表達與避免過多的附件。

Writing concise e-mails will let you get the timely, relevant responses you're looking for. A successful e-mail will largely depend on the words you choose to convey your thoughts. In addition, we have to be familiar with how to write an impressive e-mail in order to draw our reader's attention and get things done quickly. Below are 9 tips for writing great e-mails for your reference.

▌Get your e-mails noticed 如何讓你的電子郵件出類拔萃？

It's an unfortunate reality that everyone nowadays deals with dozens -- even hundreds -- of e-mails everyday. Therefore, it is easy for your message to get overlooked in all the e-mails **clamoring for attention**. Use the simple tips below to distinguish your e-mails from others, and increase your odds of getting a timely response.

　　科技進步帶動下，電腦資訊已廣泛運用於商業流程運作中，電子郵件成為企業內外部傳遞訊息與溝通的主要管道之一。今日的上班族每天必須處理數十封，甚至於上百封的電子郵件，在有限的工作時間之內，不得不選擇性地挑取重要的電子郵件優先處理。以下是幾個讓你的電子郵件能在每日淹沒的「郵海」中拔得頭籌的方法。

1. **Clear and simple subject** -- The subject of e-mail should explain what is expected. Preface your subject with a one or two word phrase that describes the action you need from the recipient. Use "**For response**" or "**Please review**" to tell your reader immediately how much attention your e-mail will require. Other good opening phrases include "**FYI** (= for your information)", "**Feedback requested**", "**Urgent**", "**Need your action**", "**Message from committee**", or "**Update**."

落標言簡意賅：一封主標簡明、具有吸引力的電子郵件，可在最短的時間內吸引收信人的注意並迅速獲得回應。由於現在有許多電子郵件容易夾帶電腦病毒，所以標示不清或沒有主題、內文卻附帶檔案的電子郵件就很容易被忽視或直接刪除。

建議電子郵件落標時可先以簡明的句子帶出，已引起收信者的注意。以下列出常用的例子供參考：

"For response"—請回覆

"Please review"—請檢核

"FYI"—訊息提供，全文是 for your information。

"FYR"—請參考，全文是 for your reference。

"Feedback requested"—期待回覆

"Urgent"—緊急

"Need your action"—需要你的行動

"Reminder"—提醒

"Message from committee"—來自委員會的訊息

"Update"—更新訊息

2. **Make your subject contents concise** -- Your subject is one of the first pieces of information your reader will see. Be as descriptive as possible, and you can convey a wealth of information in only one sentence, such as writing "**Review by Wednesday: requirements for new product promotion project**" gives the recipient enough information to accurately prioritize your message.

一目了然的主題：儘量在一個簡短的句子裡表達電子郵件內容的重點，這將讓收件者可以優先處理你的請求或訊息。例如："Review by Wednesday: requirements for new product promotion project"（星期三之前完成檢評：新產品促銷方案的需求）。

3. **Don't mark non-urgent e-mails "urgent"** -- When the e-mail is marked urgent, it will rise to the top of the inbox. *Initially*, this tactic may get your e-mails opened quickly, but *eventually*, it will only get them ignored. Instead of considering all of your correspondence urgent, the recipients will *assume* none of it. Use this word sparingly and your truly urgent messages will get the attention they deserve.

謹慎使用「緊急」一詞：若只是為了讓對方優先處理你的電子郵件，而將每封寄出的信件皆標上「緊急」一詞，終究將造成「狼來了」的效應。以後若真遇到緊急事件時，恐怕就難以再引起收件人的注意了。所以，除非真正重要且急需馬上處理，否則應避免常使用「緊急」一詞。在正式商務場合，通常發出一封「緊急」電子郵件後，常伴隨一通告知對方的電話。

■ 單字解析

initially (adv)：最初、開始

Initially we would like to purchase the printers in small quantities.

（開始我們只想採購少量的印表機。）

eventually (adv)：最後、終於

We *eventually* got the deal.

（我們終於拿到這個交易了。）

assume (v)：以為、假裝、擔任

She *assumed* the presidency of the business support division in June.

（她於六月擔任業務支援部總裁。）

4. **"cc" with caution** -- "cc" makes every recipient get to know the email addresses of all the persons that received the message which is usually not desirable. Nobody likes their email address exposed to the public. If you think an e-mail may result in *multiple* responses, only "cc" those who really need to know. Also, when responding, don't get in the habit of selecting Reply to all. Hit Reply, and only include those *critical* to the discussion.

小心使用「cc」功能：「cc」是carbon copy的縮寫，「副件」的意思。正如本章節開始時就提到的，上班族每日電子郵件繁多，為不徒增對方困擾，除非與事件有直接關係，撰寫電子郵件時應避免「cc」給公司內一大堆無直接相關的人員或部門。謹慎地回覆含有「cc」的電子信件，避免每次回信皆採用「reply to all」回覆所有人的功能。

■ 單字解析

multiple (a)：多樣的、多重的

This *multiple* purpose pocket knife enjoys a good market reputation.
（這支多功能小摺刀擁有良好的市場聲譽。）

critical (a)：關鍵的、重要的

Information technology is *critical* to customer relationship management.
（資訊技術對顧客關係管理是很重要的。）

「BCC」的全文是blind carbon copy，指電子郵件中的密件副本，其他收件者（「To」與「cc」欄位）將無法看到「BCC」欄位中收件者的詳細資料。通常使用「BCC」的情況有：(1) 收件人數過多；(2) 收件人彼此間沒有必要或是不應該互相知悉時；(3) 當你不想讓收件者知道你還寄電子郵件給哪些人時、(4) 收件人彼此之間互不相識時。

5. **Begin with what's important; end with what's needed** -- When readers choose an e-mail to read, they will ask: "How does this relate to me?" Therefore, answer the question quickly by putting the most important information in the first few paragraphs.

郵件內容切中主題：郵件內容必須讓收件者感到與他們工作內容或切身利益息息相關，所以儘量在郵件剛開始的幾句話裡，清晰表達重要訊息。

6. **Ask for a specific response** -- End your e-mail with bullets describing what's expected of each recipient. For example:

   Robert - please send me the status on the implementation of R&D project.

   Cornad - please feedback customer's requests to Hanley.

明列對不同收信人的交辦事項：若期望不同單位的收件人對郵件內容做處理進度報告，可以分別請求各主事者就其負責項目做回應。例如：

Robert - 請寄研發計畫執行現狀給我。

Cornad - 請將客戶的請求回饋給Hanley。

7. **Keep it short** -- People don't "read" text on a screen, they *skim* it. Make your e-mails are as short and direct as possible so your reader can easily pick out important information. Keep your e-mails on a single screen or two to three short paragraphs.

簡潔精要的郵件主文：非僅郵件標題要求言簡意賅，就是正文內容也須精要簡潔，防止長篇大論。郵件主文最好限制在一個電腦螢幕大小的篇幅，也就是約略二、三段左右。

■ 單字解析

skim (v)：輕輕掠過、涉獵

Birds *skim* the water looking for food.

（鳥兒掠過水面覓食。）

Marketing manager always *skims* a newspaper in the morning.

（行銷經理總是在早上略讀報紙。）

8. **Watch your tone** -- Remember to keep e-mails polite and friendly, and avoid using inflammatory statements. In some cases, humor can be easily *misinterpreted*, so play it safe and add a "smiley" face if you mean something as a joke. *Offending* someone, even unintentionally, may get you a quick response, but it may not be the one you wanted.

謙恭的語句表達：正式商用書信溝通，即使是電子郵件往來，都應以禮貌友善的語氣來撰寫。即便有時在彼此熟悉的商務關係下使用詼諧的口吻，都有可能冒犯正在進行交易的顧客。

在正式電子郵件中使用幽默詞語時，為避免對方誤解，而引起不必要的困擾，建議可在語句結束時加上一個笑臉的符號（如：☺ 、^^ 、☺），來縮短彼此的距離。有時不經意冒犯他人，而得到快速的回應，但是這絕非你所要的結果。

■ 單字解析

tone (n) 語調、音調

His manager always spoke in a *tone* of command.

（他的經理總是以命令的口吻說話。）

misinterpret (v) 誤解

Don't *misinterpret* my comments as criticism.

（請不要誤解將我的意見當作是批評。）

offend (v) 觸犯、惹惱、冒犯

In what way had Hank *offended*?

（漢克哪裡冒犯了？）

I do apologize if I've *offended* you.

（假如我冒犯你，我真的很抱歉。）

9. **Limit attachments** -- Too many attaching files can waste a lot of space under the limited mail storage size. Remember to use the shared spaces to maintain information and compress large files to reduce the size before sending.

避免過多的附件：由於多數人的電子郵件信箱或多或少有容量與頻寬上的限制，除非必要或與內容有直接相關的附件檔案，否則應避免附加太多的無相關的文件或檔案。

■ 單字解析

attachment (n) 附件

Please check your *attachments* before sending.

（在寄出前，請先檢查你的附件。）

　　再次提醒，九個讓你的電子郵件能在每日淹沒的「郵海」中拔得頭籌的方法：

1. Clear and simple subject

2. Make your subject contents concise

3. Don't mark non-urgent notes "urgent"

4. "cc" with caution

5. Begin with what's important; end with what's needed

6. Ask for a specific response

7. Keep it short

8. Watch your tone

9. Limit attachments

▌ 電子郵件範例 1 ▌

To: "Angus Ferdinand" <angus@trulyclothing.com.ca>
From: "Charlie Jones" <charlie.jones@surreytextile.co.ir>
Date: 2008/11/21 16:47
Subject: Greeting from Surrey Textile

Dear Mr. Ferdinand,

Sorry to bother you. This is Charlie Jones from Surrey Textile. While **surfing on the internet**, we **came across** your company and thought if you would be interested to learn about our products.

Please allow me to introduce our company to you. Surrey Textile was established in May 1982 and initially imported cloth from India. We soon became a **market leader** in our field and opened the first of our own textile producing factories in 1989. We now produce all kinds of cloth and have earned a good **reputation** both in Ireland and abroad.

Our latest catalog and promotion brochure are mailed to you by **express** this early morning and expected to be received within 3 days. If you need any information, please do not hesitate to contact me.

Thank you very much for your kind attention. I look forward to hearing from you soon.

Yours sincerely,

Charlie Jones

Sales Manager
Surrey Textile
GD House, Telligent Business Park
Dublin 27, Ireland
Tel: 353-1-462-7653 ext. 123
Fax: 353-1-462-7654
E-mail: charlie.jones@surreytextile.co.ir
www.surreytextile.co.ir

▌ 電子郵件範例中文翻譯 1 ▌

To（收信人）：安格斯・斐迪南<angus@trulyclothing.com.ca>
From（寄信人）：查理・瓊斯<charlie.jones@surreytextile.co.ir>
Date（日期）：2008/11/21 16:47
Subject（主題）：來自瑟瑞紡織的問候
☐urgent ☐confidential

尊敬的斐迪南先生，您好：

　　不好意思打擾您，我是瑟瑞紡織公司的查理・瓊斯。當我查看網路資訊時，找到了貴公司的訊息，覺得貴公司會對本公司的產品感到興趣。

　　請容我向您介紹本公司：瑟瑞紡織成立於1982年5月，初期從印度進口布料。不久後，我們成為紡織產業的市場領導者，並於1989年成立了屬於自己的紡織廠。現在的瑟瑞紡織生產各式各樣的布疋，擁有享譽愛爾蘭海內外的聲望。

　　今早我已將我們公司的最新目錄與促銷方案郵寄給您，預計三天後抵達。假如您需要任何資訊，歡迎與我聯繫。

　　非常感謝您的留意，期待聽到您的回音。

您最誠摯的

查理・瓊斯

銷售經理

瑟瑞紡織公司

GD House, Telligent Business Park
Dublin 27, Ireland
Tel: 353-1-462-7653 ext. 123
Fax: 353-1-462-7654
E-mail: charlie.jones@surreytextile.co.ir
www.surreytextile.co.ir

■ 單字解析

surf on the internet = surf the internet (ph.)：上網、瀏覽網路

If you *surf the Internet*, you can find our website.

（假如你上網，你可以找到我們的網站。）

come across (ph.)：偶然遇見、邂逅

The manager *came across* his old planning session files when he was clearing out his desk.

（當清空桌面時，經理找到了他的舊行動計畫檔案。）

market leader (ph.)：市場領導者

The *market leader* is dominant in its industry and has substantial market share.

（市場領導者在它所處的產業占優勢，並且擁有大的市場占有率。）

reputation (n)：名聲、聲望

A good corporate *reputation* has to be earned by the tangible products and intangible service.

（好商譽必須從有形的商品與無形的服務獲得。）

express (n)：快捷、快遞

The goods will be delivered by *express* tomorrow morning.

（貨物將於明早以快遞寄出。）

▌電子郵件範例2 ▌

To: William TONER <williamtoner@whiteorchid.com.th>
From: Goldsbrough Hotel <goldsbrough@theoaksgroup.com.au>
Date: 2008/10/30 13:35
Subject: Confirmation Letter
William Toner
482 Yawaraj Road, Bangkok, 10100 Thailand

Dear Mr. William TONER,

CONFIRMED RESERVATION NO 103567.

We would like to confirm your **reservation in** a 1 Bedroom 4 Star apartment as arriving on 11/08/2008 and departing on 11/13/2008. You have **provided us** with your credit card details, which leaves the full amount payable of $770.00. Please check these details and contact us immediately should there be any changes.

ON ARRIVAL

Accommodation charges can be paid in full or a credit card **authorisation for** the total amount will be required. If payment is made in cash, accommodation charges must be paid on arrival along with a $200 cash deposit for any incidentals. We do not accept a cheque unless it is issued on arrival and your stay is longer than 10 working days.

CHECK IN & CHECK OUT

Our check in time is 2pm and check out time is 10am, with reception open 24hrs.

CANCELLATION POLICY

If you need to change or cancel your booking, please contact us as soon as possible. If you do not give us 48 hours notice of **cancellation** or **fail to** show up, one night accommodation will be charged against your credit card.

We thank you very much for choosing to stay at The Goldsbrough Hotel on Darling Harbour and look forward to your arrival.

Best Regards
RESERVATIONS
Goldsbrough Hotel
Our address: 243 Pyrmont St, Darling harbour NSW 2009 Sydney.
www.theoaksgroup.com.au

▌電子郵件範例中文翻譯２▐

To（收信人）：威廉・通納<williamtoner@whiteorchid.com.th>
From（寄信人）：構斯伯飯店<goldsbrough@theoaksgroup.com.au>
Date（日期）：2008/10/30 13:35
Subject（主題）：訂房確認信
2008年10月30日
威廉・通納
泰國10100曼谷揚華若路482號

- -

威廉・通納先生，您好：

訂房確認號碼：103567
　　本飯店與閣下確認訂房：四星級一間臥房的公寓，2008年11月8日入宿，2008年11月13日退房。我們已取得您的信用卡資料，本次訂房費用為770澳元，請您再次確認，若有任何更動，請馬上與我們聯繫。

入住注意事項
　　住宿費必須一次付清，或以本次刷卡的信用卡付款。假如您選擇付現，住房總額必須於入住時繳清，此外還另須預支200澳元現金作為押金。我們僅接受房客住宿超過十天所開立的即期支票。

入住與退房
　　本飯店每日的入宿時間是下午二點；退房時間是早上十點，櫃檯服務二十四小時開放。

取消訂房須知
　　假如您欲改變或取消訂房，請儘速與我們聯繫。倘若我們於四十八小時前未收到您的取消訂房訊息，或是於訂房當日您未入住，我們將從您的信用卡扣除一晚的住宿費用。
　　我們非常感謝您選擇入宿坐落於達令港的構斯伯飯店，並期待您的光臨。
　　致予最深的祝福

訂房組
構斯伯飯店
地址：雪梨2009新南威爾斯達令港皮爾龐德街243號。
www.theoaksgroup.com.au

■ 單字解析

confirmation (n)：確認、批准

Confirmation letters can save companies a lot of money and time by forestalling misunderstandings.

（確認信可避免誤解，並節省公司很多的時間和金錢。）

reservation (n)：預訂、預約、保留

Let me confirm your *reservation*.

（讓我確認您的訂房。）

provide (v)：提供

We *provide* our customers one-stop service from design to merchandising.

（我們提供客戶從設計到銷售單一窗口的服務。）

accommodation (n)：住宿、宿舍

There are good *accommodations* for visitors near our office.

（在我們辦公室附近有些不錯的住宿地方。）

authorisation (n)：授權、批准

The Transport Operations Act requires all drivers of public passenger services to hold driver *authorisation*.

（運輸作業法要求所有駕駛公共旅客載運服務者須取得駕駛授權證明。）

cancellation (n)：取消、註銷

Failure to arrive Hotel before 10:00 PM may result in *cancellation* of the reservation without notice.

（如未能於晚間十點前抵達飯店，可能導致原預約被取消，而且不另行通知。）

fail to (ph.) 未能達成

The marketing manager *failed to* attend today's meeting.

（行銷經理未能出席今日的會議。）

常見美式英文與英式英文的用法列表

使用英式英文的國家除英國外,多為大英國協國家,如:愛爾蘭、紐西蘭、澳洲及印度。

	美式英文(AmE)	英式英文(BrE)
美式英文有些動詞以-ize結尾,英式英文則以-ise結尾。		
分析	analyze	analyse
授權	authorize	authorise
組織	organize	organise
私有化	privatize	privatise
摘要	summarize	summarise
英式英文有些名詞以-our結尾,美式英文則多為-or結尾。		
行為	behavior	behaviour
顏色	color	colour
海港	harbor	harbour
勞工	labor	labour
其他相異的用法如下:		
公寓	apartment	flat
開胃菜	appetizer	starter
汽車	automobile	car
行李	baggage	luggage
目錄	catalog	catalogue
手機	cell phone	mobile phone
中心	center	centre
支票	check	cheque
帳單(指餐廳)	check	bill
衣櫃	closet	wardrobe
餅乾	cookie	biscuit
行人穿越道	crosswalk	pedestrian crossing
宿舍	dormitory	accommodation
電梯	elevator	lift

茄子	eggplant	aubergine
橡皮擦	eraser	rubber
秋天	fall	autumn
水龍頭	faucet	tap
一樓	first floor	ground floor
手電筒	flashlight	torch
出租	for rent	to let
炸薯條	french fries	chips
高速公路	freeway	motorway
汽油	gasoline	petrol
休息時間	intermission	interval
詢問	inquiry	enquiry
排隊	line	queue
機車	motorcycle	bike/motorbike
國定假日	National holiday	Bank holiday
冒犯	offense	offence
長褲	pants	trousers
停車場	parking lot	car park
節目	program	programme
盥洗室	restroom	toilet
學期	semester	term
人行道	sidewalk	pavement
運動鞋	sneaker	trainer
英式足球	soccer	football
爐灶	stove	cooker
地鐵	subway	underground/tube
毛衣	sweater	jumper/jersey
計程車	taxi	cab
公共電話亭	telephone booth	phone box
卡車	truck	lorry
外帶	to go	take away
郵遞區號	zip code	post code

▲練習題③▼　請練習寫一封詢問訂房的電子郵件

　　總經理計畫利用2009過年期間全家至菲律賓宿霧（Cebu, Philippines）海濱渡假飯店Plantation Resort旅遊，為避免旺季訂不到住房，現請身為秘書的妳先行訂房。

　　以下是相關訊息：

1. Plantation Resort email: inquiry@plantation.com.ph
2. 入宿人數四人、需要兩間豪華房
3. 時間：1月14日至1月19日，共五晚

　　基於上述的背景，妳現在請Plantation Resort告知該時段是否有海景房？房價多少？房價是否含早餐？付款方式？機場接送的費用等等。

▶ 訂房小補帖

房間形式：飯店房間種類可分為「客房」（Room）與「套房」（Suite）。客房通常只有單純的臥室及衛浴設備。套房的坪數較大，隔局為一廳、一房一衛，一般飯店的套房多集中在高樓層。套房可分為總統套房（President Suite）與商務套房（Executive Suite）；商務樓層（Executive Floor）有專屬會議室與餐廳。

床的形式：床通常可分為「單人單床房」（Single Bed Room）、「雙人單床房」（Double Bed Room），及「雙人雙床房」（Twin Bed Room）三種。

早餐的形式：住房時有些飯店會附贈早餐，型式有歐陸式早餐（Continental Breakfast）、美式早餐（American Breakfast）、自助式早餐（Buffet Breakfast）以及冷盤自助式早餐（Cold Buffet）。

歐陸式早餐＝最簡單的早餐，通常只提供二、三個麵包、附帶果醬、奶油，以及一杯咖啡與果汁等，內容不豐富但足以飽食。

美式早餐＝內容相對豐盛，除了各式麵包、可頌、蛋糕之外，還可以到餐檯領取培根、火腿、炒蛋等熱食以及種類多元的果汁、咖啡或牛奶。

自助式早餐＝最豐盛的早餐，舉凡西式、中式、日式餐點一應俱全，幾乎與自助式午、晚餐的內容相當。

冷盤自助式早餐＝有些歐陸飯店僅提供冷盤自助式早餐，餐檯提供火腿肉、燻肉、冷烤火雞或是義大利臘腸等等，但是除了咖啡以外，其餘的食物皆為冷食。

飯店專業代碼：PRPN（Per Room, Per Night）每房每晚的報價。

PPPN（Per Person, Per Night）每人每晚的報價。

2.4 Price Enquiries and Proforma Invoice 詢價與報價

　　商場上企業對企業的往來通常起始於詢問，所以任何公司都很重視對這些詢問的回答。因為這些詢問者極有可能於未來會成為公司主要的客戶。詢問的內容不外乎5Ps，即People（人）、Price（價格）、Product（商品）、Place（地點）、Promotion（促銷）。但主要還是以價格為主，因為會找主動上門的客戶，某種程度上都已經對公司的產品或服務有所了解。

　　顧客想要採買的商品通常是物超所值且擁有高品質，商務人士並不像一般消費者會浪費企業的錢或預算去購置他們不需要的商品。本節就是以詢價與報價為主而整理出來，內容包含詢問與回答的例句、詢價與報價的範例書信、數字表達方式與報價單型式。

Making Enquiries：詢價

- May I have your prices, please?
  （能了解一下貴公司的價格嗎？）

- Please kindly inform your lowest price for each of the following items.
  （請針對以下商品報最低價。）

- Would you please let me know your lowest prices for the relevant goods?
  （請告知相關商品的最低價。）

- We'd rather have your quotation of F. O. B.
  （請報離岸價。）

- Please quote the price based on CIF London.
  （請以倫敦到岸價為條件報價。）

- I would like to know the availability of your air conditioner. If you have one, please let me know the price. In addition, is it suitable for different voltages?

  （我想知道貴公司目前是否有冷氣現貨，如果有，敬請報價。此外，這款冷氣可以用在不同的電壓嗎？）

- Do you supply a portable DVD player? Is this available from stock? Please quote your best air freight price for five.

  （請問貴公司有生產可攜式DVD播放機？有現貨嗎？請報價最好的空運價格，我需要五個。）

- If your prices are favorable, I can place the order right away.

  （假如價格優惠，我們可以馬上下單。）

- We are pleased to confirm our trial order as follows.

  （很高興與你確認我們試銷訂單如下。）

- We are glad to place our first order with you. Please find below details.

  （很高興第一次單下給你們，以下是訂貨詳細。）

- Please accept our confirmed order as below and issue a proforma invoice.

  （請接受以下的確認訂單，並開立預約發票。）

- Please kindly send a confirmation letter by e-mail.

  （請以電子郵件回傳確認信。）

- Please kindly handle and ship our order at your earliest convenience since we need these products urgently.

  （因產品迫切需要，希望您能儘早處理並裝運本公司的訂單。）

- If you accept US $250 per unit for Notebook Model 472, we would like to place orders for 10,000 units in 3 quarters.

  （假如貴公司可以接受筆記型電腦型號 472每台$250美金的價格，我們將分三季下單一萬台。）

- If you cannot offer widgets at a unit price of US$ 50, please kindly cancel this order.

  （若貴公司無法以產品單位價格五十美元賣出，那請取消此訂單。）

- We've already made an inquiry about your products, will you please reply as soon as possible?

  （我們已經做產品詢價，可否儘快給予答覆？）

- It's basically a matter that the quality of the ordered goods must be the same with sample received.

  （基本上訂購的貨品品質一定要達到樣品品質。）

- Please make sure that the packing follows our instructions shown on the order form.

  （請確定依照我們訂單上的指示包裝。）

- Please send me your catalog as soon as possible.

  （請儘速寄貴公司的產品目錄給我。）

- How long does it usually take to make delivery?

  （通常貴公司的交貨時間多久？）

- Please fax a copy of invoice as well as the following documents.

  （請傳真發票與下列文件。）

- Heavy inquiries prove the quality of our products.

  （大量詢價證明我們產品的品質。）

- We regret to inform you that the goods you inquire are not available at the moment.

  （很抱歉通知您，貴公司所詢問的貨品目前缺貨中。）

● Item no. ET-89 is out of stock at the moment.

（ET-89型號的產品目前無庫存。）

● Could you please tell us the quantity you require so that we can give you our offers?

（為了給貴公司報價，可否告知您所需要的數量？）

● If we receive your confirmed order before 12 of December, we will be able to dispatch the goods around the middle of next January.

（倘若於12月12日前收到確認訂單，我們將於明年1月中旬出貨。）

● Please note that this quotation is valid only within three months.

（請注意該報價僅三個月內有效。）

● Could you tell me which kind of payment terms you'll choose?

（能否告知貴公司的付款方式？）

● Would you accept the delivery spread over a period of time?

（貴公司能否接受在一段時間裡分批交貨？）

● Please kindly send us more detailed specifications.

（請寄給我們更詳細的產品規格。）

● Please send us your latest brochures at your earliest convenience.

（請儘速寄上貴公司最新的產品介紹。）

● Our engineer will need a couple of samples to test and evaluate.

（本公司的工程師需要一些樣品做測試與評估。）

● Your immediate attention to this matter would be highly appreciated.

（你們對此事立即的關注我們將十分感激。）

● Enclosed please find a specification sheet of all models for your reference.

（隨函附上所有型號之規格表，以茲參考。）

● Thank you very much for your prompt assistance.

（非常感謝您的迅速協助。）

▌ 詢價參考範例 1 ▌

Amazing Toys
168 Princess Avenue,
10504 New York
Tel: 914 499 1888 Fax: 914 499 1777

Dave Mick
Kenilworth GmbH
Katrin Wachsmith
D-80808 Munich
Germany

5 May 2008

Dear Mr. Mick,

TOY BEAR

I am writing to inform you that we have been facing some problems with one of our **suppliers** who **manufactures** toy bears. I'm pretty sure that you don't have a local distributor here. I had tried to call in the past few weeks, but you were out of country.

We require 6,500 ca of your latest model toy bears and wish the delivery can be completed by 18 June. A full specification of our requirements is given on the attached sheet, together with our company brochure.

It would be deeply appreciated if you could quote us your best price and give a full **specification** of your other products and shipping date. Of course our marketing department would need to have some samples of your toy bears to show to one of our key customers before we could place a firm order.

Assuming our customer is satisfied with your toy bear, and you can quote us a competitive price, we'd certainly be able to place more substantial orders on a regular basis.

I look forward to hearing from you soon. Should you have any enquiry, please do not hesitate to contact me.
Very truly yours,

Fred North

Purchasing Manager
Enclosed: specification and company brochure

∥ 詢價參考範例中文翻譯 1 ∥

 Amazing Toys

168 Princess Avenue,
10504 New York
Tel: 914 499 1888 Fax: 914 499 1777

Dave Mick
Kenilworth GmbH
Katrin Wachsmith
D-80808 Munich
Germany

5 May 2008

尊敬的米克先生，您好：

　　我寫這封信給您，是因為我們和一位製造玩具熊的供應商遇到了一些問題。我十分了解貴公司在紐約這兒沒有配銷商。我在數週前曾試圖與您聯繫，但是您都出國了。

　　我們需要貴公司最新款式的玩具熊六千五百隻，並希望在6月18日前可以全數收到貨。我已將我們需求的詳細規格，附在附件。附件還有本公司的簡介。

　　如果貴公司可以給我們一個好的價格，並告知其他產品規格與交貨時間將十分感激。當然，在我們可以確認下單之前，本公司的市場部需要一些玩具熊的樣本，展示給我們最重要的顧客。

　　假如我們的顧客滿意貴公司的玩具熊，貴公司且能提供具競爭力的價格，本公司將確定在未來能夠定期下大量訂單。期待能儘快得到貴公司回音，假如您有任何疑問，請與我聯絡。

你最真誠的

弗列德‧諾斯

採購經理
附件：規格與公司簡介

■ 單字解析

supplier (n)：供應商

Your new *supplier* will keep you informed when your transfer is done.

（當匯兌完成，您的新供應商將讓您知道。）

manufacture (v, n)：製造、加工

This company *manufactures* notebook computers.

（這家公司製造筆記型電腦。）

specification (n)：規格、說明書、明細單

Specification provides the necessary details about the specific requirements.

（說明書提供了有關具體規定的必要細節。）

▌報價參考範例 1 ▌

Kenilworth GmbH

Katrin Wachsmith, D-80808 Munich Germany
Telephone +49 89 / 3571 - 3500　Fax +49 89 / 3571 - 3600

Mr. Fred North
Purchasing Manager
Amazing Toy
168 Princess Avenue,
10504 New York

7 May 2008

Dear Mr. North,

Thank you very much for your inquiry. I am so sorry that I missed your call in the past few weeks since I had my business trip to Asia. We are the leading brand of manufacturing toy bears in the world so that we can definitely fit your requirements exactly.

The most suitable model for your specification is the **Amazing TB08**. This high quality item is our best-selling product in the EU countries and it is available in stock now.

Enclosed please find a detailed quotation, specifications and delivery terms, in which you will see our very competitive prices.

Our new **Amazing TB08** are purely made in Germany; therefore, our quality outperforms our competitors' products which are mainly made in China.

By the way, I have sent you 6 samples of Amazing TB08 this morning by FedEx and they are expected to be received within 2 days.

If you would like further information, please telephone or e-mail me: my extension number is 2345. I am looking forward to receiving your confirmation shortly.

Best Wishes,

Dave Mick

Sales Manager

davemick@kenilworth.com.de

▌報價參考範例中文翻譯 1 ▌

Kenilworth GmbH

Katrin Wachsmith, D-80808 Munich Germany
Telephone +49 89 / 3571 - 3500   Fax +49 89 / 3571 - 3600

Mr. Fred North
Purchasing Manager
Amazing Toy
168 Princess Avenue,
10504 New York

7 May 2008

尊敬的諾斯先生，您好：

　　非常感謝您來函詢問。真的很抱歉，上幾週因為至亞洲出差不在辦公室，未能接到您的來電。本公司是世界上製造玩具熊的領導廠牌，所以我們一定能夠完全地符合貴公司的需求。

　　本公司最符合貴公司規格的玩具熊型號是「*Amazing TB08*」，這項高品質商品是本公司在歐盟國家銷售最好的產品，而且該型號的玩具熊本公司目前有現貨。

　　隨信附上一份詳盡的報價單、規格表與交貨明細。從報價單中，您將發現我們的價格是相當具有競爭力的。

　　新產品「*Amazing TB08*」玩具熊完全是德製的，因此我們的品質將遠超過我們的競爭友商，他們的商品大多數是在中國製造的。

　　順道一提，今早我已經將六隻「*Amazing TB08*」玩具熊樣本以聯邦快遞寄出，預計在兩天之內您將收到這些貨。

　　倘若您欲知更多的訊息，請來電或寫電子郵件給我，我的分機號碼是2345。期待不久就能收到您的確認。

致予最深的祝福

戴芙·米克

銷售經理
davemick@kenilworth.com.de

▌ 詢價參考範例2 ▌

Collins Torch

32 Kenpus Highway
Cork, Germany
Tel: +49 89 3801422 Fax: +49 89 3801421
www.collins.co.de

To: Easy Access Corporation
Attn: "Mr. Peter Cobuild" <peter.cobuild@easyaccess.com.tw>
Date: 18/01/2009
Subject: **Electric Torch EA:001**

Dear Mr. Cobuild,

Thank you so much for the e-mail of Jan. 17 as well as your catalog. We are interested in your **range** of electric torch, especially the **transparent** colored ones. Please kindly inform the quotation of 5,000 pieces of model number **EA:001** in color of transparent blue, pink, yellow and green **separately**. Please also let us know your earliest delivery date after we confirm our order.

By the way, please kindly inform below enquiries by return e-mail.

1. Are these electric torches made in Taiwan? Actually, we **prefer** products made in Taiwan, not made in China.
2. How long do you provide for product warranty?
3. Could you provide a sample for our engineer to test as soon as possible?
4. Do you accept the payment by **sight L/C**?

If your prices are competitive and quality is **superior**, we plan to place quite a **substantial** order every month. We are hoping to increase our product range in the near future, so please also keep us updated with all your new products in addition to electric torch.

I look forward to hearing from you soon.

Sincerely Yours,

William Clays

Director, Collins Torch
E-mail: williamclays@collins.com.de
Tel: +49 89 3801422 * 27381

▌ 詢價參考範例中文翻譯２ ▌

Collins Torch

32 Kenpus Highway
Cork, Germany
Tel: +49 89 3801422 Fax: +49 89 3801421
www.collins.co.de

To（收信單位）：Easy Access 公司
Attn（收信人）：彼得‧柯畢爾 <peter.cobuild@easyaccess.com.tw>
Date（日期）：18/01/2009
Subject（主旨）：手電筒－型號 EA: 001

尊敬的柯畢爾先生，您好：

　　非常感謝您於1月17日寄出的電子郵件與貴公司的目錄。

　　本公司對貴公司的手電筒產品系列，尤其是透明彩色的手電筒有興趣。敬請告知型號是EA: 001的透明黃、透明藍、透明粉紅與透明綠的手電筒各五千支的報價。亦請讓我們知道貴公司在本公司確認訂單後，最快的交貨日期。

　　順道，請以電子郵件回覆下列問題：

1. 這些手電筒都是台灣製造的嗎？實際上，本公司比較喜歡台灣製造的產品，而非中國製造的商品。
2. 這些商品的保固期間是多久？
3. 能否儘快提供產品樣本供本公司工程師測試？
4. 貴公司能接受即時信用狀的付款方式嗎？

　　假如貴公司的價格具競爭力、品質優，本公司則計畫每月下大量訂單。我們也希望在不久的將來本公司能增加產品系列，故也請讓我們知道貴公司除了手電筒之外的其他新產品資訊。

　　期待很快收到您的訊息。

您最誠摯的

威廉‧克雷斯

總監 **Collins Torch**
E-mail: williamclays@collins.com.de
Tel: +49 89 3801422 * 27381

■ 單字解析

range (n)：一系列

R&D department focused on a *range* of issues on the improvement technology of product function.

（研發部門集中火力於一系列產品功能改進技術的問題上。）

transparent (a)：透明、一目了然、坦率

The CFO of Collins is a man of *transparent* sincerity.

（柯林斯公司的財務長是個坦率誠懇的人。）

separately (adv)：分別地、個別地

Japanese electronics companies Toshiba, Hitachi, and Fujitsu are *separately* developing fuel cells for cell phones.

（日本電子公司：東芝、日立和富士通，分別開發手機的燃料電池。）

prefer (v)：更喜歡、寧願

European companies *prefer* India over China for outsourcing.

（歐洲企業喜歡將委外服務設在印度更甚於設在中國。）

sight L/C (ph.)：即期信用狀

與sight L/C 相反的是Usance L/C（遠期信用狀）。

superior (a)：優秀的、上等的、較好的

EA:001 model is the torch with a reputation for *superior* quality and performance.

（EA001型號的手電筒擁有高品質與性能佳的聲譽。）

substantial (a)：大量的、堅實的、重要的

Substantial changes were made in this executive meeting.

（在此次的主管會議中作出了重大改變。）

| 報價參考範例 2 |

To: Collins Torch
Attn: "Director, Mr. William Clays" <williamclays@collins.com.de>
Subject: **RE: Electric Torch EA:001**
Date: 19/01/2009

- -

Dear Mr. Clays,

Thank you so much for your interest in our best-selling product. Concerning our transparent electric torch, the items you mentioned are popular at this moment. Therefore, the delivery date will take 8 to 10 days after the confirmed order.

As to your inquiries, please kindly **refer** to the following:

1. All Easy Access electric torches are made in Taiwan and highly **functional**, design attractive and with high quality.
2. All the product warranty of Easy Access electric torches is a year.
3. I will send you a sample of different color separately this morning by DHL.
4. **With regards to** the payment term, I am sorry to inform you that we can only accept sight L/C for orders exceeding US $50,000.

I am really grateful for your kind attention. Should you have any inquiry, please do not **hesitate** to contact me. I am looking forward to receiving your reply.

Best Regards,

Peter Cobuild

Marketing Executive
Easy Access Corporation
Peter.cobuild@easyaccess.com.tw

Tel: 886-3-568489
Fax: 886-3-568488
reply e-mail
>> To: Easy Access Corporation
>> Attn: "Mr. Peter Cobuild" <peter.cobuild@easyaccess.com.tw>

>> From: "Director, William Clays" <williamclays@collins.com.de>
>> Subject: Electric Torch EA:001

▌報價參考範例中文翻譯2 ▌

To（收信單位）：Collins Torch

Attn（收件人）：威廉‧克雷斯總監 <williamclays@collins.com.de>

Subject（主旨）：**RE**（回覆）：手電筒－型號 **EA: 001**

Date: 19/01/2009

親愛的克雷斯先生，您好：

　　非常感謝貴公司對本公司銷售最好的產品有興趣。

　　有關本公司的透明手電筒，貴公司所詢問的型號是目前本公司最受歡迎的產品。因此，該產品的交貨日期是於訂單確定後的8至10日出貨。

　　至於您的詢問，請參酌以下我們的回答：

1. 本公司所有的手電筒皆於台灣製造，功能好、外觀具吸引力、品質優。
2. 本公司所有的手電筒保固期皆為一年。
3. 今早將以DHL快遞寄出您需求不同顏色的手電筒樣本各一支。
4. 很抱歉通知您，有關付款條件方面，本公司僅接受訂單總額超過五萬美元時的支付即期信用狀。

　　非常謝謝您的留意。若有垂詢，請不要猶豫與我聯繫。期待收到您的訊息。

致予最深的祝福

彼得‧柯畢爾

行銷總監

Easy Access Corporation

Peter.cobuild@easyaccess.com.tw

電話：886-3-568489

傳真：886-3-568488

回覆電子郵件

>> To: Easy Access Corporation

>> Attn: "Mr. Peter Cobuild" <peter.cobuild@easyaccess.com.tw>

>> From: "Director, William Clays" <williamclays@collins.com.de>

>> Subject: Electric Torch EA: 001

■ 單字解析

refer (v)：參考、歸因、論及

In his speech, he *referred* to the corporate competitiveness several times.

（演講中，他多次提到企業競爭力。）

functional (a)：機能的、實用的

This new powerful hoover is a multi-*functional* machine which can be used on both dry and wet carpet.

（這新強力吸塵器具有多功能，不論乾溼地毯均可使用。）

with regard to (ph.)：關於

With regard to your request, please refer to the attached documents.

（關於您的需求，請參考附錄文件。）

hesitate (v)：猶豫、躊躇

Please do not *hesitate* to contact us if you have any further questions.

（假如您有任何其他的疑問，請不要猶豫與我們聯繫。）

▌報價參考範例3▌

Mercedes Assets

9 Pela ST., CEBU CITY, PHILIPPINES

Tel: (63) 32-2531100

Mr. William Clay

Room No. 612

Pela Commercial Center

Dear Sir/Madam:

Our records show that the **debit balance** of your account with us as of **01-31 January 2009** amount to **Peso 150,000 representing** office **dues** and other charges on your rent.

In accordance with our Asset Rules and Regulation, we take the liberty to request for a deposit today **corresponding** to the above stated balance.

We sincerely thank you for your valued **cooperation** on this matter and **assure** you the best customer service.

Very truly yours,

Pela Commercial Center

Rosemarie Bante

Accounting Department

▎ 報價參考範例中文翻譯 3 ▎

莫塞迪斯資產

9 Pela ST., CEBU CITY, PHILIPPINES

Tel: (63) 32-2531100

Mr. William Clay

Room No. 612

Pela Commercial Center

敬啟者：

　　本公司紀錄顯示，貴公司於2009年1月1日至1月31日的辦公室租金費用與其他雜項總共十五萬披索仍未繳交。

　　依據本公司的資產規章，我們有權請求貴公司今日繳交上述的費用。

　　我們誠摯地感謝貴公司對此合作的重視。本公司確保提供您最好的顧客服務。

您最真誠的

皮拉商業中心

羅絲瑪麗‧貝塔

會計部

■ 單字解析

debit (n)：借方、債目

A *debit* card is a plastic card which provides an alternative payment method.

（轉帳卡是一種塑膠卡，提供替代的付款方式。）

balance (n)：平衡

What does debit *balance* in my bill mean?

（在我帳單中的負債餘額指的是什麼意思？）

represent (v)：代表、表示

The general manager *represents* the best traditions of this company.

（這位新總經理展現了公司最好的傳統。）

due (n)：稅金、應付之款、費用（以複數表示）

We haven't received the membership *dues* from Best Security, Inc. this month.

（本月我們尚未收到Best安全設備公司的會員費。）

in accordance with (ph.)：與……一致、依照

Let's trim our proposal *in accordance with* the client's request.

（讓我們依照客戶的要求修正計畫書。）

correspond (v)：相等、相當、符合

The product's price does not *correspond* to its quality.

（這項產品價格與品質並不相當。）

The total solution provided by Best Security, Inc. exactly *corresponds* with its customers' needs.

（Best安全設備公司所提供的全方位解決方案完全符合顧客需求。）

cooperation (n)：合作、協力

The success of the project relies on the *cooperation* of all involved parties.

（這個計畫的成功仰賴所有相關部門的合作。）

assure (n)：確保、擔保

I can *assure* you of the reliability of the sales figure.

（我向你保證這個銷售統計表的可靠。）

Answering Enquiries：回覆顧客詢問或來函須知

1. 針對顧客的詢問，首先必須於回函中表示致謝

Thank the customer for their interest in your product(s) and confirm that you can (or cannot) help.

如：We will give this order our most careful attention.

（我們將對貴公司的訂單給予最深的關注。）

2. 銷售公司產品，並列舉該產品如何符合顧客的需求

'Sell' your product and explain how it is suitable for your customer's needs.

3. 告知顧客隨函附上目錄、報價單或廣告單等等

Say that you are sending a catalogue, price list, advertising literature, etc.

4. 告知顧客他們如何能取得產品的實際操作經驗

Explain how the customer can get 'hands-on' experiences of the product:

(1) offer to send samples or get a sales representative to visit with samples/demo;

（方法一：直接寄樣本給顧客，或者是派公司的業務代表帶樣品拜訪顧客或向顧客展示商品。）

(2) state the contact details of distributor near customer's address;

（方法二：告知顧客本公司在顧客所在地的配銷商聯繫方式。）

(3) announce a new product exhibition at a forthcoming trade show.

（方法三：告知顧客本公司將於即將到來的貿易展中發表新產品。）

Money Matters：數字的表達

百	100		one hundred
千	1,000	10^3	one thousand
萬	10,000		ten thousand
十萬	100,000		one hundred thousand
百萬	1,000,000	10^6	one million
千萬	10,000,000		ten million
億	100,000,000		one hundred million
十億	1,000,000,000	10^9	one billion
兆	1,000,000,000,000	10^{12}	one trillion
千兆	1,000,000,000,000,000	10^{15}	one quadrillion

Example: 8,324,946 ＝ eight million, three hundred (and) twenty-four thousand, nine hundred (and) forty-six.

小數點與百分比的表達

Invoice No. **503/18H** ＝ five zero three slash eighteen H

0.69 ＝ point six nine

0.55 ＝ point five five

Interest rate **0.69** ＝ zero-point-six-nine

A net profit of **14.97%** ＝ fourteen-point-nine-seven percent

$6.57 ＝ six dollars fifty-seven cents

1 1/2% ＝ one and a half percent

100% ＝ one hundred percent

（one hundred percent sure! 也常於口語中出現，表示非常肯定的意思。）

分數的表達

2/5 = two fifth**s**
3/4 = three quarter**s**
1/2 = a half
1/4 = a quarter
1/7 = one seventh
12/367 = twelve **over** three-six-seven
45/8 = forty-five **over** eight

比率的表達

3:11 = three out of eleven
2:7 = two out of seven
10:1 = ten to one
100: 9 = a hundred to nine

口說數字時，可以「zero」，「nought」或數字「o」（oh）來表示。「zero」是最專門與精準的說法；數字「o」的說法則較口語。

Possibility, Probability and Certainty：各種機率的表達方式

100%	75%	50%	25%	0%
certain	likely	possible	unlikely	impossible

1. **100%**

● **I'm sure that** these sales figures are accurate.
（我確信這些銷售數字是正確的。）

● The figures **must be** accurate.
（數字是正確的。）

● **There's no doubt that** the figures were carefully checked.
（數字被仔細檢查過是無庸置疑的。）

● The figures **must have been** thoroughly checked, so I'm **absolutely sure that** they're accurate.
（這些數字已被徹底核對，所以我絕對確定它們是正確的。）

2. **75%**

● Our sales in the USA **are likely to** go up next year.
（我們在美國的銷售明年很可能會增加。）

● **I expect that** our sales in Canada will go down.
（我預期我們在加拿大的銷售將下滑。）

● **I wouldn't be surprised if** our sales in Mexico went up.
（假如我們在墨西哥的銷售增加，我不會感到意外。）

● **It's quite possible that** our sales in Peru will go up.
（我們在秘魯的銷售成長是很有可能的。）

● Our sales in Argentina **may well** remain static.
（我們在阿根廷的銷售額很可能持平。）

3. **50%**

● **There's a chance that** we'll manage to break into the UK market.
（我們設法進入英國市場是有機會的。）

● **It's just possible that** your forecast is over-optimistic.
（你的預測可能過於樂觀。）

● **I'm not sure if** the figures in this report are correct.
（我不確定在這份報告中的數字是否正確。）

● **There may have been** some kind of misunderstanding.
（這可能存在某些誤解。）

4. **25%**

● **That's an unlikely** estimation.
（這個估算不太可能。）

● **It seems unlikely that** your department will achieve sales quota this
year.
（貴部門今年要達到業績似乎不太可能。）

● **It's improbable** that your client will accept this terms and conditions.
（要你的顧客接受這服務條款與細則是不太可能的。）

● The outcome of the product testing **remains in doubt**.
（產品測試結果仍然持疑。）

5. 0%

● **It is impossible** for us to launch this new product next month.

（對我們而言下個月要推出新產品是不可能的。）

● **We were unable to** connect to database server this morning.

（我們今早都無法連上資料庫伺服器。）

● That was **a thoroughly impracticable** plan.

（那根本是個無法實行的計畫。）

● The business reengineering **cannot** be done in this conservative company.

（企業再造在這家保守的公司是不可能發生的。）

What are in Proforma Invoice? 報價單內容

1. Proforma Invoice ＝ 「預約發票」，也有稱「估價單」，或「銷貨確認單」。預約發票開立於實際交易之前，可提供顧客或進口商估算進口成本、利潤等費用。可縮寫為「P/I」或「PI」。

2. No. ＝ number 編號、標明報價單的編號。

3. risk of Messrs ＝ Messrs為Mister的複數，risk of Messrs表示風險承擔人。

4. For account and risk of Messrs ＝ 貨款與風險承擔由發票受文者（即顧客）負擔。

5. freight ＝ 運輸、貨運。sea freight是海運，air freight 是貨物空運。Express為快遞。

6. quantity ＝ Qty 數量。

7. PCS ＝ pieces 貨物件數。

8. unit price ＝ U/P 單價。

9. Total ＝ total amount總價。

10. FOB ＝ Free on Board 船上交貨（價格）、離岸價格。

11. Forwarder ＝ 運輸業者。

12. C/No. ＝ carton number 紙箱編號。

13. 通常於報價單下方都會有買賣雙方業務負責人簽名欄位。出貨公司會有業務代表簽名（Confirmed 上方），以及業務主管的簽名（Authorized Signature上方），最後押上日期。買方若是接受賣方的價格與運送條件，則在訂貨公司處簽名（Confirmed and accepted by下方），即代表本契約成立。隨後，雙方必須履行出貨與付款之義務。

14. Foreign Currency 各國貨幣：

	貨幣	Currency	Symbol
1	新台幣	New Taiwan Dollar	NT$
2	日元	Japanese Yen	¥
3	韓國圓	Korean Won	W
4	香港元	Hong Kong Dollar	HK$
5	澳門元	Macao Pataca	Pat
6	人民幣	Renminbi Yuan	CNY
7	泰銖	Thai Baht	B
8	越南盾	Vietnamese Dong	D
9	馬來西亞林吉特	Malaysian Ringgit	M$
10	新加坡元	Singapore Dollar	S$
11	菲律賓披索	Philippine Peso	php
12	印度盧比	Indian Rupee	Rs
13	澳大利亞元	Australian Dollar	$A
14	紐西蘭元	New Zealand Dollar	NZ$
15	以色列鎊	Israeli Shekel	ILS
16	土耳其里拉	Turkish Lira	LT
17	美元	United States Dollar	US$
18	加拿大元	Canadian Dollar	Can$
19	墨西哥披索	Mexican Peso	Mex$
20	阿根廷披索	Argentine Peso	$a
21	歐元	EUR (Euro dollar)	€
22	瑞士法郎	Swiss Franc	SF
23	英鎊	Sterling Pound	£
24	俄羅斯盧布	Russian Rouble	Rub
25	南非蘭特	South African Rand	R

| Proforma Invoice: 報價單範例 |

COVENTRY TECHNOLOGY CO., LTD
3F, No.17 Moor Hall, Cookham
Berkshire SL9 4QH United Kingdom
Tel: +44(0)1628 426426 Fax: +44(0)1628 427427

PROFORMA INVOICE

No. A071219   Date: 21-Aug-08

INVOICE OF CCTV EQUIPMENT
For account and risk of Messrs NICOLAS KAZAN
BLOCK BANK AUDI, AUTOSRADE DORA, PO BOX 90-1234 BEIRUT, LEBNANON
Shipped by COVENTRY TECHNOLOGY CO., LTD   **per**   SEA FREIGHT
Sailing on or about 27-Aug-08   **From**   UK **To** LEBANON

DESCRIPTION OF GOODS		QUANTITY	UNIT PPRICE	AMOUNT
COVENTRY BRAND				**FOB UK**
CT-CC721	1/3" COLOR CCD CAMERA, DC12V, W/AUDIO	15 PCS	US$100.00	US$1,500.00
CT-CQ51	QUAD REAL TIME COLOR VIDEO COMPRESSOR	15 PCS	US$250.00	US$3,750.00
CT-B01	SHORT TYPE MOUNT BRACKET, PLASTIC, BLACK COLOUR	100 PCS	US$3.00	US$300.00
CT-B15A	MULTI-FUNCTION MOUNTING BRACKET, BLACK COLOUR	300 PCS	US$3.00	US$900.00
CT-BC432	1/3" B/W CCD CAMERA, W/"SONY" CHIPS & AUDIO	100 PCS	US$45.00	US$4,500.00
TOTAL FOB UNITED KINGDOM				**US$10,950.00**

SAY TOTAL US DOLLORS TEN THOUSAND NINE HUNDRED AND FIFTY ONLY.
　　　　　　1. **PAYMENT:**　T/T IN ADVANCE, 10 DAYS BEFORE THE SHIPMENT
　　　　　　2. **DELIVERY:**　27-Aug-08
　　　　　　3. **FORWARDER:** GLOBE EXPRESS
　　　　　　4. **SEA FREIGHT COLLECT**

SHIPPING MARK:

LEBANON
C/NO.
MADE IN UK

CONFIRMED AND ACCEPTED BY   COVENTRY TECHNOLOGY CO., LTD
Berry Kazan   23/08/08   *COVENTRY TECHNOLOGY*
　AUTHORIZED SIGNATURE   DAVID HUNT / SALES REPRESENTATIVE
                                                 David Hunt 2008/08/21
                                                      CONFIRMED
                                                 Sales Director : Phila Loven   8/21
                                                      AUTHORIZED SIGNATURE

▶練習題④◀

　　請練習撰寫一封商業書信，將自己扮演成筆記型電腦製造商「Go Anywhere」的業務經理，對顧客「Hanley Trading」副總Peter Roberts的來函訂購新型筆電進行答謝與回覆。

▲練習題⑤◥

　　請練習撰寫一封詢價信，以美國「Digi Device」採購經理的身分向台灣「Super Digita」詢問數位相框（digital photo frame）的報價。並分別要求一萬台及五萬台訂單的報價。

▶練習題⑥◀

　　請練習製作一張估價單(Performa Invoice)，以回覆Digi Device 對數位相框（Digital phone frame）的詢價，並以DPF-1（一吋數位相框）及DPF-2（二吋數位相框）的型號依其數量回覆。DPF-1訂購一萬台時，每台定價US $4.5；訂購五萬台時，每台定價US $3.8。 DPF-2訂購一萬台時，每台定價US $7.0；訂購五萬台時，每台定價 US $6.0。

2.5 Negotiation and Bargaining 議價與協商

　　議價與協商通常是企業對企業商務往來不可避免的過程,而且耗費時間與精力占了整個交易的一半,交易的成功與否大部分是取決於良好的議價與協商。創造雙贏是雙方共同的期待,但如無法成功也不要撕破臉,以保留下次合作的機會,俗話說:「交易不成,情意在」。

　　議價主要是針對價格的問題,而協商則較廣泛牽涉到交易內容,可包括價格、服務、保固、交貨期限等等。本節希望讀者能夠學習到不同狀況的議價與協商用法。

　　協商談判能力是從事商務相關人員必備的核心能力,成熟的協商談判技巧將有助於生意往來與業務的推廣。以下是四個精簡的談判步驟:

1. Preparation Phase (準備階段)

This is where you work out what you want and which are the main priorities.

準備階段必須找出與顧客協商的目的,以及預期達到的目標,並將這些目的或目標列出輕重緩急前後次序。

2. Debating Phase (辯論階段)

During this phase you try to find out what the other side or the customer wants. Say what you want but do not say what the final conditions. Use open questions and listen to your customer. Try to find out in what areas the other side may be prepared to move.

在協商的第二個階段,必須找出顧客的需求為何,讓顧客知悉你的期望與公司所能提供的服務內容,先不要透露出公司的底限。使用開放問句並傾聽顧客說法,試著找出對方可能的動態。

　　辯論階段可透過對顧客問問題的方式，取得所需的訊息。一般問句可分為「封閉式問句」與「開放式問句」。封閉式問句的答案侷限於「是」或「不是」，例如：「本公司所提供的優惠方案，您滿意嗎？」而開放式問句，讓顧客有更多的發揮空間，例如：「請您告訴我，針對這樣的處理方式，您的建議是？」此時，業務人員將可得到更多答案與來自顧客的心聲。研究顯示成功的業務人員在銷售過程中使用更多開放式問句。開放式問句可利用6W（what, where, when, who, why and how）來進一步獲取更完整的訊息，並進一步調整自己的策略。

3. Proposing Phase（提案階段）

This is the point at which you suggest some of the things you could trade or which you might be prepared to trade. Formulate your proposals in the form of *if..., then...* . Be patient and listen to the other side's proposals.

進入第三個協商談判階段就是讓顧客了解公司所能接受的條件與情況，以「如果……，然後就……」方式，讓顧客明白條件被滿足時，要求就會執行。此刻，多聽取不同意見是很重要的。

4. Bargaining Phase（議價階段）

This is the period or part where you indicate what it is you will actually trade. Here you exchange conditionally in turn particular points, *if..., then ...* . Remember to write down the agreement.

議價階段便是大顯身手之刻，此時貴我雙方皆擲出可接受的底限。為確保談判成功，創造「雙贏」（win-win）的策略是必要的。對於顧客的特殊要求，也必須於合約上特別載明。

▌寓言分享 ▌

　　龜兔賽跑，兔子輸掉第一場比賽後，開始自我反省，牠發現自己會輸給烏龜，完成是出自於自大和驕傲。於是牠約烏龜再比賽一次，但這一次路線須由兔子指定，烏龜同意。這次兔子選擇了一條直線跑道，並把距離縮短成原來的一半，當槍聲響起時，兔子立刻衝出，頭也不回地衝向終點，贏得勝利。

　　這回輪到烏龜自我反省了，牠發現自己會輸給兔子，是因為不懂得充分運用自身優點的緣故。想通之後，烏龜又邀兔子做第三次比賽，這次的路線由烏龜決定。

　　起跑後，兔子一如以往一路領先，因為一條河擋住了牠前進的方向而突然停下。兔子焦急地踱步，因為牠不會游泳。正著急，烏龜出現了，只見烏龜不疾不徐地爬到河邊，悠然自在下水後，游到對岸獲勝。

　　兔子一想，這樣下去會沒完沒了，就建議烏龜：「我們改變競爭關係換以策略聯盟如何？」「好呀！」烏龜爽快地答應。這次兔子背上烏龜照原來的路線再跑一次，到了河邊換兔子騎在烏龜背上過河，一上岸兔子又背烏龜跑向終點。

　　成績揭曉牠們同心協力超越了各自跑的平均值達三倍以上，是龜兔賽跑有史以來紀錄最快的一次。

（文章摘錄自：張羽良，龜兔又賽跑了，《新紀元》週刊，2008年，66期，頁64。）

　　這則寓言的確闡述了商務往來的精神所在，在企業與企業的互動中，唯有以互信互賴之誠心創造雙贏（win-win）來取代敵對競爭的零和（zero-sum）關係，才能將彼此的獲益推向頂峰，形成企業與顧客擁有彼此的終身價值（lifetime value）。

Getting It Right in Negotiation

在協商談判時，以下是幾個最常被討論的議題。

- price（價格）
  - discount（折扣）
  - good price（好價格）
  - competitive price（具競爭力的價格）
- guarantees（產品保固）
- quality（產品或服務的品質）
- the need for firm figures（提供準確的數據）

協商談判例句：Buyer 買方

- Is it possible to bring the price down a little more?
  （有可能再降價嗎？）

- I don't think we can make any profit with the price you offered.
  （我認為你們給的價格，我們無法獲利。）

- **Compared with** other suppliers, your price seems too high.
  （與其他商家相比，你們的價格似乎太高。）

- Business is closed at this price.
  （依此價交易就此敲定。）

- Your price is acceptable.
  （你的價格可以接受。）

- Your price is not competitive.
  （你們的價格沒有競爭力。）

● Your price is rather stiff.

（你們的價格太高。）

● Can you quote in US dollars?

（貴公司可以美金報價嗎？）

● I would like to know the payment terms you can accept.

（我想知道貴公司可接受的付款方式。）

● We will consider to doubling our order if Coventry Technology improves the delivery date.

（假如科芬垂科技可以改善交貨日，我們將考慮加倍訂單。）

● We can commit to place orders for the whole year.

（我們可允諾下整年訂單。）

● We need the old model this time and may consider the new model when they are ready for our second order.

（此次下訂我們需要舊型號，至於新型號在下次訂貨時，若有現貨將予以考慮。）

● Please find attached the signed Proforma Invoice. Our DHL Client No. is 15384 and we are looking forward to your samples.

（請參考回簽訂單，我們的DHL顧客編號是15384，期待收到貴公司寄來的樣品。）

● We hope you can deliver our first order by the end of month.

（我們希望本月底貴公司能將我們的首次訂單送出。）

● Please make a spare part list which is necessary for service and repair. It would be highly appreciated if you may send the necessary spares with our first shipment.

（請提供一份備件清單，以供本公司服務與維修之用。假如貴公司能夠在我們首次訂貨出貨時附上必備的零件，將十分感激。）

● Please provide us with 50 leaflets of digital cameras and another 50 of MP3 so as to enable us to distribute among our clients in a proper time.

（請提供五十份數位相機和五十份MP3的簡介，以便我們及時提供給顧客。）

● Following is a list of past problems for your reference and please assure us that they will not occur again.

（以下是過去曾發生的問題清單供貴公司參考，並請確認這些問題以後不再發生。）

■ 單字解析

compare to / compare with的差異

<u>Compare to</u> 通常用於比較兩種不同的東西。

He *compared Mary to* a summer day.

（他將瑪莉比作晴天。）

Scientists sometimes *compare* the human brain to a computer.

（有時科學家拿人腦與電腦相比。）

<u>Compare with</u> 通常用於比較兩種相似的事物。

The police *compared* the forged signature *with* the original.

（警察比對偽簽名與真人簽名。）

The committee will have to *compare* the Senate's version of the bill *with* the version that was passed by the House of Representative.

（委員會將必須比較參議院的法案版本與之前由眾議院通過的法案版本。）

▌協商談判例句：Seller 賣方

● Thank you very much for your esteemed fax dated 23-01-2009.

（十分感謝你於2009年1月23日的傳真。）

● Finally, I would like to thank you for your custom and commitment to Baxhaull over the past years and hope that you will continue to buy our products in the future.

（最後，我想感謝貴公司在過去幾年裡惠顧Baxhaull產品，並期望貴公司在未來能繼續支持我們的產品。）

● I think we can reduce the price a little bit.

（我想我們可以再降一點價格。）

● We have lowered the quotation by fifteen percent.

（本公司報價已降15%。）

● We have offered you our bottom price.

（我們已經給了最低價了。）

● We already cut the price very fine.

（我們已經降價至底線了。）

● If you can place a future order of the mobile phones, then we can have some room to cut down the price.

（假如你可以再下手機訂單，那我們就有降價的空間。）

● We regret that we have to maintain our original price.

（很遺憾我們必須維持原價。）

● Since the prices of the raw materials have been raised, I'm afraid that we have to adjust the prices accordingly.

（由於原物料價格上漲，我們不得不調漲產品價格。）

● Since the level of business in the past six months, we regret to inform you that we are unable to support you as a direct account.

（因為貴我雙方過去六個月的交易量，很抱歉告知本公司無法再視貴公司為直銷顧客。）

● Can you increase the quantity of your order?

（貴公司可以增加訂貨數量嗎？）

● I am afraid that the terms and conditions are not acceptable.

（恐怕服務條款與細則無法接受。）

練習題⑦　中翻英

1. 問：假如你能再降單價五美元，我們會將訂貨量增加到五千組。

   答：如貴公司年度訂貨量達到五千組，超過五千組之數量將提供
   單價五美元之優惠。

2. 問：產品如無法提供二年保固期（Warranty），下年度將不再下訂單。

   答：本公司產品型號HCU及DPAM將於2010開始提供二年保固。

3. 問：請貴公司於貨到裝置完畢，派工程師測試。請問收費標準為何？

   答：派工程師測試新機器是本公司的售後服務，並不會有額外收費。

4. 問：我們需要的是通用電源器（universal adopter），而不是110伏
   特（voltage）。

   答：採用通用電源器產品價格將增加二美元。

5. 問：如果貴公司堅持調漲價格，明年度我們將尋找新供應商。

   答：很遺憾新價格已經是公司的既定政策。

2.6 Complaints and Objection Handling 顧客抱怨與處理

通常危機產生，顧客是不安或是憤怒的。危機的形成不一定都是單向因公司、產品、服務或業務本身的錯誤引起，也可能是顧客自己的疏忽釀成的後果。如果此刻業務人員只是一味為自己或公司辯護，雙方易爭執不下，非但問題難解也可能種下一個不滿顧客的不定時炸彈。

針對不滿的顧客，企業很難控制其不會對公司品牌形象做出任何批評或惡意傳播，研究指出一位不滿的顧客會將不愉快的經驗告訴其他八至十位顧客。更糟糕的是，那些不滿的顧客還會帶走另一批潛在的新顧客，並使企業失去商譽，甚至競爭力。故盡力圓融不滿顧客的抱怨也是各家企業在顧客關係管理一環的當務之急。危機處理得當可成轉機，而轉機好好掌握便成商機，好壞所及其背後影響深遠。

抱怨信例句

We are concerned that the order we placed by letter on 8 June may have gotten lost in the post. What are you going to do about this?
（關於我們在6月8日所下的訂單，可能於郵寄時遺失，貴公司打算如何處理？）

The order has not yet arrived at our warehouse, even though we received advice of shipping from you a week ago. Would you check with your forwarder again?
（即使我們於一週前收到貴公司的出貨通知，本公司下的訂單至今仍未進倉，能否請貴公司與運輸業者再次確認？）

According to your price list of a single room with bath is $56 including tax. However, when I received my account statement this morning, I discovered that I was charged $68.45 per night. I hope this clarifies my position.

（根據貴旅館的價目表，有浴缸的單人房含稅價是56美元。但是，當我今早收到銀行帳單時，發現貴旅館每晚的索價是68.45美元，希望你能了解。）

On 26 July 2008 we placed an order with you for 1,200 ultra long-life batteries. When the consignment arrived yesterday, it contained only 1,100 batteries. Please make up the shortfall shortly.

（本公司在2008年7月26日的訂單中，購置了一千二百顆超長效電池。但是當昨日收到貨時，卻發現僅有一千一百顆超長效電池。請儘速將缺額補上。）

We all make mistakes - sometimes! 人難免會犯錯

If you want to complain to a person you don't know well, be careful! A direct complaint or criticism can sound very rude or aggressive.

在商務場合中，完全不出任何差錯似乎不太可能。當彼此之間的關係不是很熟悉，遇到不愉快的經驗時，用字遣詞必須十分小心，以避免不必要的誤解甚或造成顧客的流失。

■ 單字解析

aggressive (a) 侵略性的、好鬥的、有進取心的

Tom is a reliable, energetic and *aggressive* salesman.

（湯姆是一位可靠、積極和有進取心的業務員。）

It may be best to mention the problem more indirectly by saying:

儘量避免怒氣時衝口而出，如此將容易破壞商務間往來的關係。以下是幾種較委婉的表達方式：

● I'm sorry to have to say this but ...

（很抱歉我不得不說……）

● I'm sorry to brother you but ...

（很抱歉打擾你，但……）

● I think you may have forgotten ...

（我想你可能不記得了……）

● It may have slipped your mind, but ...

（你可能沒印象了，但……）

● There may have been a misunderstanding about ...

（有可能在……上有了誤解……）

Only in extreme cases, if you've already tried more polite methods, would you have to threaten someone:

極少數的情況下，強硬的口吻才能解決問題：

● Look, if you don't send your engineer to repair the machine in three days, we will be forced to cancel our next order.

（注意！如貴公司沒有在三日內派工程師來修理機器，我們將取消下張訂單。）

● Unless you pay the account within ten days, we will place the matter in the hands of our attorneys.

（如貴公司未能於十日內付款，此事將交由本公司律師處理。）

▌ 抱怨信函範例 ▌

Best Security

26 Boulton Road, Coventry, Warwickshire, CV3 7AL, UK
Telephone: (0113)986156 Fax: (0113)986765

21 Septemper 2009

Mary Lee
Precision Electronics Co., Ltd
7 Science Road,
Science-Based Industrial Park
Chunan, Taiwan 350

Dear Mrs. Lee,

I'm **enclosing** a copy of my order, dated August 3, for 500 pieces **CCD Camera**. Your sales told me that it would take four weeks to arrive in Birmingham. However, we received this shipment yesterday. When opening the carton box, we were disappointed to find that over 10% of packaging were damaged.

I think you will understand why I am upset at the manner in which this order was handled. This order had **spoiled** our company reputation.

Please inform your action plan on this, otherwise our alternative will be to find a new supplier soon.

Yours,

Sam Rewan

Product Manager
Best Security
sam_rewan@best.co.uk

▎抱怨信函範例中文翻譯 ▎

李女士，您好：

　　隨函附上本公司8月3日下的五百台監視攝影機訂單，當時貴公司業務告知貨物抵達伯明罕的時間只需四週，但是，我們直到昨日才收到這批貨。當拆箱時，又發現超過十分之一的包裝受損，我們對此感到很失望。

　　我想貴公司會了解本公司對此次訂單處理方式的不滿，這次訂單真的已經損及本公司的商譽。

　　請告知貴公司對此事件的行動計畫。否則，我們將於不久後找尋另一家新的供應商。

山姆・雷旺　謹上

產品經理

Best Security

sam_rewan@best.co.uk

■ 單字解析

enclose (v) 隨信附上

A check is *enclosed* herewith.

（隨信附支票一張。）

CCD camera (ph.) 監視攝影機

spoil (v) 損壞、糟蹋

Spare the rod, *spoil* the child.

（不打不成器。）

▌抱怨電子郵件範例 ▌

To: Leo Jones <leo.jones@foxmachines.com.tw>
From: Raymond Santamaria <raymond@goodway.com.fr>
Date: 2009/5/30 09:24
Subject: **About the Order No. 765**
■ urgent ☐ confidential

- -

Dear Leo,

As you know, we have bought several machines from your company and been quite satisfied with their performance. We have even recommended Fox Machines to many other companies here in France. Recently, however, the standard of your **after-sales service** has dropped considerably.

Our three FM88 Plus were installed in 2007 and your regular twice-yearly service together with our own maintenance programme has kept them in perfect working order. When there was a **breakdown**, your service agents used to send an engineer at 24 hours' notice.

Now the situation has changed and the engineer promises to come "in about 6 days" and is unable to tell us his exact arrival time. Last week he came at 4pm on Friday afternoon and our own maintenance engineer was unable to leave until your man had finished.

We are really discontent with your recent after-sales service. We have already spoken to your service agents, but there has been no improvement so far.

We look forward to hearing from you and hope that you can promise an immediate improvement.

Yours truly,

Raymond Santamaria

Sales Manager
Goodway Machines Co., Ltd
(33) 1 47 11 22 33
raymond@goodway.com.fr

▌抱怨電子郵件範例中文翻譯 ▌

To: Leo Jones <leo.jones@foxmachines.com.tw>
From: Raymond Santamaria <raymond@goodway.com.fr>
Date: 2009/5/30 09:24
Subject：（緊急郵件）有關765號訂單

親愛的李奧，您好：

　　正如你所知，本公司已向貴公司購買了幾台機器，並且非常滿意它們的功能。我們也推薦貴公司給在法國的很多公司。然而，最近貴公司的售後服務水準已經下滑得非常嚴重。

　　我們於2007年安裝的三台FM88 Plus機器，貴公司提供的兩年一次服務以及我們自己的維護服務方案，讓這些機器的運作狀況良好。當機器故障時，貴公司的服務代理商通常在二十四小時內派工程師前來維修。

　　現在則今非昔比，工程師允諾六天內至本公司維修，但卻無法給予確定的抵達時間。上週貴公司的服務代理商的工程師，在星期五下午四點才來，讓本公司的維修工程師，為了陪他修理機器也無法準時下班。

　　我們真的對貴公司的售後服務感到很不滿。儘管已經告知貴公司的服務代理商，但是情況直至今日仍無改進。

　　我們期待收到貴公司的回音，並且希望貴公司允諾立即改善。

你最真誠的

芮蒙‧聖塔瑪麗亞

銷售經理
Goodway Machines Co., Ltd
(33) 1 47 11 22 33
raymond@goodway.com.fr

■ 單字解析

after-sales service (ph.) 售後服務

If you have any question on the maintenance, please contact our local distributor or regional specialist for *after-sale service*.

（假如您有任何維修上的疑問，請與本公司當地配銷商或地區專員聯繫。）

breakdown (n) 故障、損壞

CMC provides comprehensive mechanical *breakdown* cover to the machine tool industry.

（CMC公司提供工具機產業全面的機器故障搶修。）

Response to Complaints：如何處理客戶抱怨

當顧客不滿呼之欲出或已爆發，應先釐清顧客不滿的原因。這時應該心平氣和，不受顧客影響自身情緒或對待顧客的態度，同理心站在對方的角度想一想，一方面表示了解並認同顧客所遭遇的困難，一方面與顧客進一步談談找出問題癥結。在找出問題所在後，若是企業疏忽應立即道歉並儘速處理或補救，將對顧客所造成的傷害降至最低；若是顧客的誤解也應委婉解釋，並進一步協助顧客解決問題。

建議此刻專心聆聽並用感性的方式處理顧客抱怨；在顧客盛怒大罵時，仍與顧客站在同一陣線，適時針對顧客的問題做回應、不急不徐。同理心傾聽（empathy listening）中，保持適度緘默（non-verbal listening）努力找出顧客的痛苦、問題的癥結以及接下來該如何協助顧客的解決方案。掌握聽的技巧能夠更清楚顧客的整體情況，對問題的解決有加分的效果，而顧客滿意度（customer satisfaction）也會提升。

If someone complains to you, or if you think they're likely to complain, it may be wise to apologize - even if it wasn't really your fault. Then you can promise to put things right.
假如客戶或是商務往來對象對你抱怨或感覺上像是抱怨，此時道歉是最聰明的方法，即便錯不在你。之後，再承諾把事情處理好，便是上上之策喔。

▶ 幾種禮貌的道歉語句

● I am very sorry, it's my fault.
（非常對不起，這是我的錯。）

● I do apologize. I didn't realize.
（很抱歉我沒注意到。）

● There has been a problem in our local agent.
（這是我們地區代理商的問題。）

● We are very sorry about the delay (mistake).
（我們對我們的延誤（錯誤）感到抱歉。）

● We wish to apologize for any inconvenience this might have caused you.
（對於此事造成您的不便，我深感歉意。）

● Please accept our apologies for losing your data.
（對於你資料的遺失，請接受我們誠心的道歉。）

● You can accept someone's apology by saying:
（回應對方的道歉）

● That's all right!
（沒事／沒關係！）

● It's perfectly all right!
（真的沒事／沒關係！）

● It really doesn't matter.
（真的不用在意。）

處理顧客抱怨書信範例

Great Ocean View, Inc.

1458 Atlantic Drive, Asbury Park, New Orleans, 70113, USA

Mr. Pat Brown
Purchasing Manager
Atlantic International

11/05/2009

Re: Your fax #0097 dated 11/04/2009

- -

Dear Mr. Brown,

Thank you so much for your fax. We are very sorry for the late delivery of your order.

We always pride ourselves on keeping to our delivery dates. In your case, it was really beyond our control owing to the natural disaster-hurricane had forced the Port of New Orleans to close for a week. That's the reason why we couldn't ship your order on time. However, I am glad to be able to say that they are packed for export now.

We will ship the goods tomorrow, and the shipment will arrive in London on November 9.

Again, we do deeply apologize for the late shipment and greatly regret any inconvenience this might have caused you.

Yours faithfully,

Francisco Handison

General Manager, Great Ocean View Suppliers

處理顧客抱怨書信範例中文翻譯

Great Ocean View, Inc.

1458 Atlantic Drive, Asbury Park, New Orleans, 70113, USA

派德・布朗先生
採購經理
大西洋國際公司
11/05/2009
主題：回覆11/04/2009貴公司 0097 號傳真

尊敬的布朗先生，您好：

　　非常感謝您的傳真。對於延遲交貨我們感到非常抱歉。

　　我們總是對準時交貨感到自豪。但是，對於貴公司的案子的確是出乎我們的控制，因為颶風的天然災害迫使紐澳良港必須關閉一週。這就是本公司無法準時交貨的原因。然而，我很高興通知您，貴公司下訂的貨物現正準備裝運。

　　我們將於明日出貨，預計貨品11月9日抵達倫敦。

　　本公司再一次針對延遲交貨致上最深的歉意，並非常抱歉任何可能已經引起貴公司的不便。

您最忠實的

法蘭西斯科・韓帝森

總經理Great Ocean View Suppliers

練習題⑧ 中翻英

A：貴公司於上個月承諾寄二個Z9電漿電視（plasma TV）的樣品，可是至今我們還沒有收到。下週我們將無法於家電展展出，你們要如何解決？

B：我們感到很抱歉，因為業務Debbie請產假沒有交代此事。我們將於今日用DHL寄出二個樣品，二日後會抵達，以供貴公司展出。祝展覽順利！

2.7 Selling, Distributing and Contract 銷售、經銷與契約

　　公司的銷售表現通常代表其營運狀況，一般的買家會信任銷售狀況良好的供應商與產品，至少他們已經獲得市場的肯定。所以，商用書信也經常會提到公司與產品的市場狀況。因為有些產品市場的範圍太大，或者企業本身不具備行銷通路，便會建立與其他企業的合作關係，成為企業的經銷商或代理商。這些與代理或經銷商的往來也成為商用英文重要之一環。本節整理相關銷售與經銷的例句與商務書信，讀者可以逐行學習。

銷售英文表達例句

● Our products are very popular in the eastern part of the USA.
（我們的產品在美國東部市場很暢銷。）

● We all understand that slippers made in Thailand are very popular in European market on account of their superior quality and competitive price.
（我們都知道泰國製的拖鞋因價廉物美而暢銷歐洲市場。）

● The new range of products launched last autumn is already selling well.
（去年秋天上市的新型產品已有很好的銷售表現。）

● This product has been a best seller for nearly one year.
（該產品成為暢銷貨已經將近一年了。）

- There is a poor market for these articles.
  （這些商品滯銷。）

- There is no market for these goods.
  （這些商品無市場。）

- Our demand for this product is steadily on the increase.
  （我們對該產品的需求穩定增長。）

- We are sure that you can sell more this year according to the marketing report.
  （根據市場報告，我們確信你們今年生意更好。）

- We are trying to find a market for this goods.
  （我們正為此商品尋找通路。）

- Taiwanese market still has great potential.
  （台灣市場仍有很大潛力。）

- There are only a few unsold pieces.
  （只剩幾件商品未售出。）

- We wish to express our sincere gratitude.
  （謹表達誠摯謝意。）

- Our company will provide our customers 100% satisfaction.
  （本公司將提供顧客完全的滿意。）

- We are given to understand that Temple Technology have interest in our promotion this quarter.
  （茲獲悉Temple科技公司對我們本季的促銷活動有興趣。）

- Please find attached descriptive and illustrated catalog for your reference.
  （請參考附件有說明與插圖的目錄。）

▌銷售電子郵件範例 ▌

To: Roster Metal
Attn: "Mr. Patrick Sean" <psean@rostermetal.com>
Subject: New Product RM-521 Launch
■ Normal　☐ Urgent　☐ Confidential
Date: 03/05/2009

- -

Dear Patrick,

Long time no see! How are you? I am writing to inform you that as a regular buyer of our metal working machines, you will be interested in our brand new model that we have just launched.

The RM-541 is a **revolutionary breakthrough** in precision engineering. This laser cutting machine uses the leading edge technology to create its precision surfaces. It is truly designed to fit any individual user. The RM-541 is easy to operate and gives one hundred percent accuracy. Attached documents are the pictures and technical information **concerning** the RM-541 for your reference.

I plan to visit your company next month and would be delighted to introduce this brand new product to you. Our first demonstration of the RM-541 will be held at the ELETROX 2009 in Berlin. It will be our great pleasure if you can **come over** to our booth B03.

Sincerely yours,

Gerald Haigh

Marketing Director
Digest Machine Co., Ltd
geraldhaigh@digest.com.jp

┃ 銷售電子郵件範例中文翻譯 ┃

To: Roster Metal

Attn: "Mr. Patrick Sean" <psean@rostermetal.com>

Subject: New Product RM-521 Launch

■ 標準　□ 緊急　□ 商業機密

Date: 03/05/2009

- -

親愛的派翠克，您好：

　　好久不見！近來可好？我寫這封電子郵件給您，是想通知身為本公司固定買主的貴公司，將對我們剛剛推出市場的新產品會有興趣。

　　新產品RM-541在精密機械是一項革命性突破，這款雷射切割機器使用前沿科技作為它的精密表面加工。RM-541也是真正為任何個別使用者所設計，它很容易操作且正確精準。請參考附件文件中對RM-541圖解與技術訊息。

　　我計劃於下個月拜訪貴公司，很榮幸將這款全新的機器介紹給您。RM-541將在2009年柏林的ELETROX第一次展示，若您能參觀本公司B3攤位，將榮幸備至。

您最誠摯的

格瑞爾德‧海

行銷總監

Digest 機器公司

geraldhaigh@digest.com.jp

■ 單字解析

revolutionary (a) 革命的、變革的、創新的

This product is a *revolutionary* innovation in pump technology.

（該項產品是泵技術的革新性創新。）

breakthrough (n) 突破

The lecturer taught us how to foster *breakthrough* thinking.

（講師教我們如何培養突破性思考。）

concerning (prep.) 關於

The committee meeting will discuss the investment amount *concerning* this joint venture.

（委員會會議將討論此合資企業的投資金額。）

come over (ph.) 順便來訪

Won't you plan to *come over* to Turkey for a business trip?

（你不計劃商務旅行來土耳其嗎？）

代理商英文表達方式

● In consideration to your extensive experience in the field, we are glad to appoint you as our *agent*.
（因貴公司在此業務範疇經驗豐富，我們很高興指定貴公司為我們的代理商。）

● I'm entitled to being appointed as your agent.
（本公司有資格被指定為貴公司的代理商。）

● We've decided to entrust you with the sole *agency* for cars.
（我們決定委託貴公司作為本公司汽車的獨家代理。）

● Thank you for your proposal of acting as our agent.
（謝謝你提議作為我們的代理商。）

● We are looking for a company like yours to act as our agent or distributor in Eastern Europe.
（我們正找尋一家像貴公司一樣擔任我們在東歐的代理商或經銷商。）

● *With reference to* your request to be our agent in the Middle East, we are very seriously considering this proposal.
（關於您要求成為我們中東的代理商，我們正審慎考量此案。）

● Many thanks for your effort to be our agent, however we already have a distributor in Hungary.
（感謝您提出要成為我們的代理商，然而我們在匈牙利已有一家經銷商。）

● We're not prepared to *take* the agency *into consideration for the time being*.
（目前我們仍不考慮代理的問題。）

- We are not yet prepared to take the question of sole agent into consideration *at present*.

  （我們目前尚不考慮有關獨家代理的問題。）

- We have to *decline* your proposal of acting as our sole agency.

  （我們必須謝絕您作為我方獨家代理的建議。）

- We are not in a position to seek an agent at present. If our situation changes in the near future, I will notify you immediately.

  （我們目前暫不考慮找代理商，若不久的將來需要，將馬上通知您。）

- Unless you increase the turnover, we can hardly appoint you as our exclusive agent.

  （除非您增加營業額，否則我們無法讓您作為我方的獨家代理。）

- Please get in touch with our agents for the supply of the goods you require.

  （請與我們的代理商聯繫您所需的商品。）

- I suggest that you contact our distributor directly.

  （我建議您直接與我們的經銷商聯絡。）

- When do you expect to sign the agency agreement?

  （您何時簽定代理協議呢？）

- Well, what annual quantity would you like to suggest for the new agreement then?

  （那麼請建議在新的協議中，年銷售量應為多少呢？）

- Our trade *is conducted* on the basis of equality and mutual benefit.

  （我們是在平等互利的基礎上進行貿易。）

● Do you have a branch office / agent / distributor in Brazil?

（貴公司在巴西有分公司／代理商／經銷商嗎？）

● I hope that your company could provide the technical support.

（我希望貴公司可以提供技術支援。）

■ 單字解析

agent (n) 代理人、經紀人（指人）

agency (n) 經銷、代辦（指地方）

General Manager made his special assistant as his *agent* while he was abroad.

（總經理請特助在他出國期間做他的代理人。）

This company has *agencies* in all parts of Middle East.

（該公司在中東各地皆有代理處。）

with reference to = concerning = regarding = with regard to 關於

take into consideration (ph.) 考慮、顧慮、體諒

When evaluating the solutions from service providers, Collins Torch Co., Ltd *took* price *into consideration*.

（假如您有任何維修上的疑問，請與本公司當地配銷商或地區專員聯繫。）

for the time being = at present (ph.) 目前、暫時

We meet the sales quota *for the time being*.

（我們暫時達到業績。）

decline (v) 婉拒、辭謝

The manager *declined* the distributor's invitation to dinner.

（經理婉拒經銷商用餐的邀請。）

conduct (v) 領導、指揮

The vice president *conducted* the price negotiation with customer yesterday.

（副總裁昨日主持與客戶的議價談判。）

代理商與經銷商範例

To: Smith Electronics Co., Ltd
Attn: "Managing Director, Mrs. Cleo Harper" <cleo@smith.com.cz>
Date: 28/12/2009
Subject: About Agent

Dear Mrs. Harper,

Thank you so much for your continuous support of our company throughout the past years. It has been a great pleasure doing business with you.

In the past couple of months, we have received many inquiries and some orders from customers based in Eastern Europe, such as the Czech Republic, Romania, Bulgaria and Poland. We feel that there is a potential and booming market in this area. We are looking for a company like yours to act as our agent or distributor in this area. Limited to the distance and few understanding, it is imperative for us to find an agent to introduce and distribute our products to this region. We are willing to provide a reasonable commission for your company and support you with samples together with after-sale service.

Please let us know your ideas and terms. We really hope that we can cooperate in the coming year.

Best Regards,

Joe Wang

CEO, Globe Vision Technology
E-mail: joewang@globevision.com.tw
Tel: 886-2-27648990 Fax: 886-2-27648991
18F, No.168, Minsheng W. Road
Ta-Tung District, 103 Taipei, Taiwan

代理商與經銷商範例中文翻譯

To: 史密斯電子公司

Attn: "克里歐‧哈柏總經理" <cleo@smith.com.cz>

Date: 2009年12月28日

Subject: 有關代理一事

尊敬的哈柏女士，您好：

　　非常感謝貴公司於過去幾年來的支持，與貴公司有生意往來是本公司的榮幸。

　　在過去幾個月內，我們收到了許多來自東歐客戶的詢問與訂單，其中有捷克、羅馬尼亞、保加利亞與波蘭。我們認為在東歐有潛在與新興的商機，我們期待找一家像貴公司一樣的企業，作為本公司在該區域的代理商或經銷商。礙於距離與缺乏了解，我們迫切希望在這個區域找一家代理商，能夠銷售本公司的產品。我們很願意提供貴公司合理的佣金與產品樣本，以及支援產品的售後服務。

　　請讓我知悉貴公司的想法與條件，真的希望貴我雙方在明年可以有合作往來。

致予最深的祝福

王　喬

全球視野科技 執行長

E-mail: joewang@globevision.com.tw

Tel: 886-2-27648990　Fax: 886-2-27648991

18F, No.168, Minsheng W. Road

Ta-Tung District, 103 Taipei, Taiwan

Contract 契約

商務契約是一特殊應用文體，重在記實，用字遣詞必須精確與嚴謹。契約牽涉到交易雙方的權利和義務，因此企業對於契約都相當重視，尤其是交易金額龐大的契約，在工作與勞務履行方面更是詳細記載。一般大型企業都有法務部門專門處理契約的內容，一般小型公司的契約則較制式簡易。有時單純的交易買賣，甚至只要回傳具有效力簽名的報價單，即可視為商業契約、買賣關係成立，並具有法律之強制力。

儘管各家公司契約內容與格式皆不盡相同，但在商務契約中，有些常用的項目是不可或缺的。而大部分的商務契約都會涵蓋特殊條款，以適用於特別情況。以下列出一般商務契約常見的條款。

(1) identify the parties：確認契約當事者或公司。
(2) addresses of parties：契約當事者或公司的聯絡地址。
(3) purposes of the contract：契約目的。
(4) contract terms：契約條款。
(5) warranties：瑕疵擔保，是指有關物或事的聲明與擔保。如擔保產品品質無瑕疵、聲明公司為合法設立且營運正常，或聲明公司無破產清算情形。
(6) disclaimers of liability：免責聲明，如聲明公司就某種服務，不負任何擔保責任。

【範例】

The information contained in this archive is provided 'as is' without warranty of any kind.

（本資料庫所呈現提供的訊息不負任何擔保責任。）

Justice Times accepts no responsibility for AD contents.

（正義時報對廣告內容不承擔任何責任。）

(7) limitations on liability：責任限制。是指發生重大災難時，事故負責人和保險人等，對受害者所提出的損害賠償請求，可限定自己的賠償責任在一定範圍內。

【範例】

Shipper agrees that the liability of SWIFT EXPRESS for any loss, damage, non-delivery or misdelivery shall only be limited to actual cost of preparation, replacement or reproduction of the shipment but not exceeding US \$3,000.

（託運人同意SWIFT EXPRESS對任何托運貨物遺失、損害、未托運或送錯時，負責有限的實際托運準備成本、替換或再生產的費用，但是不超過三千美金。）

(8) Liquidated damages：約定違約金，是指雙方在簽約時同意的一筆金額，當一方確實有違約情形產生且造成損失時，所必須支付他方的金額。

(9) Confidentiality provision：保密條款，是指當事者本誠信原則，對契約細節及經契約合作接觸而取得之各項相關資料加以保密。

(10) Indemnity agreement：賠償協議。

【範例】

In case of damage or non-delivery, claim must be submitted in writing within thirty days from date of issue of contract.

（假如貨品損害或未送達，賠償聲明應於契約簽署當日算起的三十天內提出。）

(11) Arbitration clause：仲裁條款，係屬當事人以約定之機關、方式
　　 等解決其糾紛。

(12) Venue of lawsuits involving the contract：訴訟法院之載明。

【範例】

Parties agree that any action that may arise out of this Contract shall
be filed only in the Courts of Taipei alone to the exclusion of all other
courts.

（雙方同意若契約有任何爭議時，僅以台北法院為訴訟法院。）

(13) Signatures of authorized signatories：雙方當事人簽字。

【範例】

By affixing your signature hereunder, you agree to the terms and
conditions of this contract.

（依此簽名後，你同意本合約的服務條款與細則。）

公文慣用副詞

　　商務契約為具有法律效力的文件，所以英譯時必須使用公文語詞，尤其是使用公文語慣用副詞，這樣結構將更嚴謹，且達到言簡意賅的作用。

　　公文語慣用副詞是由副詞，如here再加上 after、by、in、of、on、upon等字，構成一體化形式的公文語副詞。例如：

在上文中、在以上部分	hereinbefore	關於這個	hereto
在下文、在以下部分	hereinafter	關於此點	hereof
於此	hereon / hereupon	此後、今後	hereafter
依此、在下文	hereunder	隨即、立即	hereon
在上文中	hereinbefore	在下文中	hereinafter
特此、藉此、茲	hereby	藉以	whereby

● This contract will come into force from the date of execution hereof by the Buyer and the Supplier.

　　（本契約自買方和供應方簽署之日生效。）

● The undersigned hereby agrees that the services requested as shown below shall be performed by the staff.

　　（下述簽署人特此同意以下所要求的服務應由工作人員執行。）

契約中容易犯的錯誤

契約的重要項目，如：金錢、時間以及數量是不容出錯的。為避免犯錯，撰寫契約時必須使用一些有限定作用的語句，來界定所指定項目的明確範圍。

1. 責任

契約中明確規範雙方兩造的責任。在雙方責任的許可權與範圍，常使用連接詞和介繫詞。

(1) and/or：「甲和乙」/「甲或乙」，如此可避免遺漏其中一方

- The shipper shall be liable for all damage caused by such goods to the ship *and/or* cargo on board.

（如果上述貨物對船舶和（或）船上其他貨物造成任何損害，托運人應負全責。）

(2) by and between：當事雙方有義務履行契約責任

- This contract is made *by and between* the Buyer and the Seller, whereby the Buyer agrees to buy and the Seller agrees to sell the undermentioned commodity subject to the terms and conditions stipulated below.

（買賣雙方簽訂本合約，藉以買方同意按照下列條款購買商品，賣方同意出售商品。）

2. 時間

契約擬定必須審慎處理時間相關字眼，契約中時間的準確性通常以下述結構來表達。

(1) include：含當日在內的時間

● This credit expires *till* January 15 (*inclusive*) for negotiation in Taipei.

= This credit expires till and including January 15 for negotiation in Taipei.

（本證在台北議付，有效期至1月15日。）

※若不包括1月15日在內，可表示為 till and not including January 15。

(2) not (no) later than：後面加日期，意即「不得晚於某年某月某日」

● Party B shall ship the goods within one month of the date of signing this Contract *not later than* March 3.

（乙方須於契約簽字日一個月內出貨，即不得晚於3月3日。）

(3) on or before 或 on or after：以雙介詞表示含當日在內的起迄時間

● Party A shall be unauthorized to accept any orders *on and after* September 20.

（自9月20日起甲方無權接受任何訂單。）

● Our payment terms are cash within three months *on or before* January 1, 2010.

（本公司的付款條件是，顧客不得晚於2010年1月1日的三個月內，支付現金。）

3. 金額

契約中為避免金額誤植或被塗改，通常表示方式如下：

(1) 以大寫文字書寫金額

契約中的金額通常以大寫文字表示。大寫文字前加上**"SAY"**或是**"SAY TOTAL"**，意為「大寫」；在最後加上**"ONLY"**，意為「整」。書寫時要注意小寫與大寫的金額總數必須一致。

● Party A shall pay Party B a monthly salary of US $800 (**SAY EIGHT HUNDRED US DOLLARS ONLY**).

（甲方須每月支付乙方八百美元整的薪資。）

(2) 正確使用貨幣符號

契約中必須詳列並正確使用不同貨幣的名稱與符號。$可代表「美元」，亦可為其他國家的幣別；而£不僅代表「英鎊」，也可能是其他地方的貨幣。所以，為避免往後無謂的爭議，契約中必須清楚書寫幣別。如：US Dollars（美金）、Sterling Pounds（英鎊）。

另外，撰寫金額時仍須注意：數字金額緊靠貨幣符號，例如：Can $891,568（加拿大元）；以及正確使用小數點「.」與逗號「,」。因為此兩符號容易造成筆誤，稍有疏忽，後果將不堪設想。

▎契約書信例句

● We'll have the contract ready for signature.
（我們將準備好契約以備簽字。）

● We had signed a contract for medicines.
（我們簽訂了一份藥品契約。）

● Mr. Chang signs the contract on behalf of Henrich Company.
（張先生代表漢理契公司在合約上簽字。）

● It was because of you that we landed the contract.
（因為你的關係，我們才簽署那份合約。）

● Our competitor offered a much lower price, so they got the contract.
（由於競爭者的報價非常低，所以他們拿到了合約。）

● The seller should draw up a contract and the buyer has to sign it.
（賣方應擬出一份合約而買方必須簽署。）

● We both want to sign a contract, and we have to make some concessions.
（貴我都想簽定合約，所以我們必須作出一些讓步。）

● We are here to discuss a new contract with you.
（我們來這是要和您談談新合約。）

● As per the contract, the construction of factory is now under way.
（根據合約規定，建廠現進行中。）

● By affixing your signature hereunder, you agree to the conditions on the back of this contract.
（於下方簽名後，你即同意本契約背面所述之條件。）

● The shipper hereby certifies that all information is true, correct and complete.
（貨主特此證明所有提供的資訊都是真實、正確並完整的。）

▌ 貨運簡易合約範例 ▌

SWIFT EXPRESS INC.

SWIFT BLDG., General Aviation Center

Domestic Road, Domestic Compound, Pasay City

(632) 854-5858

Official Receipt No. A13124	Tracking No: 181972924 HCL
Shipper: Osmena Seafood, Inc.	Care of: SWIFT - Manila
Address: 234 Rizal Boulevard, Cebu City	Address: 95 San Francis, Quezon City

Tran. Date: 08/17/2009

Time: 10:42:08 AM

Area Destn: Metro Manila

Tran. Type: Door-to-Door Delivery

Cut-Off Time 3:30:00 PM

No. of item(s): a case of carton

Wt: 25 Kg

SWIFT EXPRESS

Declared Value: 15,000

Freight: 2,010 Peso

Discount: 0.00

Mode: Cash

Content: Dried Fish

To Track your package, call 632-8548888 ext. 1234
or log on to www.SWIFTEXPRESS.com.

By affixing your signature hereunder, you agree to the conditions on the back of this contract. The shipper hereby certifies that all information are true, correct and complete.

Francis Vicedor	*Juna Dy*
Signature of Shipper	Authorized Signature

▌貨運簡易合約範例中文翻譯 ▌

SWIFT EXPRESS INC.

SWIFT BLDG., General Aviation Center

Domestic Road, Domestic Compound, Pasay City

(632) 854-5858

貨運證明收據號碼：A13124　　貨運追蹤號碼：181972924

　　　　　　　　　　　　　　　　　　HCL

寄貨人：Osmena Seafood, Inc.　貨運站：SWIFT - Manila

地址：234 Rizal Boulevard,　　地址：95 San Francis,

　　　Cebu City　　　　　　　　　　Quezon City

　　　　　　　　　　　　　　　貨運日：08/17/2009

　　　　　　　　　　　　　　　貨運時間：10:42:08 AM

　　　　　　　　　　　　　　　貨運目的地：馬尼拉

　　　　　　　　　　　　　　　貨運種類：送貨到址

　　　　　　　　　　　　　　　交件時間：3:30:00 PM

　　　　　　　　　　　　　　　托運數量：一個紙箱

　　　　　　　　　　　　　　　淨重：25 公斤

SWIFT EXPRESS

　　　　　　　　　　　　　　　貨物價值：15,000披索

　　　　　　　　　　　　　　　運費：2,010 披索

　　　　　　　　　　　　　　　折扣：0.00

　　　　　　　　　　　　　　　付款方式：現金

　　　　　　　　　　　　　　　內容物：魚乾

追蹤貨物請撥電話632-8548888分機1234，或線上查詢

www.SWIFTEXPRESS.com

依此簽名，寄貨人同意該合約背面的條款。貨主特
此證明所有提供訊息皆為真實、正確並完整。

法蘭西斯・汎德　　　　　　　胡瓦娜・戴
_____　　　　　_____
　寄貨人簽名　　　　　　　　　授權簽名

練習題⑨　中翻英

1. 這個產品將是未來三年的明星商品。

2. 我們生產的太陽能暖氣（solar power heater）世界上的市占率達四成。

3. 本公司可以邀請您擔任在台灣的配銷商嗎？

4. 自10月20日起授權乙方成為北美地區的代理商。

5. 本契約自6月1日買方與賣方簽署後生效。

Section ③

測驗與解答
Quiz and Answers

▶▶ 第一回測驗

翻譯題

1. 【　】 Should you have any inquiry, please do not hesitate to contact me.

 (1) 若有垂詢，請不要猶豫與我聯繫。

 (2) 你應該有疑問，請不要猶豫與我聯繫。

 (3) 若有垂詢，直接打電話給我。

 (4) 你應該有疑問，不要客氣找我。

2. 【　】 Our product is second to none and is outstanding value for money.

 (1) 我們的產品是第二好，而且很有價值。

 (2) 我們的產品首屈一指，而且物超所值。

 (3) 我們的產品目前市面上找不到，而且很棒。

 (4) 我們的產品首屈一指，而且非常貴。

3. 【　】 Thank you very much for your prompt service and courtesy in this manner.

(1) 非常謝謝你的促銷服務與有禮貌。

(2) 非常感謝你迅速的服務與禮貌的舉止。

(3) 非常感謝你的服務項目和行為舉止。

(4) 非常感謝你對這個案子的幫忙。

4. 【　】 A moment, please. I will put you through to John.

(1) 請稍候，我為你轉接給約翰。

(2) 請稍候，我幫你把約翰抓過來。

(3) 一刻鐘後，我為你轉接給約翰。

(4) 一刻鐘後，我將轉達你的訊息給約翰。

5. 【　】 He clarified his stand on this issue.

(1) 他說明他的故事。

(2) 他清潔在事件地點的攤位。

(3) 他澄清在該議題上的立場。

(4) 他是事件發生的主導者。

6. 【　】 My presentation will take about two hours. But, there will be a twenty minute break in the middle.

(1) 我的演講將在兩小時後發生。但是中間有東西破了。

(2) 我的演講已在兩小時前發生。但是，中場會休息二十分鐘。

(3) 我的演講將為時兩小時。但是，在會場中間有一個時鐘提醒我時間。

(4) 我的演講將為時兩小時。但中場會休息二十分鐘。

7.【　】　We apologize for the mistake.

(1) 我們的錯誤是不小心的。

(2) 我們對所犯的錯誤感到抱歉。

(3) 我們向你說聲對不起。

(4) 你們所犯的錯誤，我們感到抱歉。

8.【　】　Notice is hereby given that the annual meeting of the shareholders will be held at Sun Moon Hotel.

(1) 特此函告：年度股東會將於日月飯店舉行。

(2) 特此函告：一年一度的會議將於日月飯店舉行。

(3) 特此公告：年度股東會在日月飯店建立。

(4) 特此公告：一年一度的會議在日月飯店建立。

9.【　】　We wish to set up business relationship with your company.

(1) 我們希望在　貴公司建立一項商業產品。

(2) 我們的生意希望　貴公司的陪伴。

(3) 我們希望與　貴公司建立生意往來關係。

(4) 我們懇求與　貴公司的友好關係。

10.【　】　I do apologize for any inconvenience this might have caused you.

(1) 與你們做生意很不便。

(2) 很抱歉這已經造成你的不便。

(3) 我對你的不便感到抱歉。

(4) 與你們做生意很不便，為此我道歉。

文法測驗

1. 【　】 Customer service is　(1) **regarding**　(2) **taken**　(3) **deem** (4) **saw** as the priority of this company.

2. 【　】 （選出錯的片語）I am　(1) **take charge of**　(2) **in charge of**　(3) **responsible for** sales department in this company.

3. 【　】 （選出錯的片語）I am　(1) **delighted to**　(2) **glad to** (3) **happy to**　(4) **pleasing to** introduce our brand new product to you.

4. 【　】 It's our great　(1) **pleasing**　(2) **pleasure**　(3) **pleased** (4) **pleasant** to have you here.

5. 【　】 Hi Tech Co., Ltd　(1) **majoring in**　(2) **major in**　(3) **majors in**　(4) **is majoring** notebook design.

6. 【　】 Nobody actually wants to　(1) **cause**　(2) **caused**　(3) **causing**　(4) **be caused** offence in business practice.

7. 【　】 Good manners in France　(1) **requires**　(2) **require**　(3) **is required**　(4) **requiring** that a manager shakes hands with everyone in the meeting.

8. 【　】 The more you know of the culture of the country you are dealing with,　(1) **the few**　(2) **the fewer**　(3) **the limited** (4) **the less** likely you get into difficulties.

9. 【　】 一個漫不經心的評論 ＝ a　(1) **lighting-heart**　(2) **light-hearting**　(3) **light-hearted**　(4) **lighted-heart** comment.

10. 【 　】 We always refer CEO, CFO, CIO, CKO as executives in an enterprise, what C & O means are (1) **Chief & Officer** (2) **Cheat & Open** (3) **Cheer & Operation** (4) **Confirm and Operate**.

字彙測驗

1. 【 　】 He has learnt to deal (1) **at** (2) **with** (3) **through** (4) **in** all kinds of complicated situations.

2. 【 　】 First, I'd like to say a few (1) **letters** (2) **words** (3) **vocabularies** (4) **phrases** about the terms and conditions of this transaction.

3. 【 　】 (1) **According to** (2) **according to** (3) **According with** (4) **According at** the specification, this wire should go into that hole.

4. 【 　】 A new marketing campaign has just been (1) **launch** (2) **launching** (3) **launched** (4) **lunched**.

5. 【 　】 We wish to express our sincere (1) **thank** (2) **gratitude** (3) **thankful**.

6. 【 　】 Through the (1) **polite** (2) **answering** (3) **courtesy** (4) **inform** of the Taipei World Trade Center, we have obtained your company name.

7. 【 　】 We regret to tell you that the shipment will not be delivered (1) **in time** (2) **at time** (3) **on time** (4) **through time**.

8. 【 　 】 （選出意義相反的字彙）They are 　 (1) **nowhere** 　 (2) **well-known** 　 (3) **famous** 　 (4) **famed** in cycling circles.

9. 【 　 】 We are writing to you in order to 　 (1) **establish** 　 (2) **sets up** 　 (3) **had** 　 (4) **have made** business relationship.

10. 【 　 】 You have provided us 　 (1) **at** 　 (2) **with** 　 (3) **by** 　 (4) in your credit card details.

句型測驗

1. 【 　 】 當我們在正式場合中做自我介紹，可用以下何種方式表達？
   (1) I am so glad to have this opportunity to introduce myself to you.
   (2) It's a pleasure for me to be here to present myself.
   (3) I welcome the opportunity to introduce myself to you.
   (4) all of above.

2. 【 　 】 （選出錯誤的句子）當我們於商用書信結尾提到「隨信附件」，應如何表達？
   (1) Please find enclosed ...
   (2) Enclosed please find ...
   (3) Enclose: ...
   (4) Enclosing: ...

3. 【　】　（選出錯誤的句子）If you want to give someone information, you can say:

(1) I'd like you to know that ...

(2) I think you should know that ...

(3) That's interesting.

(4) I'd like to give you an overview of ...

4. 【　】　假如Mary的電話忙線中，下述何種表達方式是錯誤的？

(1) Mary is in the meeting now.

(2) Mary is on another line right now.

(3) Her line is busy at the moment.

(4) Her line is engaged right away.

5. 【　】　在商用書信中撰寫感謝對方的文句，下述何者不適？

(1) Thank you very much for your kind assistance.

(2) If you need any help, please let me know.

(3) Your help is really appreciated.

(4) Your assistance is highly grateful.

6. 【　】　It's important to take brief explanatory comment in business conversation. Rather than replying on your memory, we can call such kinds of brief explanatory comments as:

(1) notes

(2) report

(3) memorandum

(4) all of the above

7. 〔　〕　在正式英文書信中，若稱謂以"Dear Mr. Johnson,"開頭，則禮貌性常以何為結尾？

　　(1) Yours sincerely,

　　(2) Yours truly,

　　(3) Yours faithfully,

　　(4) Yours ever,

8. 〔　〕　In a meeting, you'd like to ask somebody to explain what he/she just said again, you can **NOT** ask:

　　(1) Could you explain it in detail?

　　(2) Pardon. I couldn't catch that. Could you repeat it?

　　(3) Does this make sense?

　　(4) I don't get your points.

9. 〔　〕　In a meeting, when the topic is off track, we can say:

　　(1) I think we are getting off-topic now.

　　(2) We have a bad connection. Let me call you back.

　　(3) Let's see.

　　(4) Excuse me. There is some noise on the line.

10. 〔　〕　I'll be　(1) **not**　(2) **out of**　(3) **with**　(4) **in not** office for a couple of weeks from tomorrow.

▶▶ 第二回測驗

翻譯題

1. 【 　 】 抱歉，他現在不方便接聽電話。

(1) Excuse me. He is not available to take the phone just now.

(2) I am sorry. He is able to take the phone now.

(3) Excuse me. He is unable to take the phone right now.

(4) I am sorry. He is not available to take the phone just now.

2. 【 　 】 （選出錯誤的句子）我將請他回來後與你聯絡。

(1) I will ask him not to call when he is at office.

(2) I will ask him to call you back when he is available.

(3) I will ask him to call you back when he is back.

(4) I will ask him to phone you back when he is free.

3. 【 　 】 （選出錯誤的句子）我們公司提供物美價廉的產品。

(1) Our company provides good quality and expensive products.

(2) We are offering a sound article at popular price.

(3) Our company provides great products at cheap price.

(4) We are offering nice goods with high quality.

4. 【 　 】 這家餐廳提供免費的礦泉水供客人飲用。

(1) This restaurant have complimentary mineral water to customers.

(2) This restaurant complimenting mineral water to customers.

(3) This restaurant is provided free mineral water to customers.

(4) This restaurant provides complimentary mineral water to customers.

5. 【　】　請給我們的貴賓熱烈掌聲。

(1) Please gives a big hand for our guest speaker.

(2) Please giving a big hand for our guest speaker.

(3) Please give a warm round of applause for our guest speaker.

(4) Please be given a warm round of applause for our guest speaker.

6. 【　】　（選出錯誤的句子）我的演講題目是國際行銷。

(1) The subject of my presentation is International Marketing.

(2) The theme of my talk is International Marketing.

(3) The title of my speech is International Marketing.

(4) International Marketing are my lecture subject.

7. 【　】　（選出錯誤的句子）請儘速給我數位相機的報價。

(1) Please let me have the prices on digital camera as soon as possible.

(2) Please give me the prices of digital camera ASAP.

(3) Please provided the quotation of digital camera as soon as possible.

(4) Please provide the quotation of digital camera ASAP.

8. 【　】　期待能很快收到你的回覆。

(1) Look forward to hearing from you soon.

(2) Look forward to hear from you soon.

(3) Look forwards to heard from you soon.

(4) I looks forward to hearing from you soon.

9. 【　】　（選出不對的句子）請問大衛在嗎？我是聖卡洛斯大學的布蘭達。

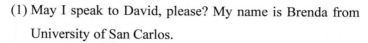

(1) May I speak to David, please? My name is Brenda from University of San Carlos.

(2) May I speak to David, please? I am Brenda at University of San Carlos.

(3) Is David available, please? This is Brenda from University of San Carlos.

(4) Is David available, please? My name is Brenda from University of San Carlos.

10. 【　】 打斷別人的話是不禮貌的。

(1) It is a bad manners to interrupt.

(2) Interrupting are bad manners.

(3) It is bad manners to interrupt.

(4) Interrupting are a bad manners.

文法測驗

1. 【　】 For the (1) **fiscal** (2) **finance** (3) **financing** (4) **financed** year 2007 it was over 8 billion dollars.

2. 【　】 Let's (1) **to call** (2) **calling** (3) **call** (4) **called** the meeting to order.

3. 【　】 I call this session to (1) **be addressed** (2) **address** (3) **addressing** (4) **have addressed** this crash issue.

4. 【　】 The chairman thinks we're (1) **run** (2) **having runned** (3) **running** out of time.

5. 【　】 We have trouble in (1) **supplied** (2) **supplying** (3) **ha-**

ving supplied the metal working machines.

6. 〔 　〕 International trade is the　(1) **sell**　(2) **sold**　(3) **exchanged**　(4) **exchange** of goods and services across international boundaries.

7. 〔 　〕 He is used to　(1) **working**　(2) **work**　(3) **worked**　(4) **being working** hard.

8. 〔 　〕 That's where I used to　(1) **living**　(2) **live**　(3) **lived**　(4) **am living** when I was a child.

9. 〔 　〕 Customers' needs are always　(1) **demand**　(2) **demanded**　(3) **demanding**.

10.〔 　〕 You will be　(1) **interested in**　(2) **interesting in**　(3) **interested**　(4) **interesting** our brand new machine.

字彙測驗

1. 〔 　〕 If the attached files of your email are too big, you should　(1) **compress**　(2) **shorten**　(3) **smaller**　(4) **enlarge** them before sending.

2. 〔 　〕 We would certainly be able to　(1) **have placing**　(2) **placing**　(3) **place**　(4) **be placed** substantial orders on a regular basis.

3. 〔 　〕 Please　(1) **make surely**　(2) **sure make**　(3) **make sure**　(4) **making sure** that the packing follows our strict instructions.

4. 〔 　〕 We have bought several machines from your company and been quite satisfied　(1) **with**　(2) **at**　(3) **in**　(4) **on** their

performance.

5. 【　】 A　(1) **stamped**　(2) **stamp**　(3) **stamping**　(4) **stamps** envelope is enclosed for reply.

6. 【　】 We enclosed an account statement for your remittance at your (1) **earliest**　(2) **early**　(3) **earlier**　(4) **rapid** convenience.

7. 【　】 In the past few years, Surrey Trading has done a lot of trade (1) **at**　(2) **through**　(3) **with**　(4) **as well as** IBN.

8. 【　】 （選出錯誤的單字）I　(1) **draw**　(2) **pay**　(3) **request** (4) **have** your attention to below signature.

9. 【　】 We will　(1) **contracted**　(2) **sign**　(3) **write**　(4) **do** a triangle trade agreement next week.

10. 【　】 We shall　(1) **welcomed**　(2) **available**　(3) **availably** (4) **welcome** a chance to renew our friendly relationship.

句型測驗

1. 【　】 Which meaning of the sentence is different from others?
   (1) Your price is not competitive for us to order.
   (2) Your price is rather stiff.
   (3) Your price is acceptable.
   (4) Your price is too expensive.

2. 【　】 If your customer complains to you, it may be wise to apologize. Which one is not suitable to use?
   (1) Look! If you follow the manual, the problem will not exist.
   (2) I'm very sorry. I will check it up as soon as possible.

(3) I do apologize for any inconvenience this might have caused you.

(4) There has been a problem in our shipping department.

3. 【　】　下列哪個單字或片語不代表「公司」？

    (1) company

    (2) Co., Ltd

    (3) corporation

    (4) cooperation

4. 【　】　下列哪個片語意義與其他三者相異？＿＿＿＿＿＿＿ our sales representative, we enclose a brochure of our new products.

    (1) Referring to

    (2) As to

    (3) With reference to

    (4) In response to

5. 【　】　（選出不對的答案）Thank you so much for your ＿＿＿＿.

    (1) email of Nov. 17

    (2) email dated on Nov. 17

    (3) email which was dated on Nov. 17

    (4) email in Nov. 17

6. 【　】　（選出不對的答案）＿＿＿＿＿ you have any enquiry, please do let me know.

    (1) Should

    (2) If

    (3) Providing that

(4) Do

7.【　】　（選出不對的答案）

(1) 3:10 = three out of ten

(2) 2:7 = two out of seven

(3) 10:1 = ten to one.

(4) 10:7 = ten out of seven

8.【　】　（選出不對的答案）＿＿＿＿＿, it would be a head start for us if we could secure a deal with you.

(1) To be perfectly honest

(2) Honest

(3) Honestly

(4) Honestly speaking

9.【　】　（選出意義相反的選項）When we want to start a meeting, We cannot say:

(1) Let's call the meeting to order.

(2) Let's get things under way.

(3) Shall we start?

(4) We will stop here.

10.【　】　（選出意義相反的選項）When you agree with someone, we cannot say:

(1) You're right there.

(2) Exactly!

(3) That's not how I see it.

(4) I'm in complete agreement.

▶▶ 第三回測驗

翻譯題

1. 【　】　我認為你們給的價格我們無法獲利。

   (1) I don't think we can make profits with the price you offered.

   (2) I think we cannot make profits at your offer price.

   (3) I don't think we can make profits at your offered price.

   (4) I think we can make profits with the price you offered.

2. 【　】　請接受我們的確認訂單，並於收到此訂單後開立預約發票。

   (1) Please accepts our confirmed order and issues a proforma invoice as soon as you receive it.

   (2) Please accept our confirmed order and issue a proforma invoice as soon as you receive it.

   (3) Please accept our confirming order and issue a proforma invoice as soon as you receive it.

   (4) Please accept our confirmed order and issue proforma invoice as soon as you receive it.

3. 【　】　史密斯先生現正忙於會議中，他將隨後回你電話。

   (1) Mr. Smith will phone you right back, he's tied up in a meeting right now.

   (2) Mr. Smith will phone you right back, he's tie up in a meeting right now.

   (3) Mr. Smith will phone you right back, he's tieing up in a meeting right now.

(4) Mr. Smith will phone you right back, he's tying up in a meeting right now.

4. 【 　 】 那我們就先討論一下第一個問題。

　　(1) Well then, let's to toss the first problem around a little.

　　(2) Well then, let's tossing the first problem around a little.

　　(3) Well then, let's tossed the first problem around a little.

　　(4) Well then, let's toss the first problem around a little.

5. 【 　 】 目前CO-28型號產品無庫存。

　　(1) Item no. CO-28 find a ready market at the moment.

　　(2) Item no. CO-28 is out of stock at the moment.

　　(3) Item no. CO-28 has found a poor market at the moment.

　　(4) Item no. CO-28 does out of stock at the moment.

字彙測驗

1. 【 　 】 While browsing on the internet, we (1) **came across** (2) **came on** (3) **come in** (4) **come at** your company.

2. 【 　 】 Our computer mouse is compatible (1) **with** (2) **at** (3) **in** (4) **by all** PCs and operating systems.

3. 【 　 】 You will not believe the software's performance (1) **that** (2) **until** (3) **what** (4) **in which** you see the demonstration.

4. 【 　 】 It will be our great (1) **please** (2) **pleasing** (3) **pleasure** (4) **pleased** if you can come to our booth in the exhibition.

5. 【 　 】 The engineer (1) **illustrated** (2) **describe** (3) **read** (4) **given** his presentation with the pictures.

6. 【　】 We're not prepared to take the agency into　(1) **consider**　(2) **consideration**　(3) **think**　(4) **thinking** for the time being.

7. 【　】 I know your company is　(1) **look**　(2) **looking**　(3) **seeing** (4) **watching** to tap into the market here in Taiwan.

8. 【　】 I will be in charge of the first　(1) **around**　(2) **about**　(3) **running**　(4) **round** of negotiations.

9. 【　】 SANYOO enlarged their product　(1) **rows**　(2) **columns** (3) **string**　(4) **lines** to include washers, dryers, and ovens.

10. 【　】 Which option do you believe is　(1) **the best**　(2) **best** (3) **most**　(4) **the most**.

句型測驗

1. 【　】 選出正確的句子。

(1) I suggested that he take off his jacket.

(2) I suggested that he takes off his jacket.

(3) I suggested that he took off his jacket.

(4) I suggested that he had taken off his jacket.

2. 【　】 選出正確的句子。

(1) I'll take him right to the hotel, so he can get some shuteye.

(2) I'll take him right to the hotel, therefore he can get some shuteye.

(3) I'll take him right to the hotel, so he could got some shuteye.

(4) I'll take him right to the hotel, therefore he could got some

shuteye.

3. 【 　 】 選出正確的句子。

(1) This flight was uneventful, except for a little turbulence here and there.

(2) This flight was uneventful, except a little turbulence here and there.

(3) This flight was uneventful, except for there was a little turbulence here and there.

(4) This flight was uneventful, except there were a little turbulence here and there.

4. 【 　 】 選出正確的句子。

(1) I'll pick you at the hotel at 9:30am.

(2) I'll pick up you at the hotel at 9:30am.

(3) I'll pick you up at the hotel at 9:30am.

(4) I'll be picking you at the hotel at 9:30am.

5. 【 　 】 We will save money by placing a large order of watches - 1500ca _____ 400ca.

(1) replace

(2) instead of

(3) replaced

(4) instead

6. 【 　 】 選出不適的答案。

Peter: Well, three other companies make these chairs for the same price. I need another reason to buy your chairs.

Chris: Then I'm glad you called. _____ answer any questions you may have.

(1) It will not be my place

(2) I'd be happy to

(3) I am ready to

(4) I am willing to

7.【 】 選出不適的答案。

Peter: I want to ask about the delivery.

Chris: We'll send your order by ship, then have it trucked to your warehouse.

Peter: That's not exactly what _____.

(1) I was getting up

(2) I was getting at

(3) I was thinking about

(4) I had in mind

8.【 】 The new employees don't know how to use the computer. Someone will have to _____ them.

(1) practice

(2) train

(3) education

(4) take

9.【 】 I estimate it will _____ four hours to drive there, but I'm really not sure. All cars are similar in many ways, but of course a sport car has better quality than a van.

(1) cost

(2) spend

(3) give

(4) take

10. 【　】 選出不對的答案。

    (1) Sunny and Steve found an old, inexpensive house they could afford, so they bought it.

    (2) They wanted a newer house, but they bought an old apartment.

    (3) Sunny and Steve applied for a loan to fix up the dilapidated building though the lender approved it.

    (4) They replaced the old toilet in the bathroom upstairs, but the bathtub fell through the rotted floor into the kitchen below.

閱讀測驗

Doing Business in Europe: Good Manners, Good Business

(Source: Jones, Leo and Richard Alexander (1996) New International Business English. Cambridge: Cambridge University Press. p.10)

Nobody actually wants to cause offence but, as business becomes ever more international, it is increasingly easy to get it wrong. There may be a single European market but it does not mean that managers behave the same in Greece as they do in Demark.

In many European countries handshaking is an automatic gesture. In France, good manners require that on arriving at a business meeting a manager shakes hands with everyone present. This can be demanding.

Handshaking is almost as popular in other countries - including Germany, Belgium and Italy. But Northern Europeans, such as the British and Scandinavians, are not quite so fond of physical demonstrations of friendliness.

In Europe, the most common challenge is not the content of the food, but the way you behave as you eat. In France, it is not good manners to raise tricky questions of business over the main course. Business has its place: after the cheese course.

Italians give similar importance to the whole process of business entertaining. In fact, in Italy the biggest fear, as course after course appears, is that you entirely forget you are there on business. If you have the energy, you can always do the polite thing when the meal finally ends, and offer to pay. Then, after a lively discussion, you must remember the next polite thing to do – let your host pick up the bill.

In Germany, as you walk sadly back to your hotel room, you may wonder why your apparently friendly hosts have not invited you out for the evening. Don't worry, it is probably nothing personal. Germans do not entertain business people with quite the same enthusiasm as some of their European counterparts.

The Germans are also notable for the amount of formality they bring to business. As an outsider, it is often difficult to know whether colleagues have been working together for 30 years or have just met in the lift. If you are used to calling people by their first names this can be a little strange. To the Germans, titles are important. Forgetting that someone should be called Doktor or Direk might cause serious offence. It is equally offensive to call them by a title they do not possess.

In Italy the question of title is further confused by the fact that everyone with a university degree can be called Dottore – and engineers, lawyers and architects may also expect to be called by their professional titles.

These cultural challenges exist side by side with the problems of doing business in a foreign language. But the more you know of the culture of the country you are dealing with, the less likely you are to get into difficulties. It is worth the effort. It might be rather hard to explain that the reason you lost the contract was not the product or the price, but the fact that you offended your hosts in a light-hearted comment over an aperitif. Good manners are admired: they can also make or break the deal.

1. 【　】 What we call good manners here in Taiwan might be different from its acts in the USA.
   (1) True
   (2) False
   (3) Neither true nor false
   (4) No answer

2. 【　】 As business becomes more globalized and complicated, it is easy for us to cause offense.
   (1) True
   (2) False
   (3) Neither true nor false
   (4) No answer

3. 【　】 In which country do good manners require a manager to shake hands with everyone in the meeting?
   (1) Germany
   (2) Belgium
   (3) France
   (4) Italy

4. 〔　〕 According to this article, which country is not fond of physical demonstration of friendliness?

    (1) Germany

    (2) Belgium

    (3) France

    (4) Finland

5. 〔　〕 In which country does business always come after the cheese course?

    (1) Germany

    (2) Belgium

    (3) France

    (4) Italy

6. 〔　〕 In which country should you remember that the host will pay the bill?

    (1) Germany

    (2) Belgium

    (3) France

    (4) Italy

7. 〔　〕 In which country could you hardly know whether colleagues have been working together for 30 years or have just met in the lift?

    (1) Germany

    (2) Belgium

    (3) France

    (4) Italy

8. 〔　〕 In Germany, you should bear the titles of your customers in mind. Otherwise it will cause serious offence.

(1) True

(2) False

(3) Neither true nor false

(4) No answer

9. 〔 〕 The more you know of the culture of customers you are dealing with, the less likely you are to get it wrong.

(1) True

(2) False

(3) Neither true nor false

(4) No answer

10. 〔 〕 Before doing business with other countries, it is NOT necessary for us to study their culture in advance since we will not cause any offence.

(1) True

(2) False

(3) Neither true nor false

(4) No answer

▶▶ 第四回測驗

翻譯題

1. 【　】 我們必須謝絕您作為我方獨家代理的提案。

(1) We have to decline your proposal of acting as our sole agency.

(2) We have to incline your proposal of acting as our sole agency.

(3) We have to recline your proposal of acting as our sole agency.

(4) We have to accept your proposal of acting as our sole agency.

2. 【　】 我們簽訂了一份藥品契約。

(1) We have draw up a contract for medicine.

(2) We have to draw a contract for medicine.

(3) We have signing a contract for medicine.

(4) We have signed a contract for medicine.

3. 【　】 我們真的很抱歉整件事超出我們所能控制。

(1) We do apologize, but it was beyond our control.

(2) We are really sorry for it beyond our control.

(3) We do apologize, but it does beyond our control.

(4) We are really sorry since it did beyond our control.

4. 【　】 業務代表將電腦比作蘋果。

(1) The sales representative compared the computer with an apple.

(2) The sales representative compared the computer to an apple.

(3) The sales representative comparing the computer with an apple.

(4) The sales representative comparing the computer to an apple.

5. 【 】 貨主特此證明所有提供訊息皆為真實、正確並完整。

(1) The shipper hereby certifies that all information are true, correct and complete.

(2) The consignee hereby certifies that all information are true, correct and complete.

(3) The shipper hereby believes that all information are true, correct and complete.

(4) The shipper hereafter certifies that all information are true, correct and complete.

文法測驗

1. 【 】 (1) **At** (2) **In** (3) **On** (4) **By** this, we inform you that we have paid Mr. Henry US $15 million today.

2. 【 】 We are delighted to (1) **assistance** (2) **helping** (3) **serve** (4) **serving** you at any time.

3. 【 】 I do think this will be a (1) **memorial** (2) **memorize** (3) **memorable** (4) **memory** trip.

4. 【 】 The operation manual of your working machines is too

complicated　(1) **too**　(2) **to**　(3) **in**　(4) **for** understand.

5. 〔　〕　Multicolored woodcuts must be printed with as many blocks as　(1) **they are**　(2) **many**　(3) **some of**　(4) **it is** colors in the composition.

6. 〔　〕　The greater an object's mass, the more difficult it is

(1) to speed it up or slow it down.

(2) its speeds up or slows down.

(3) than speeding it up or slowing it down.

(4) than speeding up or slowing down.

7. 〔　〕　Which one is wrong?

(1) 0.67 = zero-point-six-seven

(2) $5.54 = five dollars fifty-four

(3) 508/19G = nineteen G oblique five zero eight

(4) 100% = one hundred percent

8. 〔　〕　Which one is right?

(1) 2/5 = two fifth

(2) 2/5 = two fifths

(3) 2/5 = two five

(4) 2/5 = second five

9. 〔　〕　If we want to express 100% possibility, which of the following sentence is right?

(1) I expect that these sales figures are accurate.

(2) There is a chance that these sales figures are accurate.

(3) It's quite possible that these sales figures are accurate.

(4) I'm sure that these sales figures are accurate.

10. 〖　〗 Which sentence is different from others?

(1) We have semimonthly direct sailing from Keelung to San Francisco.

(2) We have two direct sailing a month from Keelung to San Francisco.

(3) We have one direct sailing every two months from Keelung to San Francisco.

(4) We have one direct sailing every two weeks from Keelung to San Francisco.

字彙測驗

1. 〖　〗 Phone me right away if you (1) **happen** (2) **happen to** (3) **happening** (4) **have happened to** see him.

2. 〖　〗 Let's go see the movies, (1) **should we?** (2) **am I?** (3) **shall we?** (4) **will you?**

3. 〖　〗 Unless she agrees, (1) **touch** (2) **don't be touching** (3) **don't touch** (4) **touching** the books on her desk.

4. 〖　〗 Somebody (1) **help** (2) **need help** (3) **helps** (4) **helping** me I have too much work to do.

5. 〖　〗 We sent three (1) **shipments** (2) **ships** (3) **shipment** (4) **ship** of toys to our overseas agents.

6. 〖　〗 I prefer going dancing, but she prefers (1) **going to** (2) **to go to** (3) **to go** (4) **goes** see a movie. We always disagree with each other!

7. 【 　】 When somebody says: "Could you please explain the present situation?" He or she can also address:

(1) Can you clean the present situation?

(2) Can you take notes of the present situation?

(3) Could you clarify the present situation?

(4) Could you help the present situation?

8. 【 　】 We would like payment (1) **superior** (2) **prior** (3) **first** (4) **before** to the delivery, since this is your first order.

9. 【 　】 請選出正確的句子。

(1) North Americans seem to be pretty laid-back about most rules of etiquette, from what I've seen.

(2) North Americans seem to be pretty laid-back about most rules of etiquette, according to what I've seen.

(3) North Americans seem to be pretty laid-back about most rules of etiquette, as to what I've seen.

(4) North Americans seem to be pretty laid-back about most rules of etiquette, since what I've seen.

10. 【 　】 請選出正確的句子。

(1) Each of the other presenters follows as scheduled.

(2) Each of other presenters follows as scheduled.

(3) Each of the other presenters follow as scheduled.

(4) Each of other presenters follow as scheduled.

句型測驗

1. 【　】 In order to make the best impression on your potential employer, you need to _____ these three things in mind: dressing appropriately, doing some homework on the company, and punctuality.

   (1) bearing

   (2) bore

   (3) bear

   (4) be bearing

2. 【　】 I used to work in the accounting _____, but now I'm a salesman.

   (1) department

   (2) session

   (3) part

   (4) apartment

3. 【　】 One president and two vice presidents form the top level of _____ at my company.

   (1) manager

   (2) management

   (3) managing

   (4) manage

4. 【　】 A friendly, respectful relationship is more effective _____ an aggressive, competitive one.

   (1) then

   (2) below

   (3) than

(4) to

5. 【　】　選出不對的答案。

A: What jobs have you had already?

B: I have done three jobs. _____, I was working as a salesman in a department store. _____ I got a sales marketing offer from 7-11. The third job I'm doing now is a computer programmer.

(1) In Fast, Then

(2) First, Second,

(3) First, Then,

(4) Firstly, Secondly,

6. 【　】　下述哪個句子非表達「建議、提案」？

(1) Let's put this issue to the vote.

(2) I think it's time to adjourn the meeting.

(3) I propose we go to station to meet our guests.

(4) My recommendation is that we should go to station to meet our guests.

7. 【　】　下述哪個句子非表達與「會議主題已經離題」相關？

(1) We have a bad connection. Let me call you back.

(2) We get off track.

(3) I think we are getting a bit off-topic now.

(4) We should get back to the subject at hand.

8. 【　】　請選出一句與其他意義不同的句子。

(1) My instructions are to negotiate hard on this deal.

(2) I've been told to negotiate hard on this deal.

(3) I'm obliged to negotiate hard on this deal.

(4) I can make any decisions on this deal.

9.【 】 若要建議對方以另一種態度看問題，下列哪個句子不宜？

(1) Let's look at this from another angle.

(2) Let's look at this in a different way.

(3) That's about all for the time being.

(4) Let's look at this from another points of view.

10.【 】 若針對會議結果持「反對或不同意」的態度時，下列哪個句子不對？

(1) We are hoping for a different answer.

(2) That makes sense.

(3) That might work, but I'm afraid it's not a final solution.

(4) This is a good idea, but we need an official statement, not a work-around.

填空測驗

To: Greenworld, Inc.

Attn: "Mr. Renato Isidro" < renato@greenworld.com >

Subject: New Product GW/007 Launch

■ Normal ☐ Urgent ☐ Confidential

Date: 01/05/2010

_____(1)_____ Renato,

I am sure that as a regular buyer of Greenworld LED products, you will be interested _____(2)_____ a new high-power LED that we have just _____(3)_____ .

The GW/007 is a revolutionary _____(4)_____ in chip design. This precise package technique is the _____(5)_____ step toward the creation of high luminous efficiency and long endurance. It is truly designed _____(6)_____ the twenty-first century. It is easy to install and give _____(7)_____ high power. You won't believe it _____(8)_____ you see it! The next page shows the pictures and technical information about our GW/007 _____(9)_____ .

Our sales representative will visit your company next month and would be delighted to introduce this brand new product to you. The first public demonstration of the GW/007 will take place at the ELETROX 2010 in Berlin. It will be our great pleasure if you can come to our booth C007.

_____(10)_____

Gerald Haigh

Marketing Director

Digest Electronics Co., Ltd

geraldhaigh@digest.com.tw

1. 【　】　選出正確答案。

  (1) Hello

  (2) Dear

  (3) He!

  (4) Yes

2. 【　】　選出正確答案。

  (1) with

  (2) at

  (3) in

  (4) by

3. 【　】　選出正確答案。

  (1) launched

  (2) launch

  (3) lunched

  (4) lunch

4. 【　】　選出正確答案。

  (1) break-over

  (2) breakthrough

  (3) break-up

  (4) break-down

5. 【　】　選出正確答案。

  (1) newest

  (2) most new

  (3) latest

  (4) late

6. 【　】　選出正確答案。

    (1) for

    (2) with

    (3) to

    (4) by

7. 【　】　選出正確答案。

    (1) one hundred percent

    (2) two hundreds percent

    (3) ninety-nine percent

    (4) only one percent

8. 【　】　選出正確答案。

    (1) through

    (2) until

    (3) at

    (4) when

9. 【　】　選出正確答案。

    (1) for your refer

    (2) with referring

    (3) for your reference

    (4) referring to

10.【　】　選出正確答案。

    (1) Your sincerely

    (2) your sincerely,

    (3) sincerely

    (4) Sincerely yours,

▶第 1 章◀ 練習題參考範例

【練習題①】請寫下你的應徵信函

May 23, 2009

Mr. Austin Tai
Director of Personnel
Great Times, Inc.
8 Chung- Shiao East Road
Taipei 100

- -

Dear Mr. Tai,

I am writing to express my interest in Great Times, Inc. My name is Tom Wang and I will graduate from Taipei Institute of Technology this June with a Master degree in Computer Science.

In consideration of your recent recruitment advertisement, I have noted that your job position of software engineer strongly appeals both to my academic background and personal goals.

At TIT, I am a teaching assistant of Professor Ricardo Tang who has taken part in many national science projects. From these experiences, my software development techniques have been cultivated. Additionally, I have worked as an intern for the past three summers with Best Technology, the Software Engineering Department where my skills to construct, code and test computer software programs have been developed.

I will welcome a personal interview at your convenience to learn more about this opportunity. I can be reached by below contacts and look forward to hearing from you soon.

Thank you for your time and consideration.

Yours Sincerely,

Tom Wang

0938-7654321
tom_wang@gmail.com

【練習題②】請撰寫自己的英文履歷表

Curriculum Vitae

Name: Pat Rollyn	Female
Date of Birth: May 20 1983	
Address: 65 Duke Street, Taipei 100 Taiwan	
E-mail: Pat_rollyn@gmail.com	Tel: 02-25630947 Mobile phone: 0910-123456

Academic Background

2006 June	Bsc - Business Management University of West Anglia (England)
2002 June	Hsinchu Girls Senior High School

Work Experiences

	Truth Publishing Ltd, Editor
2007 Aug - Present	Job descriptions: Originated **TRUTHFULNESS**, a monthly newsletter focused on human rights development and public affairs. Topics included life planning, worldwide human rights status, book and film reviews and job satisfaction. Address: 15 Chung-Cheng Road, Taipei 100

2006 Aug - 2007 Aug	**University of West Anglia, Assistant to Conference Coordinator** Job descriptions: Assisted conference co-coordinator at the University of West Anglia Conference Centre in planning and putting on more than 100 conferences. Co-coordinated activities of convention personnel in preparing banquet and convention rooms and erecting displays and exhibits. Address: University of West Anglia, Melbury, Wills, UK

Competence and Qualifications

1. **Conference Management:** assist organizations to plan details, programmes, display space and facilities.
2. **Programme Development:** arrange publicity, brochure design, co-ordination of direct mail, public relations, location selection and space negotiations.
3. **Leadership Abilities:** train and supervise staff.

【練習題③】請寫下身為主持人時，你將使用的介紹語詞

If you are a host and chair, write down your opening.

Ladies and gentlemen. May I have your attention, please! It is our great pleasure to invite the president from Carbon Materials, Mr. Baclon Mercury to give us a speech. Mr. Mercury has been well known for starting his business from 200 dollars and now has over 80 branches all over the world. The topic today is "How to create your blue ocean strategies". Let us give him a warm welcome before his speech. (Applause...)

【練習題④】

▶ 情境一

Elly：您好，我是Goody食品公司行銷部的Elly，請問David Cheng在嗎？

Hello! This is Elly from the marketing department of Goody Food. May I speak to David Cheng?

David：我就是，有什麼可以為您效勞的嗎？

Speaking! What can I do for you?

Elly：David，你好嗎？好久不見！

Hi, David. How are you? Haven't seen you for a long time.

David：Elly，我很好，您呢？是呀，從去年台北食品展到現在都沒碰面。

Hi, Elly, I am fine, and you? Yes, since we met at the Food Taipei Show last year.

Elly：我也很好，只是最近忙著準備食品展。

I am OK too, only too busy in preparing for the Food Show currently.

對了，我想和你約個時間見面以討論本次展覽的細節。

By the way, I am calling to make an appointment with you to discuss the details about this Show.

David：好的。請等一下，我拿一下我的工作日誌。（約略30秒）

OK! Wait a minute. I am going to get my diary. (silent for 30 seconds)

回來了，我6月11日到22日會去台北。

Here I am, I will go to Taipei from 11th to 22nd in June.

Elly：太好了！您 6月12日下午能到本公司來討論嗎？

Great. Would you please visit our office for further discussion in the afternoon of 12th of June.

David：沒問題！

No problem at all.

Elly：好，會後我請您去陽明山用餐並享受溫泉浴。

OK. I will take you to have dinner at the Yangming Mountain and to enjoy spring spa after the meeting.

David：我已經迫不及待地想去台北了！

Really! I can't wait to go to Taipei.

Elly：我會在您出發前，以email與您討論細節。謝謝您！

I shall discuss the details with you through e-mail before your departure. Thank you.

David：不客氣，台北見。

You are welcome! See you in Taipei.

Elly：再見，台北見囉。

Bye. See you then.

David：再見，保持聯絡。

Bye. Keep in touch.

▶ 情境二

Ariel：你好，我是Perkins科技的Ariel。請問維修部門的工程師Joey在嗎？

Hi, this is Ariel from Perkins Technology. May I speak to engineer Joey of Repair Department?

Coreson：對不起，Joey外出開會，不在辦公室。我能幫妳嗎？

Sorry. Joey is out of office for a meeting. How can I help you?

Ariel：下午他會進辦公室嗎？

Will he come in this afternoon?

Coreson：我想他今天應該不會再進辦公室了。

I think he will not come into office today.

Ariel：我可以留個訊息給Joey嗎？

May I leave a message to Joey?

Coreson：沒問題，請說。

Sure! Please go ahead.

Ariel：我們的網路系統不穩定，想請他來檢查。我是Perkins科技公司的資管經理Ariel，手機號碼是0910-000888。

The internet system is unstable in our company. So we want Joey to have an on-site check. This is Ariel, IT Manager of Perkins Technology and my mobile is 0910-000888.

Coreson：我已寫下，並將請Joey儘快與您聯繫。

I've written down and will ask Joey to contact you as soon as possible.

Ariel：謝謝。可以請教你的名字嗎？

Thank you so much for your help. May I have your name, please?

Coreson：我是Coreson。

My name is Coreson.

Ariel：麻煩你了，Coreson。再見！

Thank you, Coreson. Good-bye!

Coreson：不客氣。再見！

You are welcome. Bye!

【練習題⑤】 請依據下列狀況編寫備忘錄

2009年9月24日你出差到德國漢諾威（Hannover）參加
Computex，遇到義大利廠商Vespian Computer的採購經理Mr. Lucas
Pavaradi，詢問本公司Tiny Notebook的規格與報價，並把此備忘錄寄
回台灣，請業務助理Tata Tsai與工程師Willy Tu協助後續事宜。（請
自行運用8 Ws）

To: Tata Tsai (Sales Dept.) & Willy Tu (Engineer Dept.)

Time: 24/09/2009, 2:45pm

Place: Computex, Hannover, Germany

Who I met: Mr. Lucas Pavaradi, Purchasing Manager from Vespian Computer, Italy

Event: Inquiry for our product－Tiny Notebook. Need detail information of specifications and quotation.

Following actions:

1. Tata prepares proforma invoice

2. Willy prepares lists of Spec. and technical statement.

3. Send a sample to Vespian Computer via Fedex by 30/09

4. Inform Mr. Lucas Pavaradi when our sample is sent.

▶第 2 章◀ 練習題參考範例

【練習題①】中翻英

1. 本公司從安全雜誌上看到貴公司的廣告訊息，想藉此機會與貴公司建立生意往來關係。

   We read your AD from Security Magazine and hope to build business with you.

2. 據悉貴公司正在找尋太陽能電視的供應商，很榮幸通知您本公司的產品正屬於此範疇。

   It is learned that your company is looking for the supplier of sola-powered Television. It is our pleasure to inform you that our products are what you need.

3. 特此通知，本公司自下個月起將移至新廠房辦公。

   I would like to inform you that our office will move to a new factory next month.

4. 很抱歉至今才回覆貴公司上週三的來函。

   I am very sorry for the late reply of your letter sent last Wednesday.

5. 茲附上本公司最新產品目錄，以供參考。

   Please see the attached latest product catalog for your reference.

6. 想與您確認貴公司剛剛寄來訂單的電子郵件內容。

   I would like to double check with you the latest email concerning your new order.

7. 隨函附上本月的貨款明細。

Please refer to the attached for the details of payment in this month.

8. 非常感謝您的協助。

I am very grateful for your assistance.

= It is kind of you to help. = Thank you very much for your assistance.

9. 謝謝貴公司訂貨。

Your order is appreciated! = Thank you so much for your order.

10. 我們一直對在北歐投資感到興趣。

We are always interested in investing in Northern Europe.

【練習題②】Write a reply letter in accordance with enquiry from overseas customer

　　請練習撰寫一封完整的英文信函，描述Mercia Tech公司的業務經理Helen Wu答謝Roster公司副總裁Fred Dabenson於2009年3月18日來函決定下訂五萬台最新款的數位相機。Helen Wu並於信中允諾可以優惠價格並於兩週之內交貨。

Mercia Tech

Your definite choice!

Tel: 00-886-4-23230000 Website: www.merciatech.com.tw

- -

Mr. Fred Dabenson
Roster Co., Ltd
11 Thame Road West,
Nottingham, UK
NG2 3AC.

19/03/2009

- -

Dear Mr. Dabenson,

Thank you very much for your letter dated on 18/03/2009. It is highly appreciated that you decide to order 50,000 new digital cameras. We promise to provide you competitive price and ship the order within two weeks as you requested.

Sincerely,

Helen Wu

Sales Manager, Mercia Tech
Tel: 00-886-4-23230000 ext.168
E-mail: helen.wu@merciatech.com.tw

No. 1 Kuan-Yeh Road, Taichung Industrial Park, Taichung City 407 Taiwan

【練習題③】請練習寫一封詢問訂房的電子郵件

　　總經理計劃利用2009過年期間全家至菲律賓宿霧（Cebu, Philippines）海濱渡假飯店Plantation Resort旅遊，為避免旺季訂不到住房，現請身為秘書的妳先行訂房。

　　以下是相關訊息：

1) Plantation Resort email: inquiry@plantation.com.ph

2) 入宿人數四人、需要二間豪華房

3) 時間：1月14日至1月19日，共五晚

　　基於上述的背景，妳現在請Plantation Resort告知該時段是否有海景房？房價多少？房價是否含早餐？付款方式？機場接送的費用？

To: inquiry@plantation.com.ph

From: maggie_chu@hi-speed.com.tw

Date: 12/12/2008

Subject: Hotel Reservation

■ Normal □ Urgent □ Confidential

- -

Dear Sir/Madam,

I am writing to make an inquiry about my reservation for two luxury rooms for 5 nights during 14th to 19th of January. This reservation is for a family of four. Here are some inquires about this reservation:

1. Do you still have sea view rooms available, and how much is the rate?

2. Is breakfast included in the room rate?

3. How about the payment terms?

4. Do you provide airport pick up service? How much is the cost of airport pickup service?

Thank you very much for your kind attention. Should you need any information, please do not hesitate to contact me. I look forward to hearing from you soon.

Sincerely,

Maggie Chu

Secretary to CEO, Hi-Speed Co., Ltd

Tel: 00-886-87661234

e-mail: maggie_chu@hi-speed.com.tw

【練習題④】

　　請讀者練習撰寫一封商業書信，將自己扮演成筆記型電腦製造商「Go Anywhere」的業務經理，對顧客「Hanley Trading」副總 Peter Roberts的來函訂購新型筆電進行答謝與回覆。

GO ANYWHERE

No. 1813 Marco Tower
Juana Osmena Extension
300 Hsiu-Chu, Taiwan
00-886-3-556600

7th March, 2009
Ref. No. TJX 4236 Notebook

- -

Dear Mr. Roberts,

Thank you so much for your order of our new Notebook PC TJX 4236. This order has been delivered by air cargo today, and is expected to arrive tomorrow. We are looking forward to serving you anytime.

Should you require any information, please feel free to call me.

Sincerely yours,

Joseph Adre

Sales Manager
Go Anywhere Co., Ltd
e-mail: Joseph.adre@goanywhere.com.tw
mobile: 00-886-928-876795

【練習題⑤】

請讀者練習撰寫一封詢價信電子郵件，以美國「Digi Device」採購經理的身分向台灣「Super Digita」詢問數位相框（digital photo frame）的報價。並分別要求一萬台及五萬台訂單的報價。

To: sales@superdigita.com.tw

From: ben_hamin@digidevice.com

Date: 07/06/2009

Subject: (Enquiry) Digital Picture Frame

☐ Normal ■ Urgent ☐ Confidential

- -

Dear Sir/Madam,

We have come across your promotion AD in the latest Digital World magazine, and we would like to inquire about the price of the digital photo frame from Super Digita. Would you please kindly provide the quotations with an order of ten thousand and fifty thousand respectively? Your prompt reply will be deeply appreciated since we will accommodate these products to one of our main customers here in the States shortly.

I look forward to starting a business with you. Should you need any information from Digi Device, please let me know. Thank you very much for your kind attention.

Truly yours,

Ben Hamin

Digi Device

Purchasing Manager

Tel-00-1-850-9340808

Fax-00-1-850-9340809

e-Mail-ben_hamin@digidevice.com

603 Silverthorn Avenue, Gulf Breeze, FL 32561, USA

【練習題⑥】

　　請讀者練習製作一張估價單（Performa Invoice），以回覆Digi Device對數位相框（Digital phone frame）的詢價，並以DPF-1（一吋數位相框）及DPF-2（二吋數位相框）的型號依其數量回覆。DPF-1訂購一萬台時，每台定價US $4.5；訂購五萬台時，每台定價US $3.8。DPF-2訂購一萬台時，每台定價US $7.0；訂購五萬台時，每台定價US $6.0。

To: ben_hamin@digidevice.com
From: sales@superdigita.com.tw
Date: 07/07/2009
Subject: RE: (Enquiry) Digital Picture Frame
☐ Normal ■ Urgent ☐ Confidential

- -

Dear Mr. Hamin,

Thank you so much for your inquiry letter of 07/06/2009 and interest in our product - digital photo frame. In fact, we have manufactured two models of digital photo frame. **Product No. DPF-1** is a one-inch frame, while Product **No. DPF-2** is a two-inch frame.

Because we have no idea which product you would prefer, a proforma invoice containing two different models as well as various quantities were made under your request. Please refer to the attached proforma invoice for your reference, in which you could sum up the total amount according to the product and quantity you choose.

Thank you again for choosing Super Digital products. We hope to hear from you soon.

Sincerely,

Andrew Lin

Sales Director

Super Digita

Tel: 00-886-7-5668726
Mobile: 00-886-933-123456
e-mail: sales@superdigita.com.tw

8F, No.88 Chi-Chang Road, Ling-Ya District, Kaohsiung 802 Taiwan

>> To: sales@superdigita.com.tw
>> From: ben_hamin@digidevice.com
>> Date: 07/06/2009
>> Subject: (Enquiry) Digital Picture Frame
   ☐ Normal ■ Urgent ☐ Confidential

【Attachment：附件】

Super Digita

3F, No.88 Chi-Chang Road Ling-Ya District
Kaohsiung 802 TAIWAN
Tel: +00-886-7-5668726 Fax: +00-886-7-5668727

PROFORMA INVOICE

No. DPF(1)(2)070709   *Date:* 7-Jul-09

INVOICE OF Digital Photo Frame
For account and risk of Messrs DIGI DEVICE MR. BEN HAMIN
603 Silverthorn Avenue, Gulf Breeze, FL 32561, USA
Shipped by SUPER DIGITA CO., LTD   *per* AIR FREIGHT
Sailing on or about 18-Jul-09   *From* TAIWAN *To* USA

DESCRIPTION OF GOODS		QUANTITY	UNIT PPRICE	AMOUNT
SUPER DIGITA BRAND				**FOB USA**
DPF-1	1-Inch Digital Photo Frame	10,000 PCS	US$4.50	US$4,500.00
DPF-1	1-Inch Digital Photo Frame	50,000 PCS	US$3.80	US$190,000.00
DPF-2	2-Inch Digital Photo Frame	10,000 PCS	US$7.00	US$70,000.00
DPF-2	2-Inch Digital Photo Frame	50,000 PCS	US$6.00	US$300,000.00
TOTAL FOB UNITED STATES OF AMERICA				US$564,500.00

SAY TOTAL US DOLLORS FIVE HUNDRED SIXTY-FOUR THOUSAND AND FIVE HUNDRED ONLY.
    1. PAYMENT: T/T IN ADVANCE, 5 DAYS BEFORE THE SHIPMENT
    2. DELIVERY: 18-Jul-09
    3. FORWARDER SPEEDY EXPRESS
    4. AIR FREIGHT COLLECT

SHIPPING MARK:

USA
C/NO.
MADE IN TAIWAN

CONFIRMED AND ACCEPTED BY   SUPER DIGITA CO., LTD

                                                  Super Digita
_____   VIVIAN CHANG / SALES REPRESENTATIVE
  AUTHORIZED SIGNATURE   *Vivian Chang* 2009/07/07
                                                  CONFIRMED

【練習題⑦】中翻英

1. 問：假如你能再降單價五美元，我們會將訂貨量增加到五千
   組。

   If you could bring the price down by $5 per unit, we would increase
   our order to 5,000 units.

   答：如貴公司年度訂貨量達到五千組，超過五千組之數量將提
   供單價五美元之優惠。

   If the amount of yearly order excesses 5,000 units, we would like to
   provide further concession for those orders by $5 per unit.

2. 問：產品如無法提供二年保固期(Warranty)，下年度將不再下訂
   單。

   If you could not provide a two-year warranty, we would not place
   orders next year.

   答：本公司產品型號HCU及DPAM將於2010開始提供二年保
   固。

   Our products, Model HCU and Model DPMA will provide a two
   year warranty starting from 2010.

3. 問：請貴公司於貨到裝置完畢，派工程師測試。請問收費標準
   為何?

   Please send an engineer to test machine/system/operation after
   installation by receiving the goods. And would you please inform the
   cost for this service?

答：派工程師測試新機器是本公司的售後服務，並不會有額外收費。

It is a part of after sales service to send an engineer to test the newly installed machine. There will be no extra charge for this service.

4. 問：我們需要的是通用電源器(universal adopter)，而不是110伏特(voltage)。

We need a universal adopter rather than a 110V adopter.

答：採用通用電源器產品價格將增加二美元。

For those products with universal adopters, we will add two dollars in the price.

5. 問：如果貴公司堅持調漲價格，明年度我們將尋找新供應商。

We would search for new suppliers next year, if you insist to increase the price.

答：很遺憾新價格已經是公司的既定政策。

I am sorry that these new prices are a firmed policy of company.

【練習題⑧】中翻英

A：貴公司於上個月承諾寄二個Z9電漿電視（plasma TV）的樣品，可是至今我們還沒有收到。下週我們將無法於家電展展出，你們要如何解決？

> Your company promised to deliver two samples of Z9 Plasma TVs last month, but we haven't received them till now. We might have no Plasma TV exhibits in the Home Appliance Exhibition next week. What are you going to do about this?

B：我們感到很抱歉，因為業務Debbie請產假沒有交代本部門同事此事。我們將於今日用DHL寄出二個樣品，二日後會抵達，以供貴公司展出。祝展覽順利！

> We feel very sorry for all the inconveniences caused because our account sales representative Debbie did not inform anyone at our department before her maternity leave. Two samples will be delivered by DHL today, and they shall be arrived within two days just in time for your demonstration. Wish every success in your Exhibition.

【練習題⑨】中翻英

1. 這個產品將是未來三年的明星商品。

   This product is going to be the best-selling goods in the coming three years.

2. 我們生產的太陽能暖氣（solar-powered heater）世界上的市占率達四成。

   Our solar-powered heater has a 40% market share in the world.

3. 本公司可以邀請您擔任在台灣的配銷商嗎？

   May we invite you as our distributor in Taiwan?

4. 自10月20日起授權乙方成為北美地區的代理商。

   Party B shall be authorized as the agency in North America on and after October 20.

5. 本契約自6月1日買方與建造方簽署後生效。

   This contract will come into force from first of June hereof by the buyer and the builder.

▶第 3 章◀ 測驗題解答

第一回測驗

翻譯題

1. (1)　2. (2)　3. (2)　4. (1)　5. (3)　6. (4)　7. (2)　8. (1)
9. (3)　10. (2)

文法測驗

1. (2)　2. (1)　3. (4)　4.(2)　5. (3)　6. (1)　7. (2)　8. (4)
9. (3)　10. (1)

字彙測驗

1. (2)　2. (2)　3. (1)　4. (3)　5. (2)　6. (3)　7. (3)　8. (1)
9. (1)　10.(2)

句型測驗

1. (4)　2. (4)　3. (3)　4. (1)　5. (2)　6. (4)　7. (1)　8. (3)
9. (1)　10.(2)

第二回測驗

翻譯題

1. (4)　2. (1)　3. (1)　4. (4)　5. (3)　6. (4)　7. (3)　8. (1)
9. (2)　10. (3)

文法測驗

1. (1)　2. (3)　3. (2)　4. (3)　5. (2)　6. (4)　7. (1)　8. (2)
9. (3)　10. (1)

字彙測驗

1. (1)　2. (3)　3. (3)　4. (1)　5. (1)　6. (1)　7. (3)　8. (2)
9. (2)　10. (4)

句型測驗

1. (3)　2. (1)　3. (4)　4. (2)　5. (4)　6. (4)　7. (4)　8. (2)
9. (4)　10. (3)

第三回測驗

翻譯題

1. (1)　2. (2)　3. (1)　4. (4)　5. (2)

字彙測驗

1. (1)　2. (1)　3. (2)　4. (3)　5. (1)　6. (2)　7. (2)　8. (4)
9. (4)　10. (1)

句型測驗

1. (1)　2. (1)　3. (1)　4. (3)　5. (2)　6. (1)　7. (1)　8. (2)
9. (4)　10. (3)

閱讀測驗

1. (1)　2. (1)　3. (3)　4. (4)　5. (3)　6. (4)　7. (1)　8. (1)
9. (1)　10. (2)

單字解析

manners (n)：禮貌、規矩、習慣

It is bad *manners* to interrupt others when speaking.

（打斷他人說話是不禮貌的。）

Good *manners* are good for business.

（有禮貌助於商務。）

demanding (a)：苛求的、高要求的、

Customers are a lot more *demanding* today than ever before.
（現今顧客的需求比以前更多。）

counterpart (n)：相對物、配對者

enthusiasm (n)：熱心、熱忱

CEO's proposal was greeted with great *enthusiasm*.
（執行長的提案受到熱情的回響。）

light-hearted (ph.)：輕鬆的、無憂無慮的

This restaurant offers *a light-hearted* environment.
（這家餐廳提供愉悅的用餐環境。）

aperitif (n)：開胃酒

Aperitif is a before-dinner drink to stimulate the appetite.
（開胃酒是餐前為增加食慾所飲用的飲料。）

第四回測驗

翻譯題
1. (1)　2. (4)　3. (1)　4. (2)　5. (1)

文法測驗
1. (4)　2. (3)　3. (3)　4. (2)　5. (1)　6. (1)　7. (3)　8. (2)
9. (4)　10. (3)

字彙測驗
1. (2)　2. (3)　3. (3)　4. (1)　5. (1)　6. (1)　7. (3)　8. (2)
9. (1)　10. (1)

句型測驗
1. (3)　2. (1)　3. (2)　4. (3)　5. (1)　6. (2)　7. (1)　8. (4)
9. (3)　10. (2)

填空測驗

1. (2)　2. (3)　3. (1)　4. (2)　5. (3)　6. (1)　7. (1)　8. (2)

9. (3)　10. (4)

附錄1：貿易英文辭彙
Glossary of International Trade Terms

中文	英文
一切險	all Risks
三角債	chain debts
工廠交貨價	Ex Factory
工廠或現場交貨價	Ex Works
不合理競爭	unfair competition
中間商／經紀人／掮客	middleman
中斷業務往來關係	to interrupt business relationship
分批裝運	partial shipment
分期付款購買	hire purchase
反傾銷	antidumping
水漬險	WA／WPA (With Average or With Particular Average)
世界貿易組織	WTO (World Trade Organization)
出口	export
出口退稅	tax rebate
出口商	exporter
出口許口證	export license
加工貿易	processing trade
加速業務往來關係	to speed up business relationship
北美自由貿易區	NAFTA (North American Free Trade Area)
平安險	F. P. A. (Free from Particular Average)
未完稅交貨	DDU (Delivered Duty Unpaid)
正式申報／完整申報	make a complete entry
世界貿易組織	World Trade Organization
交貨	delivery

全損險	FAA (free from all average)
回扣	return commission
多邊貿易	multilateral trade
存貨／庫存量	stocks
成本加運費價	CFR (Cost & Freight)
成本加運費價	C&F (Cost and Freight)
托運單／裝貨單	shipping order
收貨人／收件人	consignee
有形貿易	visible trade
佣金	commission
免賠額	franchise
兵險	War Risks
含佣價	price including commission
完稅後交貨／稅訖交貨價	DDP (Delivered Duty Paid)
技術合作	technology cooperation
技術性貿易壁壘	TBT (Technical Barriers to Trade)
批發	wholesale
批發價	wholesale price
折扣	discount / allowance
改善業務往來關係	to improve business relationship
到岸價／保險費運費在內價	CIF (Cost, Insurance and Freight)
卸貨費	landing charges
受讓人	concessionaire / licensed dealer
承運人	carrier
承運貨物收據	cargo receipt
東南亞國協	ASEAN
東盟自由貿易區	AFTA (ASEAN Free Trade Area)
空白背書	blank endorsed

信用狀	L/C (Letter of credit)
保持業務往來關係	to present business relationship
保稅倉庫	bonded warehouse
保險費在內價	C&I (Cost & Insurance)
保險運費及佣金在內價	CIF&C (Cost, Insurance, Freight & Commission)
保險運費及利息在內價	CIF&I (Cost, Insurance, Freight & Interest)
保險運費及匯費在內價	CIF&E (Cost, Insurance, Freight & Exchange)
保險運費及關稅在內價	CIF Duty Paid
保險運費卸地價	CIF Landed
促進業務往來關係	to promote business relationship
恢復業務往來關係	to resume business relationship
訂貨／下單	order
消費者	consumer
海運提單	marine bills of lading
海關估價	customs valuation
海關擔保	customs bond
臭味險	Risk of Odor
託收	Collection
偷竊及未送達險	TPND (Theft, Pilferage and Non-delivery)
區域貿易協定	RTA (Regional Trade Arrangements)
參考價格	indicative price
商行／商號	business house
商品目錄	catalog / catalogue
商業糾紛調解	mediation of dispute
國內貿易	inland trade / home trade / domestic trade
國際市場價格	world market price / international market price

國際貨幣基金組織	IMF (International Monetary Fund)
國際貿易	international trade
淡水雨淋險	F. W. R. D. (Fresh Water Rain Damage)
清關	customs liquidation
混雜與玷污險	Risk of Intermixture and Contamination
淨價	net price
現行價格／時價	current price
現金交易	cash sale
現貨價格／即期價格	spot price
組裝貿易	assembling trade
船上交貨／目的港船上交貨價	DES (Delivered Ex Ship)
船邊交貨價	FAS (Free Alongside Ship)
貨交承運人價	FCA (Free Carrier)
貨運代理	freight forwarder
貨幣貿易理事會	CTG (Council for Trade in Goods)
通關交貨價	CIF Cleared
提貨單／提單	Bill of Lading
港口稅／港埠捐稅	port dues
無形貿易	invisible trade
短缺險	Shortage Risk
結關	customs clearance
買主／買方	buyer
買回	buy-back
買賣／交易	commercial transaction
貿易	commerce / trade / trading
貿易平衡	trade balance
貿易合作	trade cooperation
貿易協定	trade agreement

貿易協會	trade association
貿易展	trade fair / trade show
貿易逆差	unfavorable balance of trade
貿易條款	trade terms / trade clause
貿易順差	favorable balance of trade
貿易夥伴	trade partner
貿易管制	restraint of trade
貿易磋商	trade consultation
進口	import
進口附加稅	import surcharge
進口差價稅	import variable duties
進口商	importer
進口許口證	import license
傾銷	dumping
傾銷差價 / 傾銷差額	dumping profit margin
瑕疵貨	condemned goods
經銷商	dealer / distributer
經銷管道	distribution channels
詢價	inquiry
運費	freight
運費付訖條件	CPT (Carriage Paid To)
運費保險費付訖條件	CIP (Carriage and Insurance Paid To)
達成交易	to make a deal
達成協議	reach an agreement
零售業	retail
零售價	retail price
對外貿易	foreign trade / overseas trade
滲漏險	Risk of Leakage
製造商	manufacturer

價目表	price list
價格術語	price term
歐洲自由貿易聯盟	EFTA (European Free Trade Association)
碼頭交貨／目的港碼頭交貨價	DEQ (Delivered Ex Quay)
碼頭費	wharfage
罷工險	Strikes Risk
整批銷售／躉售	bulk sale
銹蝕險	Risk of Rust
優惠關稅	special preferences
總值	total value
聯合國貿易與發展會議	UNCTAD (United Nations Conference on Trade and Development)
講信用做生意	to do business in a sincere way
購買	purchase
擴大業務往來關係	to enlarge business relationship
轉口貿易	transit trade
離岸價／船上交貨價	FOB (free on board)
雙邊貿易	bilateral trade
壞帳	bad account
邊境交貨價	DAF (Delivered at Frontier)
關稅	customs duty / tariff
關稅壁壘	tariff barrier
繼續業務往來關係	to continue business relationship
顧客／客戶	client, customer

附錄2：台灣駐外商務代表處
Overseas Offices of Bureau of Foreign Trade

亞太地區	
駐日本代表處經濟組	Economic Division, Taipei Economic and Cultural Representative Office in Japan
駐韓國代表處經濟組	Economic Division, Taipei Mission in Korea
駐越南代表處經濟組	Economic Division, Taipei Economic and Cultural Office in Hanoi, Vietnam
駐胡志明市辦事處商務組	Commercial Division, Taipei Economic and Cultural Office in Ho Chi Minh City
駐泰國代表處經濟組	Economic Division, Taipei Economic and Cultural Office in Thailand
駐新加坡代表處經濟組	Economic Division, Taipei Representative Office in Singapore
駐馬來西亞代表處經濟組	Economic Division, Taipei Economic and Cultural Office in Malaysia
駐印尼代表處經濟組	Economic Division, Taipei Economic and Trade Office in Indonesia
駐菲律賓代表處經濟組	Economic Division, Taipei Economic and Cultural Office in The Philippines
駐澳大利亞代表處經濟組	Economic Division, Taipei Economic and Cultural Office in Australia
駐紐西蘭代表處經濟組	Economic Division, Taipei Economic and Cultural Office in New Zealand
駐索羅門群島大使館經濟參事處	Economic Counsellor Office, Embassy of the Republic of China (Taiwan), Honiara, Solomon Islands

駐印度代表處經濟組	Economic Division, Taipei Economic and Cultural Center in New Delhi
行政院大陸委員會香港事務局商務組（遠東貿易服務中心駐香港辦事處）	Far East Trade Service, Inc. Hong Kong Branch Office
美洲地區	
駐加拿大代表處經濟組（駐加拿大台北經濟文化辦事處經濟組）	Economic Division, Taipei Economic and Cultural Office in Canada
駐美國代表處經濟組（駐美國台北經濟文化代表處經濟組）	Economic Division, Taipei Economic and Cultural Representative Office in the United States
駐美投資貿易服務處（駐美投資貿易服務處）	Investment and Trade Office, Taipei Economic and Cultural Representative Office in the United States
駐亞特蘭大辦事處商務組（駐亞特蘭大台北經濟文化辦事處商務組）	Commercial Division, Taipei Economic and Cultural Office in Atlanta
駐休士頓辦事處商務組（駐休士頓台北經濟文化辦事處商務組）	Commercial Division, Taipei Economic and Cultural Office in Houston
駐芝加哥辦事處商務組（駐芝加哥台北經濟文化辦事處商務組）	Commercial Division, Taipei Economic and Cultural Office in Chicago
駐洛杉磯辦事處商務組（駐洛杉磯台北經濟文化辦事處商務組）	Commercial Division, Taipei Economic and Cultural Office in Los Angeles
駐波士頓辦事處（駐波士頓台北經濟文化辦事處）	Taipei Economic and Cultural Office in Boston
駐墨西哥代表處經濟組（駐墨西哥台北經濟文化辦事處經濟組）	Division Economica, Oficina Economica y Cultural de Taipei en Mexico

駐瓜地馬拉大使館經濟參事處（駐瓜地馬拉共和國大使館經濟參事處）	Oficina del Consejero Economico de la Embajada de la Republica de China en Guatmala
駐宏都拉斯大使館經濟參事處（駐宏都拉斯共和國大使館經濟參事處）	Oficina del Consejero Economico, Embajada de la Republica de China
駐薩爾瓦多大使館經濟參事處（駐薩爾瓦多共和國大使館經濟參事處）	Oficina del Consejero Economico, Embajadad de La Republica de China
駐尼加拉瓜大使館經濟參事處（駐尼加拉瓜共和國大使館經濟參事處）	Oficina del Consejero Economico, Embajada de la Republica de China
駐巴拿馬大使館經濟參事處（駐巴拿馬共和國大使館經濟參事處）	Oficina del Consejero Economico, Embajada de La Republica de China (Taiwan)
駐委內瑞拉代表處經濟組（駐委內瑞拉台北經濟文化辦事處經濟組）	Division Economica, Oficina Economica Y Cultural de Taipei en Venezuela
駐哥倫比亞代表處經濟組（駐哥倫比亞台北商務辦事處經濟組）	Division Economica, Oficina Comercial de Taipei en Colombia
駐多明尼加大使館經濟參事處（駐多明尼加共和國大使館經濟參事處）	Office of the Economic Counsellor, Embassy of the Republic of China in Santo Domingo, Dominican Republic
駐秘魯代表處經濟組（駐秘魯台北經濟文化辦事處經濟組）	Oficina Economica y Cutlural de Taipei Division Economica

駐巴西代表處經濟組（駐巴西台北經濟文化辦事處經濟組）	Divisao Economica, Escritorio Economico e Cultural de Taipei no Brasil
駐智利代表處經濟組（駐智利台北經濟文化辦事處經濟組）	Economic Division, Taipei Economic and Cultural Office in Chile
駐巴拉圭大使館經濟參事處（駐巴拉圭共和國大使館經濟參事處）	Oficina del Consejero Economico, Embajada de la Republica de China
駐阿根廷代表處經濟組（駐阿根廷台北商務文化辦事處經濟組）	Division Economica, Oficina Comercial y Cultural de Taipei en la Republica Argentina
歐洲地區	
駐芬蘭代表處商務組（駐芬蘭台北代表處商務組）	Commercial Division Taipei Representative Office in Finland
駐丹麥代表處經濟組（駐丹麥台北代表處經濟組）	Economic Division, Taipei Representative Office in Denmark
駐英國代表處經濟組（駐英國台北代表處經濟組）	Economic Division, Taipei Representative Office in the United Kingdom
駐荷蘭代表處經濟組（駐荷蘭台北代表處經濟組）	Economic Division, Taipei Representative Office in the Netherlands
駐歐盟兼駐比利時代表處經濟組（駐比利時台北代表處經濟組）	Economic Division, Taipei Representative Office in the EU and Belgium
亞洲貿易促進會駐巴黎辦事處（亞洲貿易促進會駐巴黎辦事處）	C. A. P. E. C. (Centre Asiatique de Promotion Economique et Commerciale)
駐西班牙代表處經濟組（駐西班牙台北經濟文化辦事處經濟組）	Division Economica, Oficina Economica y Cultural de Taipei

駐德國代表處經濟組（駐德國台北代表處經濟組）	Economic Division, Taipei Representative Office in the Federal Republic of Germany
駐慕尼黑辦事處商務組（法蘭克福）（駐德國台北代表處慕尼黑辦事處商務組）	Taipeh Vertretung in der BRD, Buero Muenchen, Handelsabteilung Frankfurt/M, Germany【Taipei Trade Office Frankfurt】
駐俄羅斯代表處經濟組（台北莫斯科經濟文化協調委員會駐莫斯科代表處經濟組）	Economic Division, Representative Office in Moscow for the Taipei-Moscow Economic and Cultural Coordination Commission
駐波蘭代表處經濟組（駐波蘭台北經濟文化辦事處經濟組）	Economic Division, Taipei Economic and Cultural Office in Poland
駐捷克代表處經濟組（駐捷克台北經濟文化代表處經濟組）	Economic Division, Taipei Economic and Cultural Office in the Czech Republic
駐奧地利代表處經濟組（駐奧地利台北經濟文化辦事處經濟組）	Economic Division, Taipei Economic and Cultural Office in Austria
駐義大利代表處經濟組（駐義大利台北代表處經濟組）	Ufficio Rappresentanza Di Taipei in Italia (URTI), Divisione Economica【Ecomomic Division, Taipei Representative Office in Italy】
駐瑞士代表處經濟組（駐瑞士台北文化經濟代表團經濟組）	Economic Division, Delegation Culturelle et Economique de Taipei
駐斯洛伐克代表處經濟組（駐斯洛伐克台北代表處經濟組）	Economic Division, Taipei Representative Office in Bratislava, Slovakia Republic
駐匈牙利代表處經濟組（駐匈牙利台北代表處經濟組）	Economic Division, Taipei Representative Office in Hungary

駐土耳其代表處經濟組（駐安卡拉台北經濟文化代表團經濟組）	Economic Division, Taipei Economic and Cultural Mission in Ankara
駐希臘代表處經濟組（駐希臘台北代表處經濟組）	Economic Division, Taipei Representative Office in Greece
中東、非洲地區	
駐沙烏地阿拉伯王國代表處經濟組（駐沙烏地阿拉伯王國台北經濟文化代表處經濟組）	Economic Division, Taipei Economic and Cultural Representative Office in the Kingdom of Saudi Arabia
駐吉達辦事處（駐沙烏地阿拉伯王國台北經濟文化代表處吉達分處）	Taipei Economic and Cultural Representative Office in the Kingdom of Saudi Arabia, Jeddah Office
駐以色列代表處經濟組（駐台拉維夫台北經濟文化代表處經濟組）	Economic Division, Taipei Economic and Cultural Representative Office in Tel Aviv
駐約旦代表處經濟組（駐約旦中華民國（台灣）商務辦事處經濟組）	Economic Division, Commercial Office of the Republic of China (Taiwan), Amman, Jordan
駐南非代表處經濟組（駐南非共和國台北聯絡代表處經濟組）	Economic Division, Taipei Liaison Office in the Republic of South Africa
遠東貿易服務中心駐象牙海岸辦事處（遠東貿易服務中心駐象牙海岸辦事處）	Far East Trade Service Inc. Branch Office in Cote d'Ivoire (Bureau Economique de Taiwan)
駐史瓦濟蘭大使館經濟參事處（駐史瓦濟蘭王國大使館經濟參事處）	Economic Counsellor Office, Embassy of Republic of China (Taiwan) in the Kingdom of Swaziland

資料來源：國際貿易局。

■ 附錄3：國際機場代碼
International Airport Codes

國際機場	英文全名	機場縮寫
亞洲		
台灣桃園國際機場	Taiwan Taoyuan International Airport	TPE
日本東京成田國際機場	Narita Airport	NAA
日本大阪關西國際機場	(Osaka) Kansai International Airport	KIX
日本中部國際機場	Central Japan International Airport (Centrair)	NGO
韓國首爾國際機場	(Seoul) Incheon International Airport	ICN
韓國釜山國際機場	(Busan) Gimhae International Airport	PUS
香港國際機場	Hong Kong International Airport	HKG
中國北京首都國際機場	Beijing Capital International Airport	PEK
中國上海浦東國際機場	(Shanghai) Pudong International Airport	PVG
中國廣州白雲國際機場	Guangzhou Baiyun International Airport	CAN
新加坡樟宜機場	Singapore Changi Airport	SIN
泰國曼谷蘇汪納蓬機場	(Bangkok) Suvarnabhumi International Airport	BKK
泰國普吉島國際機場	Phuket International Airport	HKT
馬來西亞吉隆坡國際機場	Kuala Lumpur International Airport	KUL

馬來西亞檳城（峇六拜）國際機場	Penang (Bayan Lepas) International Airport	PEN
印尼雅加達蘇加諾—哈達國際機場	(Jakarta) Soekarno-Hatta International Airport	CGK
菲律賓馬尼拉尼諾阿奎諾國際機場	(Manila) Ninoy Aquino International Airport	MNL
澳洲雪梨機場	Sydney Airport	SYD
澳洲墨爾本機場	Melbourne Airport	MEL
澳洲凱恩斯國際機場	Cairns International Airport	CNS
紐西蘭奧克蘭國際機場	Auckland International Airport	AKL
紐西蘭基督城國際機場	Christchurch International Airport	CHC
紐西蘭威靈頓國際機場	Wellington International Airport	WLG
關島國際機場	Guam International Airport	GUM
印度新德里國際機場	(New Delhi) Indira Gandhi International Airport	DEL
印度孟買國際機場	(Mumbai) Chhatrapati Shivaji International Airport	BOM
斯里蘭卡可倫坡機場	Colombo Bandaranaike Airport	CMB
美洲		
加拿大蒙特利爾杜魯多國際機場	Montréal-Trudeau Airport	YUL
加拿大溫哥華國際機場	Vancouver International Airport	YVR
加拿大多倫多皮爾森國際機場	Toronto Pearson International Airport	YYZ
美國波士頓洛根國際機場	(Boston) Logan International Airport	BOS
美國克里夫蘭霍普金斯國際機場	Cleveland Hopkins International Airport	CLE
美國達拉斯沃爾斯堡國際機場	Dallas-Fort Worth International Airport	DFW

美國華盛頓杜勒斯國際機場	Washington Dulles International Airport	IAD
美國紐約甘迺迪過國際機場	(New York) John F. Kennedy International Airport	JFK
美國拉斯維加斯馬卡倫國際機場	(Las Vegas) McCarran International Airport	LAS
美國洛杉磯國際機場	Los Angeles International Airport	LAX
美國芝加哥中央國際機場	Chicago Midway International Airport	MSW
美國路易斯阿姆斯壯紐奧良國際機場	(New Orleans) Louis Armstrong New Orleans International Airport	MSY
美國檀香山國際機場	Honolulu International Airport	HNL
美國聖地牙哥國際機場	San Diego International Airport	SAN
美國西雅圖塔科馬國際機場	Seattle-Tacoma International Airport	SEA
美國舊金山國際機場	San Francisco International Airport	SFO
美國聖荷西國際機場	(San Jose) Mineta San Jose International Airport	SJC
墨西哥墨京機場	(Mexico City) Benito Juarez International Airport	MEX
巴拿馬市圖庫曼國際機場	Tocumen Panama International Airport	PTY
阿根廷皮斯塔拉尼國際機場	(Ezeiza) Ministro Pistarini International Airport	EZE
巴西里約熱內盧國際機場	Rio de Janeiro-Galeão (Antonio Carlos Jobim International Airport)	GIG
智利聖地牙哥阿圖洛美利諾貝尼代國際機場	(Santiago) Arturo Merino Benítez International Airport	SCL
厄瓜多爾基多國際機場	(Quito) Mariscal Sucre International Airport	UIO

祕魯利馬豪爾赫查韋斯國際機場	Jorge Chávez Lima-Callao International Airport	LIM
委內瑞拉西蒙玻利瓦爾國際機場	Caracas Maiquetía International Airport (Simón Bolívar)	CCS
歐洲		
挪威奧斯陸國際機場	Oslo Airport	OSL
瑞典斯德哥爾摩亞蘭達國際機場	Stockholm Arlanda Airport	ARM
芬蘭赫爾辛基萬塔國際機場	Helsinki-Vantaa Airport	HEL
丹麥哥本哈根國際機場	Copenhagen Airport	CPH
冰島凱佛拉維克國際機場	Keflavik International Airport	KEF
英國倫敦希斯洛國際機場	London Heathrow Airport	LHR
英國伯明罕國際機場	Birmingham International Airport	BHX
英國愛丁堡國際機場	Edinburgh Airport	EDI
愛爾蘭都伯林國際機場	Dublin Airport	DUB
法國戴高樂國際機場	Paris Roissy Charles de Gaulle Airport	CDG
德國法蘭克福國際機場	Frankfurt Airport	FRA
德國柏林國際機場	Berlin-Tegel Airport	TXL
德國慕尼黑國際機場	Munich Airport	MUC
瑞士日內瓦國際機場	Geneva International Airport	GVA
荷蘭阿姆斯特丹國際機場	Amsterdam Airport Schiphol	AMS
荷蘭諾特丹國際機場	Rotterdam Airport	RTM
奧地利維也納國際機場	Vienna International Airport	VIE
比利時布魯塞爾國際機場	Brussels Airport	BRU
葡萄牙馬德拉國際機場	Madeira Airport	FNC

西班牙馬德里國際機場	Madrid Barajas Airport	MAD
義大利米蘭國際機場	Milan Linate International Airport	LIN
馬爾他國際機場	Malta International Airport	MLA
捷克布拉格國際機場	Prague Ruzyne Airport	PRG
匈牙利布達佩斯國際機場	Budapest Ferihegy Airport	BUD
保加利亞瓦爾納國際機場	Varna International Airport	VAR
希臘雅典國際機場	Athens Eleftherios Venizelos International Airport	ATH
土耳其伊斯坦堡國際機場	(Istanbul) Atatürk International Airport	IST
俄羅斯莫斯科多莫傑多沃國際機場	(Moscow) Domodedovo International Airport	DME
中東、非洲		
以色列特拉維夫國際機場	(Tel Aviv) Ben Gurion International Airport	TLV
科威特國際機場	Kuwait International Airport	KWI
沙烏地阿拉伯利雅德國際機場	Riyadh King Khaled International Airport	RUH
卡達國際機場	Doha International Airport	DOH
杜拜國際機場	Dubai International Airport	DXB
阿拉伯聯合大公國阿布達比國際機場	Abu Dhabi International Airport	AUH
埃及開羅國際機場	Cairo International Airport	CAI
摩洛哥卡薩布蘭卡國際機場	(Casablanca) Mohammed V Airport	CMN
衣索比亞國際機場	Addis Ababa Bole International Airport	ADD
科託卡國際機場	Accra (Kotoka International Airport)	ACC

奈及利亞國際機場	Lagos Murtala Muhammed International Airport	LOS
肯亞國際機場	(Nairobi) Jomo Kenyatta International Airport	NBO
模里西斯國際機場	(Mauritius) Sir Seewoosagur Ramgoolam International Airport	MRU
突尼西亞國際機場	Tunis Carthage International Airport	TUN
南非約翰尼斯堡國際機場	(Johannesburg) O R Tambo International Airport	JNB
南非角城國際機場	Cape Town International Airport	CPT

附錄4：網頁縮寫國碼

　　一般企業網址的呈現是：www.公司英文名稱.com.國家縮寫碼。以下列出各國縮寫碼，供讀者參考。

網頁縮寫國碼	代表國家英文	代表國家中文
ar	Argentina	阿根廷
au	Australia	澳洲
at	Austria	奧地利
be	Belgium	比利時
br	Brazil	巴西
ca	Canada	加拿大
cn	China	中國
cz	Czech Republic	捷克
dk	Demark	丹麥
eg	Egypt	埃及
fi	Finland	芬蘭
fr	France	法國
de	Germany	德國
gr	Greece	希臘
hk	Hong Kong	香港
hu	Hungary	匈牙利
is	Iceland	冰島
in	India	印度
id	Indonesia	印尼
ie	Ireland	愛爾蘭
il	Israel	以色列
it	Italy	義大利

jp	Japan	日本
kw	Kuwait	科威特
my	Malaysia	馬來西亞
mx	Mexico	墨西哥
nl	Netherlands	荷蘭
nz	New Zealand	紐西蘭
no	Norway	挪威
pe	Peru	祕魯
ph	Philippines	菲律賓
pl	Poland	波蘭
pt	Portugal	葡萄牙
ru	Russia	俄羅斯
sa	Saudi Arabia	沙烏地阿拉伯
sg	Singapore	新加坡
za	South Africa	南非
kr	South Korea	南韓
es	Spain	西班牙
lk	Sri Lanka	斯里蘭卡
se	Sweden	瑞典
ch	Switzerland	瑞士
tw	Taiwan	台灣
th	Thailand	泰國
tr	Turkey	土耳其
uk	United Kingdom	英國
—	United States	美國
vn	Vietnam	越南

附錄5：量度 Measurements

Abbreviation	Measurement	Chinese
in	inch	吋
ft	foot/feet	呎
yd	yard	碼
mile	mile	哩
mm	millimeter	公釐
cm	centimeter	公分
—	meter	公尺
km	kilometer	公里
sq in	square inch	平方吋
sq ft	square foot/feet	平方呎
sq yd	square yard	平方碼
—	square mile	平方哩
mm^2	square millimeter	平方公釐
cm^2	square centimeter	平方公分
m^2	square meter	平方公尺
km^2	square kilometer	平方公里
cu in	cubic inch	立方吋
cu ft	cubic foot/feet	立方呎
cu yd	cubic yard	立方碼
mm^3	cubic millimeter	立方公釐
cm^3	cubic centimeter	立方公分
m^3	cubic meter	立方公尺

附錄6：時間的表達方式　Time of Day

時間	英文表達方式
12:00	twelve o'clock ＝ noon ＝ midday ＝ midnight
1:10	ten after one ＝ one ten
2:15	a quarter past two ＝ two fifteen ＝ a quarter after two
3:30	half past three ＝ three thirty
4:45	a quarter to five ＝ four forty-five
5:25	twenty-five past five ＝ five twenty-five
6:35	twenty-five to seven ＝ six thirty-five
7:57	three minutes to eight ＝ seven fifty-seven
8:03	three minutes past eight ＝ eight oh three

■ 英文索引

English	Page
attitude	2, 33, 94
account	12, 35, 88, 124, 130, 133, 173, 182, 196, 199, 200, 211, 245, 263, 289, 300
active listening	4
agent	203, 207, 216-220, 261
agreement	42, 44, 89, 125, 189, 217, 223, 245, 247, 298, 299
application letter	17
appreciate	69, 84, 105, 115, 126, 130, 132, 161, 162, 193, 239, 278, 279, 283
attention	38, 39, 78, 84, 95, 115, 138, 139, 141, 148, 161, 170, 176, 245, 272, 281, 283
autobiography	9
bargaining	188, 189
brochure	5, 106, 129, 130, 148, 161, 162, 246, 271
business etiquette	94, 95
business letter	103
catalog	106, 118, 128, 148, 154, 160, 167, 176, 212, 277, 297
CIF	158, 296, 297, 298
communication	2, 4, 24, 101, 114
company	5, 14, 33, 45, 54, 67, 70, 77, 78, 82, 95, 98, 111, 112, 115, 121, 122, 124, 126, 127, 132, 148, 162, 164, 175, 181, 201, 203, 212, 213, 216, 218-220, 235-237, 241, 244, 246, 249, 250, 263, 266, 275, 277, 288, 289

中文索引

國家圖書館出版品預行編目資料

商用英文／劉鴻暉、林秀璟著.--二版--.--臺
北市：五南圖書出版股份有限公司, 2011.08
　面；　公分.
ISBN 978-957-11-6384-0（平裝）
1.商用英文　2.讀本
805.18　　　　　　　　　　100014949

1065

商用英文

作　　　者 ― 劉源暉、林秀璟

發 行 人 ― 楊榮川

總 經 理 ― 楊士清

總 編 輯 ― 楊秀麗

主　　　編 ― 侯家嵐

責任編輯 ― 侯家嵐

文字編輯 ― 劉禹伶

封面設計 ― 侯家嵐、盧盈良

出 版 者 ― 五南圖書出版股份有限公司

地　　　址：106台北市大安區和平東路二段339號4樓

電　　　話：(02)2705-5066　　傳　　真：(02)2706-6100

網　　　址：https://www.wunan.com.tw

電子郵件：wunan@wunan.com.tw

劃撥帳號：01068953

戶　　　名：五南圖書出版股份有限公司

法律顧問　林勝安律師事務所　林勝安律師

出版日期　2008年12月初版一刷
　　　　　2011年8月二版一刷
　　　　　2021年9月二版二刷

定　　　價　新臺幣350元